W9-ALM-233

A Girl
Becomes
a Comma
Like That

a novel

Lisa Glatt

Simon & Schuster
New York London Toronto Sydney

SIMON & SCHUSTER
Rockefeller Center
1230 Avenue of the Americas
New York, NY 10020

SIMON & SCHUSTER and colophon are registered trademarks
of Simon & Schuster, Inc.

For information regarding special discounts for bulk purchases,
please contact Simon & Schuster Special Sales:
1-800-456-6798 or business@simonandschuster.com

Designed by Karolina Harris

Manufactured in the United States of America

10   9   8   7   6   5   4   3   2   1

Library of Congress Cataloging-in-Publication Data
Glatt, Lisa.
  A girl becomes a comma like that / Lisa Glatt.
  p. cm.
  1. Parent and adult child—Fiction. 2. Mothers and daughters—Fiction. I. Title.
PS3607.L375G57 2004
813'.54—dc22   2003070356
ISBN 0-7432-5775-8

Acknowledgments

Portions of this novel appeared in altered form in *Many Mountains Moving* ("Egg Girls"), *Mississippi Review* ("The Clinic That Ella Built"), *Other Voices* ("A Girl Becomes a Comma Like That"), and *Swink* ("Cream"). "Geography of the Mall" won first place for the 2003 *Mississippi Review* Prize.

I am grateful to many people and organizations: to Yaddo, MacDowell, Fundación Valparaiso, Djerassi, Headlands Center for the Arts, the Ludwig Vogelstein Foundation, and the California Arts Council for the gift of time and support. To Marilyn Johnson, Leelila Strogov, Mia Pardo, and David Hernandez, who read the manuscript and offered wisdom. With love to my family, especially my father and stepmother, Aaron and Fredda Glatt, to Andrew Glatt and Katherine Thompson, and to my fabulous in-laws, James and Nancy Hernandez. To Jessica Ware, Gwen Dashiell, and C. J., who spent more than one evening with me at "Ruby's Room" doing research. To Jenna, Maria, Lauren, Scott, Mr. Mark, Holly, Todd, and Stan Stanton, who were there. To my students, who surprise and inspire me, especially those I see on Sundays. To Diana Athill, Gerald Locklin, Joan Jobe Smith, Patrick Pardo, and Nick Carbó, who encouraged my early efforts with fiction. To Denise Duhamel and Kim Addonizio for their poetry and friendship. To my loyal agent Andrew Blauner, who said he would *open the door* and who did. And finally, to Tara Parsons and David Rosenthal at Simon & Schuster—and a special thank-you to my perceptive and talented editor, Marysue Rucci.

For my mother, Iris Stanton
and
my love, David Hernandez

Contents

Rachel Spark

1999

Dirk or Derrick or Dick

My mother is sick at home, and I am downtown, full of beer, kissing a long-haired man in the pizza place next door to Ruby's Room.

His name is Dirk or Derrick or Dick. I make a mental note to find out which one before I let his hand into my skirt.

I met him at the bar next door less than an hour ago.

His hands are huge, one of them making its way to my blouse's top button.

It's early May, and even at this late hour the Southern California heat is something to talk about.

"It's hot," he'd said at the bar, fanning himself with one of those hands.

I watched the long fingers flip back and forth in front of his face. "You'd never even know it was night," I said.

"Too many people in here breathing all at once," he said. "Want to go next door?"

I shook my head no, but smiled at him.

"You're ambivalent," he said.

"I'm not," I said, turning away from him and looking out the front door. A girl with pink hair held a cigarette, leaned against a streetlight, and a skinny boy stood next to her, pulling on her sleeve. She brushed his hand off and shook her head. I turned back to Dirk or Derrick or Dick, who now spoke with a rubber band between his lips and was using both hands to gather his hair behind his head. "You know them?" he mumbled.

"No," I said.

He pulled the band from his mouth and put his hair back in a ponytail. Several dark strands fell into his face and he pushed them away. "Come on, let's go," he said.

"Bacco's?" I wavered.

He nodded.

"Isn't it closed at this hour?"

"I work there." He picked up a set of keys that had been sharing a napkin with his beer.

"No, really, I can't," I said.

It is my mother's second recurrence of breast cancer, a pesky piece of disease showing up in her hip, appearing two Sundays ago as an annoying limp, nothing more—no pain, just a slight shift to the left, an inability to find balance in her body, which has become increasingly unruly.

My mother, on her way to the high school where she's been teaching twelfth-grade English for the past twenty years, wobbled out the front door on Monday with her book bag over her shoulder, wondering out loud, *What is this limping about?*

When she returned home, we sat together on the couch— my mother full of optimism, me full of denial—and discussed the possibilities: arthritis, muscle strain, perhaps even osteo-porosis. Maybe she'd broken her hip and didn't even know it.

"It happens," I said. Wasn't there some distant cousin who'd done just that? We pitched diseases against each other, feeble bones and constant joint pain—nothing, when compared to what was actually happening.

Exactly how I changed my mind and ended up in the pizza place with Dirk or Derrick or Dick, I'm not exactly sure. I know my best friend, Angela, had run into an old boyfriend on her way to the bathroom and never returned to her stool. I know there were several tall glasses of cold beer involved, and I know that my new pal was talking about breast cancer, his mother sick too, good God, dying on some farm in the middle of Maine, and then an impassioned speech—by me, of course—about living in the moment, carpe diem, and all of that hooey.

Now, we're in the back of the restaurant, in the kitchen, my ass exactly where the pies had been earlier, where this man, all perfect torso and bad teeth, had stood in his white shirt and funny square hat, pounding the dough and spreading tomato sauce and sprinkling cheese and proudly scattering little rounds of pepperoni on five pies at once. The two of us are as ferocious and unconcerned about public safety as cancer itself, holding on and moving and panting and kissing and sucking as if we are each other's much-needed medicine, like we are the experimental treatment that might finally work.

Bare-chested in his boxers, he slips his hands inside my blouse, holds my breasts like they are the first and last breasts in the world, and all I keep thinking about is how breasts are the enemy, armed, dangerous, two ticking bombs, how my mother's are killing her right this moment, and he of all people should be afraid of them, should refuse them, slip them back inside the black bra from whence they came, but oh, oh, maybe Dirk's or Derrick's or Dick's thoughts are better, more accurate and optimistic than mine—his lips and tongue and heat, they certainly *feel* better.

His fingers are making their way into my tights when I say, "Spell your name."

"Huh?"

"Please," I say.

"You don't know my name?"

"Just spell it."

His name is Dirk. He spells it for me. "D-I-R-K," he says, rolling his pretty brown eyes.

"Dirk," I say.

"Your name is Rachel Spark."

"First *and* last. Impressive."

"You teach, right? Your eyes are green and you've got one dimple, on the left side of your face."

"Now you're just showing off."

Dirk reaches behind him and lets his ponytail free in one swift pull.

"What about you?" I ask.

"Story's messy," he says.

"And sad?"

He nods and his hair falls to his bare shoulders. He looks at me and leans in. "Your mother is sick," he says quietly.

I reach for his chest. "D-I-R-K," I say. "Dirk," I whisper into his neck.

He collects old cars and toasters. He owns two Studebakers, a Nash, and a Sunbeam. He's thinking about buying a Triumph; there's one for sale on Fourth and Cherry. He owns more than one toaster that's older than his great-grandfather. "I've got a Triple Banger worth over five grand," he says, beaming.

A lot of vehicles, plenty of places to stick his sliced bread, but no home; Dirk lives in a shack behind the restaurant and bar. He uses the bathroom and sink in the restaurant when he wants to wash up. It's been this way for months, and he doesn't remember the last time he paid rent.

"I couldn't live like that," I say.

"It's fine," he says. "It's convenient. I practically live at my work. Who wouldn't like to do that?"

I picture myself living in a tent on campus. "Me," I say.

Earlier tonight I sat with my mother on her bed, sharing one phone. Our skulls knocked, our ears touched, and neither of us would let go of the receiver. "I'll hold it," I said. "I've got it," I whispered. "So do I," she whispered back. Reluctantly, we decided to share.

The doctor's voice was upbeat and straining to remain so, even when the words came: metastasis, diameter, radiation, and maybe some more chemo.

"Oh, well," my mother said when we'd hung up. She was smiling. "We know now what we're up against."

"Yeah," I said.

"I feel better," she continued, standing up. "It's good to know what we're dealing with." She paused. "And I didn't want osteoporosis anyway."

I shook my head.

"He said that there's a chance . . ."

"What now?" I said.

"A few zaps of radiation and I'll be fine, Rachel. Don't get all dramatic on me. Don't look at me like that."

"Like what?"

"Like I'm disappearing," she said. "I'm still here."

"I know," I said.

"It's just my hip," she continued. "No one ever died from a sore hip. Do you know anyone who ever died because of such a thing?" She picked up a blouse from her dresser and held it in front of her face, checking for wrinkles. "Do you think I can wear this one more time?" she asked me.

"Probably," I said.

"Worry if it goes to my liver. They say that's when you're supposed to worry." My mother opened her closet and took out some hangers. She set the hangers on the bed next to me, holding on to one of them.

"That would be worrisome, yes," I said.

"They say you've got to fight. You've got to be strong."

"Okay, okay," I said, annoyed.

"They say a good attitude makes a big difference." She had the blouse on the hanger now and was putting it in the closet. Her back was to me.

"You *have* a good attitude," I said, "and it's recurred. What's your good attitude done for you?"

"Well, they say—"

"Who are *they*?" I said.

"You know, *them*," she said.

"Oh, *them*," I said angrily. "Let's certainly listen to them. The invisible them."

Dirk's shack has a metal roof and a little metal door that he holds open for me. I stand leaning, torso forward, with my boots half in and half out, peering in, until Dirk insists with a gentle nudge of his hip that I move inside. He uses a flashlight to show me around. I get most of the tour standing in one spot. He has cats, three of them. Two look out at me from under a table, four glowing eyes, and one circles Dirk's pant leg. He's got an old mattress on the floor he calls a bed. There are toasters lined up on shelves like fat silver books. "Check them out," he says.

I step past Dirk and the cat. I bend down and feign interest. "Wow," I say. "Nice," I tell him.

Yes, he is thirty-six, but he's been grieving—for nearly ten years. It's pathetic, sure, but behavior that I recognize and can empathize with—the inability to move on, get on with things, foreseeable in my own future. In addition to the dying mother, Dirk had two sisters who'd come to visit him in California eight years ago and were killed in a car accident. It was Thanksgiving, and the three of them were on their way to Palm Springs to visit an uncle. Somewhere near that ridiculous dinosaur on Route 5 a woman swerved into their lane and killed the girls instantly. Dirk survived with a scratch on his forehead, a bruised hip, and a twisted toe. So, because of this, I'm guessing, he didn't finish college and he's never held a decent job, and once, he wants me to know, he lived for three months without a working toilet. This is all wonderful news and if, in my drunk and needy state, I'd had any intention of seeing Dirk again, the confessions are dimming the possibility, especially the bit about living without a toilet.

"I need to get going," I say, stepping outside.

"Now?" he says.

I look at my watch. "It's after three."

He shrugs.

"I've got a class tomorrow."

"Let's sit on the curb and look at the moon—it's full," he says.

"No, I—"

"What time's your class?" he interrupts.

"One-thirty, but I've got to prepare," I say.

"Sure," he says, doubtful.

"I told you that earlier, remember?"

"But the moon's full," he says.

"It'll be full again," I say.

In the alley Dirk holds my hand and leads me toward the Studebaker—a big, ridiculous car. Salmon pink. He painted it himself, he wants me to know, when his girlfriend threw him out.

He leans down and puts the key in. "Color's classic—titty pink," he says, smiling, opening the door. "It's the only door that works," he tells me, "and sometimes it gets jammed. Then I've got to use the window." He climbs over the passenger seat and emergency brake and sits huffing behind the wheel. He pats the seat next to him. "Come on," he says.

We drive up Pine Avenue and down Broadway and he chats about the toasters. He loves that Triple Banger and his Toasterlater Model #7, which is one of the most unusual toasters made, he informs me. It has a sawtooth conveyor belt that jiggles the toast through and a porthole for viewing progress.

"Does it make good toast?" I ask.

"Hell, no," he says.

"No?"

"It's a merciless burner."

I laugh. "What about the porthole for viewing progress?"

"It doesn't matter."

"You'd think it would matter," I say, getting serious. "If you could see the bread burning, you'd think you could save it."

He shakes his head.

"I mean, the bread's moving along and you're watching it, right?"

"Right."

"Push stop, hit a button, do something."

"Not that simple."

At a red light we sit silently. "Oh, yeah," he says, remembering, "there's even a darker/lighter control switch that adjusts toast travel speed in seven increments, but still you're left with a charred mess."

"It's green."

"What?"

"The light," I say.

Dirk pushes the gas pedal and we lurch forward.

"Make a right here," I say.

He turns onto Ocean Boulevard. "What do you teach again?"

"Writing."

"Journalism, that kind of thing?"

"No."

"What then?"

"Poetry workshops."

"Where?"

"At the University."

"Damn," he says. "A professor . . . you don't act like a professor."

"Maybe not," I say.

"I thought maybe you taught high school, maybe grade school—but college, huh? A professor," he says again, clicking his tongue.

"A lecturer, actually."

"What's the difference?" he asks.

"Never mind," I say wearily. "I'm tired."

In front of my mother's high-rise, he turns off the engine. We look at each other. "Must be nice to live by the ocean," he says.

"I like the way it sounds more than anything," I say. "I mean, looking at it is fine, but listening is the best."

"I went surfing once," he says.

"Just once?"

"Sometimes that's all there is—the one time," Dirk says, leaning toward me.

I kiss his face and neck. I touch his hair, which smells of sweat and tomatoes and yeast. "Good-night," I tell him.

"Yeah," he says.

"Good luck with the Triple Banger and Toasterlater #7." I turn to the door and try the handle. It won't budge. I try it again, then again. For a moment it is funny—a woman like me, a teacher, a writer, stuck in a pink Studebaker with a toaster-collecting man like him—and then it isn't funny, and I am pounding on the door, wanting suddenly to get out of there, wanting to get to my mother's apartment, up the elevator and down the hall, into her room and warm sheets. Suddenly I want to hold my sick girl more than anything, and I begin to whimper.

Dirk is nervous, saying, "Shh, wait, sometimes the door jams, remember?" He reaches over me and rolls down the window.

"Fuck," I say.

He gently nudges my thigh.

"No," I tell him.

"It's easy," he says.

"I'm not climbing out that window," I say stubbornly.

"Come on," he says.

"I can't, I don't . . ."

"I'm sorry—about the door, I mean. I wish it worked."

"So do I."

"When it's just me—I climb in, I climb out—sometimes I use the window without even checking the damn door. You can do it."

"Don't tell me what I can and can't do." I am crying now and shaking my head.

"It's okay."

"It's not. It's too damn much."

"I won't look," he says. "I'll face the building across the street. Pretend that you're alone," he says.

"I *am* alone," I say.

"I'll cover my eyes. See?" he says through open fingers.

I make him turn around. I make him promise. I make him keep his hands in front of his face, those fingers closed, and then I take a deep breath and hoist my leg, one black boot, then the other, moving my hips and torso and shoulders and head out of the car window and into the night, making my way back to her.

A Girl Becomes
a Comma Like That

1.

It was a Saturday morning in early December, and I was deciding exactly what it was that I wanted. I wanted my mother healthy and I wanted a husband or at least a boyfriend or at least a dinner date for Friday night. Right now, though, I was in bed with one more man I barely knew. He was sleeping and I was wondering how to get out of bed without waking him. The two of us were on our sides, his soft crotch up against my back. I faced the wall. His arms were wrapped around my body, his fingers intertwined, locked under my breasts. It felt good and suffocating at once, the position I was in, and I thought that if this man were my husband he would know when I wanted him like this, bundled around me, and when I didn't. But he wasn't and he didn't.

I was gently picking Rex's fingers apart while making a list in my head, resolutions aimed at changing things. I wasn't waiting for New Year's Day this time because it never worked for me. I knew it wasn't always enough, just deciding what I wanted; there were necessary steps. And even then, if I took those steps—if I slept only with men who knew my full name, if I signed up for dance classes, if I ate more fruit—even then there was no guarantee I'd get what I wanted, or if I got it, that it would be what I really wanted after all. Also, there were things I could control and things I couldn't. Say, if I was approachable, dressed in denim, tennis shoes, a smile on my face, I might be approached. Then there was my mother's health that I couldn't control, and it didn't matter if I screamed and sobbed and shook in my sheets all night long, if I ran my fingernails across my bare thighs, drawing blood, or if I behaved like other people who loved their mothers, yes, but had healthier perspectives, ones that enabled them to *get on with things*. What I *wanted* didn't decide anything: cancer disappeared or came back on its own.

I was thinking that with a husband or boyfriend or date for Friday night I would have someone to soothe me when she died. Who knows, if I had a husband, I might turn from him with a scowl on my face. Everything he said and did not say in response to my mother's dying might be all wrong. He might run off with Mark and Billy and Darrin to get a beer because my sorrow was too great and ugly, filling every room and cup in the house. He might sit across the table from me, shrug his shoulders and say nothing. He might tear the bread without imagining its effect on my heart. He might try, "She's in a better place, Rachel," or "She's with Jesus," or worse: "God's got a special plan for her." And I might hate him suddenly, asking, "Yeah, what's that? What sort of plan does God have?" And when he mumbled something else, I might wish him dead instead of her. I might barter in my head with that God I don't believe in for my mother's life back: *Take this from me, take that, take my mumbling, bread-tearing idiot and my adjunct jobs, but please let me have her sitting in her blue chair, sewing, let me have her standing in the hall, modeling one of her hand-made dresses.*

But now, I was prying at Rex's fingers, convinced that a husband might make the unbearable a little less so.

Depending on what magazine I opened or what relative I talked to, there were specific things a woman needed to do to deserve a husband: lose weight, balance cucumber slices over her eyes for an hour a day, smile, don't smile too much, keep the number of former lovers she's had to herself, learn to cook a perfect brisket, pretend she's sweeter than she is, less educated, more educated, younger, taller, learn to drive a stick shift, talk during sex, scream during sex, shut up during sex, take him into her mouth because he'll love it, don't take him into her mouth because it's a whorish act, listen and nod, listen and nod, and above all, stop cussing.

"Fuck," I said softly, just now breaking Rex's hands apart and getting free. I turned and looked at him. It was still early, and the sun was coming in a bit at a time, lighting the sheets and half of his face. One half was mashed into the pillow, but the half I could see looked fine, full lips and long girlie eyelashes. Still, he wasn't my future. The reasons were numerous: he lived on another continent, outside London, he had a violent ex-wife, a new girlfriend, there was his baby boy and teenage girl, but mostly, I slept with him after two days, two brief meetings, which was one thing magazines and my relatives agreed on: you shouldn't offer up the dressing unless he buys the salad.

I was still a little drunk from last night's cider and feared my heart was somehow visible, puffed up, obvious and eager inside my chest.

"Coffee?" I said, waking him.

"Yes," he said, groggily. "Is your mum still here?"

"No," I told him.

"Where'd she go? I was hoping to meet her," he said, winking.

"She buys ointment on Saturday mornings."

"For what?"

"The radiation burns her skin."

He frowned.

"Monday they did her shoulder. It'll just now begin to
crack," I said, unable to stop myself.

"Christ," he said. "Jesus," he said.

I stepped out of bed and pulled the sheet with me. I
turned at the door, knotting the sheet at my chest. His dick
was curled and humble on his thigh.

"Your room is chilly," he said, yanking the blanket up and
around his body. He shivered or pretended to.

"What did you expect?"

"I thought Los Angeles would be warm. Isn't it always
warm? Isn't that what you people like best?"

"We're at the beach, remember? It's not always warm."

He smiled. "Did you mention coffee?"

"Right away," I told him, opening the bedroom door,
thinking that I must look like a ghost, wrapped in white, moving down the hall, away from him.

The kitchen tile was cold, sticky in spots where last night we
spilled nightcaps. I understood it was playing house, all of it,
fixing drinks, leaving him in a bedroom I called mine, this
couple stuff, this dressing in sheets. I was on tiptoe at the cupboard, reaching for cups, sugar cubes, imagining him. Perhaps
he turned and stirred now in a bed I didn't even own. Perhaps
he was stretching to the window, parting the blinds, looking at
the sea.

Last night I stifled my sobs into the pillow. I was either grieving or coming lately, the sounds themselves blending into one strange cry. Sometimes I didn't know the difference, how to identify or name my very own bells. I wondered if my mother heard me from her own bedroom, sleeping or trying to, perhaps being jolted awake by the noises I made at night.

Six months earlier I had met this guy at a bar downtown who couldn't have been over twenty. I remembered insisting on his ID before I let him touch my face with his fingers. I was sitting in a booth alone, and he slid up like a snake or cowboy, boots on, smelling like tobacco and mint and musk, a Southern accent—something I thought I hated—but when he said, *Hey girl, hey sad girl,* my knees pulled apart from each other and I began talking myself into him.

He was nervous or drunk, babbling, questions and comments coming at me like bullets: *Let's go. You live around here? I'm from Alabama. Where you from? I got me a horse at home. I ride. You ride? How old are you anyway? You married, engaged, got a boyfriend? Mind if I chew?* I shook my head and he rolled his fat tongue in his mouth, then flipped the dark wad onto a cocktail napkin he held in his palm. "It's mint flavored," he told me. "At first I did cherry, now I do mint. Pretty soon I won't need flavors at all."

"Great," I said.

"What?"

"You're advancing," I said, smiling.

"Let's go," he said.

On the way out the door I stopped him, my hand around his upper arm like a mother's. "Let's be quiet," I said. "Let's not make a mess."

He didn't understand. He was just a boy. "A mess?" he said. "We're not even in bed yet."

"That's right," I said. "Fine," I told the boy.

Sometimes I'd meet a guy and bring him to the beach in front of my mother's apartment building rather than go to his home or risk waking her. I imagined the stretch of sand was mine, and I'd kiss whoever he was, as if I owned it, as if it was where the two of us belonged, outside with the chill and broken bottles, with the cigarette butts and seaweed, the tiny bits of shells, outside, ten stories away from my life. But this one I brought into my mother's home, up the elevator and down the hall, and I knew he was important that way, that after him, there'd be others.

I don't remember the elevator itself, but I must have been in there with him, four walls, mirrors, harsh light, the terrible sounds it made then, struggling up to the tenth floor. Perhaps he said, "Your elevator needs fixing," or maybe he just sighed. Perhaps he couldn't look at me. Perhaps his palms were on my hips and he stared hard into my eyes. Maybe I wanted to do it right there and he had to convince me to wait. Perhaps I wanted to be standing up, stuck between floors like bad luck or an accident. Perhaps he said, "Hey girl, hey sad girl, I need a bed to get this right."

I do remember laughing in the living room, my sandals hanging from two curled fingers. Then I was leading the way. He kissed me while I led, his lips cemented to my own. We were two sick twins, connected at the mouth like that, drunk in my mother's apartment at two in the morning. My back was against my bedroom door and he was slipping a palm into my skirt when I heard my mother's voice. "Rachel, what are you doing? Who's with you?" she wanted to know. And her voice was deep, masculine, guttural, thick with sleep and chemo, worry or anger, and he said, "Hey, come on, I didn't know you were married, you didn't tell me you were married, I asked you at the bar and you didn't say a thing."

I laughed, his thinking my mother was a man, my husband. I opened my mouth to set him straight, to tell him the voice was my mother's and that my mother was sick, but what came out was, "He's not my husband. He's just a friend."

He was shaking his head, voicing his reluctance. "I don't know," he said. "I don't like this. Are you a liar?" he asked.

I rolled my eyes. "Come on," I said.

"Are you a liar?" he repeated. "Maybe you're a freak, one of those girls who brings a guy home just to make her husband jealous. I've heard about girls like you. Things get rough at home, you don't like the way he looked at you over dinner or something, and you head to the neighborhood bar to bring back the competition—is that what I am, the competition?" He was pointing at his chest now, backing away.

"That doesn't make sense," I said.

"Oh yeah?"

"Yeah," I said. "I wouldn't bring you here if I was married."

"I'm not so sure," he said.

"I wouldn't need you," I said softly, almost to myself.

"I don't know," he said. "You chicks get weird. Who knows how weird you could get."

"That might be true, about being weird," I said. "You might have a very good point there," I told him.

I left my mother's competition in the hall and went to wash my face. When I returned, he was gone, vanished. It was as if he flew away, and I remember imagining him doing just that, growing wings and flying off. The front door was open, cool air from the building's hallway filling the living room. It was the middle of the night and I was drunk still, my panties damp with wanting, my mouth still buzzing from his minty tobacco.

In the morning, about the flying guy, my mother tried to stay quiet. Outside on the balcony, she was sitting in a plastic chair, wearing a floral robe and a pink scarf on her head. A wig sat in her lap, the morning paper spread out on top of the wig, red hairs fanning out behind the news. I was pacing the living room, hung over, sweaty and shy and guilty. I was looking at my mother. Every now and then she glanced up at me and smiled.

"*What?*" I finally said.

"You're a grown-up," she said.

"And?"

"I was just thinking about nature and what you need."

"Don't start," I said.

"Still," she said, "you need—"

I cut her off. "It won't happen again," I lied.

"You're thirty. Of course you need *connection*."

"Please," I said. "It's too early for this. I'm going to make eggs now. Do you want a couple fried eggs?" I asked my mother.

She lifted the newspaper from her lap and shook it out, pretending to read.

I tried again. "Are you hungry?"

My mother shook her head. She folded the newspaper up and rested it on her swollen belly. "I was young once," she said. "I was healthy. Remember when I used to visit you in that apartment on Belmont Street?"

"They weren't really *visits*," I said.

21

"I visited you," she insisted. "I came by every Friday."

"You came by, yes."

"That's not a visit? What's a visit?"

"You wouldn't put your purse down," I said. "You walked from room to room and the damn thing swung from your shoulder."

"I had things to do, people to see."

"That boyfriend in Anaheim."

"That's right," she said, smiling, obviously reminiscing. "The podiatrist who loved Disneyland—talked about specific rides the way other people talk about movies or books. 'The Pirates of the Caribbean, now that's a ride,'" she said.

"You saw a lot of the park that summer."

"I did."

"You complained that it was all he talked about."

"Russell talked about feet, too. Thought mine were especially healthy, not a bunion or corn anywhere, no dry skin, clear nails. He was very happy with my feet," she said.

"I'm hungry. I'm going to cook something," I said, but instead of turning around, I stood there, looking at her.

My mother picked up the wig. She spun the wig on two fingers. "Remember those toys that spun around?"

"Tops," I said.

"You liked the wooden ones. If I brought home plastic, you'd scream. You were picky. You were so very picky," she said.

And the word "picky" stayed with me even after I turned away from her and went to the kitchen. I was standing at the stove, watching the eggs bubble in the frying pan. I was thinking that a picky child does not necessarily grow into a picky adolescent, does not necessarily become a picky adult. She might move from boy to boy, from dark backseat to dark bar,

from drowsy man to drowsy man. "Picky," I said softly, deciding I'd write a poem later about last night's mess, about the
flying boy and his minty chew. I picked up the saltshaker and
tipped it this way and that, watching the grains fall through
the air.

I was over thirty years old, living with my mother because
she was sick and because I was poor. It was an exchange. It was
love, yes, but need was a part of it too. I wanted to pretend I
was still an adult, that returning to my mother wasn't an indication I'd gone backwards: thumb sucking, dependency,
crawling, fear, and breast milk.

Later, while I showered, my mother stood at the bathroom
sink, pulling an extra toothbrush from a shopping bag. She
punctured the package with a fingernail and tossed the wrapper into the trash. She slipped the toothbrush into the ceram-
ic holder shaped like a hand. I could see my mother through
the clear curtain, giving the brush a slot. "For guests," she
shouted. "In case a good one stays."

Her comment startled me and I nicked my calf. I slammed
the razor down on the edge of the tub and looked out at her
from behind the shower curtain. "*Mom,*" I said, in the same
exasperated tone I'd used on her as a teenager. "Get out of
here."

My calf bled and bled. The cut was tiny, but deep. I
propped my foot up on the closed toilet and stopped the
bleeding with tissue and pressure. I placed a Band-Aid on the
cut, wrapped a towel around myself, and sat down on the edge
of the tub, staring at the new toothbrush. My mother had
placed it in the thumb slot, while our own brushes occupied
the pinkie and ring finger. It was blue, a boy's color, big and
clean, with uneven bristles, better quality, more expensive, I
could tell, than either of ours. I ran my finger over the bristles

and thought about that flying guy and his fake ID, pretending.

I have a problem with my imagination. I might be doing something with someone and I'll be nodding or moving my torso or handing him a beer, but inside my head I am with someone else, doing something else entirely. Like skiing or surfing (which I've never been able to do) or bathing in a claw-foot tub with that husband I don't have. From far away, the husband is unique, an individual, but when I come in close to focus on his features, they are indistinct; he is anyone.

Sometimes I'll be *with* the person I am with, but I'll have scooted the two of us ahead in time so that we are better, tighter friends than we actually are, or longtime lovers, or maybe even on our way down the aisle, although it isn't an ordinary aisle, with sisters and mothers weeping to the left and right, and little girls dressed like grown women with glossy lips and elaborate hair, but an empty room that isn't a church, and my dress is black and tight and low-cut, and my legs are three inches longer than they really are.

Like right then, I was there, but I wasn't, standing at the kitchen counter, wrapped like a mummy, making coffee for Rex. I wanted it strong. It was one of the steps I was going to take, drinking one cup of strong coffee instead of four cups of regular. I'd save time, and perhaps with a little less caffeine I wouldn't be edgy and impatient. The men I met might have a better chance.

While I was scooping the fifth tablespoon of beans from the can, it occurred to me that I hadn't learned one damn thing in seventeen years of fucking. Since that first wrong boy on the bathroom tile took my new nipple between his teeth. I was worried even then about being unlovely, unloved, and on that black-and-white floor of his, everything was slick and cold. Within minutes of my first kiss I was stripped like a squid and knew he didn't care whether I was Carol from third period or Christine from sixth or bad Brittany who didn't even go to school anymore, and something inside me hardened, turned into a chunk of cement.

A girl becomes a comma like that, with wrong boy after wrong boy; she becomes a pause, something quick before the real thing. Even now, I am certain that the light coming from his parents' room was a warning that the sincere lovers of the world existed elsewhere, not where I was, and that it would always be like that, the light on the other side not seeping in enough to illuminate his thin cheeks or the stubble I felt with a curious teenage palm.

We couldn't see each other in that bathroom, and now, making coffee for a man I barely knew in my ailing mother's kitchen, I realized that I was stirred by darkness, bars and rooms and clubs, by movie theaters where my date's hand might rest on my thigh without responsibility, without complete admission—without light. And a man who was traveling interested me *because* he was traveling. I imagined Rex's plane waiting for him right now, the tunnel he'd move through as easily as he moved through me. He'd pull his bags behind him, and the tunnel would fill with people walking too slowly or too quickly, but no one—here's the thing—no one would match his exact stride. The flight staff would look like mannequins, would sound robotic, saying, *Hello, how are you?* and then one starched blonde would point her ridiculously long nail in the direction of his seat before he had the chance to answer, before he had the chance to even wonder how he was.

When the plane landed he'd be across the world from me, and we'd both be relieved. No chance of him interrupting me during a class. No chance of me having to explain who he was, what I was doing, to my students. No chance of me showing up at his studio, where he'd surely be annoyed. Where he'd answer the door with a paintbrush between his teeth, rubbing his palms on his jeans. *What are you doing here?* he'd mumble through the brush. *I mean, really, just what do you think you're doing?* There'd be spots of yellow, green, and blue paint on his T-shirt, splattered everywhere, on his walls, chairs, and doors, on his chin and forehead, those full lips, so that he'd look like just one more painted thing, a piece of furniture or art equipment, but with a face.

Sometimes I went with my mother to the radiation clinic and my imagination worked in another way. I kept my sunglasses on and tried not to look at people. I tried not to smell the Chinese noodles the receptionist was eating. I tried not to notice the few noodles hanging out of the girl's mouth. I tried not to hear the slurp as she brought the noodles inside.

I picked up that kids' magazine *Highlights* and followed the path to the defined words: *delusion, destruction, feline, reiterate, problematic.* I pretended I wasn't thirty, but younger, that my mother wasn't ill at all, that I was there for someone else, someone I loved less—a pushy friend, my slowest cousin, a dull and needy neighbor, and that's about the time my mother would come bouncing out of the double doors, all smiles and bright wig.

When the doctor came out of surgery six weeks ago, I asked him what the cancer looked like, what color it was. He tugged on a bushy eyebrow and looked at me. "What?" he said. "*Why?*"

Four years ago, when he took my mother's first breast and a dozen nodes, I was twenty-six and fell to the floor after he spit out her prognosis. I was a panting heap, wiping my nose with the hem of my skirt. I was drooling and sobbing, an animal. This last time I was someone else, new, in Italian shoes and silk blouse. I looked directly at him. I was curious, wanted to see, wanted a color, a shape, a texture to the disease. "What color is it?" I said again.

"I remember," he said, nodding. "You're the writer, aren't you? Your mother is very proud—" he began.

"Fine," I said, cutting him off. "I just want to know what color it is."

"It's gray," he said.

"Light gray?"

He scowled.

"Pencil lead or lighter?"

"Just gray."

"Cloudy-day gray or like metal?"

"Jesus," he said, tugging on that eyebrow one last time. "Are you okay?"

2.

Rex had interviewed me just four days earlier about my first book of poems. He sat in the leather chair by the window. I sat on the couch. It was tense, sexy. He had me read my poems into a microphone. Rex drank a diet cola, crossed and uncrossed his legs, nodded while I read. From his body language and the small sounds he made in between poems, I knew he preferred the ones that mentioned parts of my body. Even when those poems dealt with cancer and fear, knives and cuts and fate, I sensed they turned him on. It was on his face, his excitement, and at the end of the reading I looked up from my book and caught it.

He blushed then, his already pinkish face going pinker,

and looked out the window at the ocean and bike path below. "Would you look at that?" he said. "Bike riding in December. Half naked in the dead of winter. Families bobbing by in boats. The sun out, not one cloud. Some life you got here, Rachel. Some great life."

"If weather was enough."

"It's beautiful."

"Sometimes it gets monotonous," I tried.

"You don't like the sun?"

"I like the sun, it's not that."

"What then?"

"Sometimes I want to be surprised."

"Surprised?"

"I want to wake up and not know what sort of day it's going to be."

"I don't think you know how lucky you are." He was grinning, shaking his head.

"My friend Angela has allergies," I offered. "She lives here because of her job, but the weather is killing her. She's got welts and hives—they won't go away."

He wasn't listening. He was standing at the window with his glasses on now. He was pressed up against the window, watching. "People on skates," he said.

"Rollerblades," I corrected him.

"Rollerblades, huh? You do that, Rachel? You skate on those things?"

"No."

"Why not?"

I pointed at the red bike in the corner.

"Very good, then." He leaned forward, hitting the button on the recorder.

I got up from the couch and went to the bike. I rang the

little metal bell for him with my thumb. I was thinking about the weather, the envy coming at California from other lands, and I was thinking about my friend Angela, how in early November the hives completely covered the left side of her body, one arm, one leg, one breast, half her neck, one cheek. I was thinking about a few years ago when her lips swelled to ten times their normal size. Her doctor blamed Angela's allergies on the weather, the climate and moisture, the mold and thriving dust mites. I was ringing the bell and thinking about that.

"Wonderful," he said.

"What?"

"Bells are terrific."

I nodded.

"When do you ring it? I mean, on what occasion might you ring it like you are now?"

I looked down at my finger, which was still going at the bell. I wrapped my hand around the handlebars to keep myself from ringing. "When a kid doesn't know he's a kid, when he thinks he's a bike."

"I don't understand." He cocked his head like a puppy.

"One time I was riding by and a couple of little boys were playing jacks. Remember jacks?" I said. "Right on the bike path, two little boys in shorts, sitting there, playing jacks. I rang the bell that morning. My bell made those two jump."

"What else?" he said.

"I rode over a jack and popped a tire. It was awful. Those boys pissed me off."

He was nodding, leaning toward me. I wanted to lean forward too, but felt my body tilting backward, away from Rex. "The bell is like a horn, a warning," I said, suddenly nervous, stating the obvious.

"Of course. Yes," he said.

He kissed my cheek before he left, quickly, awkward in his boots, moving a piece of hair away from his eyes. When the door closed behind him I went to the phone. I called Angela, who had lived in London for a year, with questions.

"How are your hives?" I asked first.

"Everywhere."

"Is the lotion helping at all?"

"I keep scratching it off," she said.

"What are you going to do, Ang?"

"I'm going to get my shot, and maybe I'll move to the desert, somewhere hot and dry. I look awful."

"What about your job?"

"I can't work like this anyway. I'd scare the kids."

"Is it on your face?"

"At my jawline," she said. She paused. "Enough about my allergies," she said. "What's going on with you?"

"That journalist-artist guy just left," I said.

"Oh yeah, how was your interview?"

"He kissed my cheek."

"He kissed you?"

"Just my cheek."

"Still."

"Do they kiss strangers there? In London, I mean."

"Never," she said. "They're cold."

"Not even on the cheek? It was just a peck," I explained. "He leaned down and then—"

"Look," she interrupted, "you're lucky if a Brit kisses you after he fucks you—*before* he fucks you, for that matter. You're lucky if he pats you on the back the morning after, that's how removed and distant they are. You think American men are distant? Goddamn, good luck with this one."

"It was probably nothing," I said.

"Doesn't sound like nothing to me."

"He's a friendly guy, that's all. He's here for a short while, and he wants to make friends."

"Right," Angela said, sarcastically.

"Friendly," I repeated.

"I should know. I fucked a whole bunch of them."

"I remember the stories, Angela."

"They were cute."

"I know."

"Icy and seductive at the same time."

"I'm sure it was meaningless. The kiss," I said.

"And then there's that whole thing about land and territory, ownership and war. It's all about jealousy, rage. We hate each other and are curious as hell." She was talking more to herself now than to me. "I remember one," she continued, "tall, big, hair to his shoulders, and a pierced tongue. Do you know what a skillful man can do with a little gold stud in his mouth?"

"I should go."

"A pierced tongue," she repeated. "I'm telling you, Rachel, there's nothing quite like it. A pierced nipple on a guy is worthless—all about ego. I mean, how's he going to make you shake with a decorated nipple? A tongue, though, is something else altogether. A man who pierces his tongue is a generous king," she said, emphatically.

"I have to go."

"Imagine the pain."

"I'm imagining."

"The sacrifice," she continued.

"I have to go," I tried again.

"How's your mom? Still upbeat? Still cheerful?" she wanted to know.

. . .

Angela was convinced that my mother was in denial, that her smile and good mood was a front, and had suggested to me more than once that I intervene, help her open up and discuss her fears and anger. When I asked my mom about the smiling, the shopping, the continuing to teach through the chemo, she said that Angela was well-meaning but still young, that her hives were one thing, but illness was something else altogether. She looked at me hard and said, "I understand a thing or two about time, and I'm not going to waste it on worry." She'd leave that to me. I did it well, she said. I was an expert.

And she wouldn't waste time in long lines, either, especially in department stores. She'd look at the line, then at me, and I'd shake my head no, *Don't you dare, let's just wait,* and she'd nod yes, and she'd grin, and sometimes she'd even wink, and then she'd start reaching for her wig, and when her hand went up, I'd dart across the store and hide behind a rack of jackets, pretending not to know her.

Sometimes, the people in line were especially stubborn and didn't respond to her lifting the wig up and revealing her smooth forehead, so she'd pull it off completely. She'd stand there, holding the wig at her hip, head shiny, and lean in. She'd whisper that she had cancer, that it had metastasized, and no, she wasn't in a lot of pain yet, but the pain was probably coming, and she didn't have a lot of time, would they mind so much if she moved to the front, she only had this one sweater to buy or this bra or this pretty watch.

On the way home, she'd confide, "I don't know why people let me cut in front of them. It really doesn't *hurt.* When is it supposed to hurt, Rachel?"

And I'd look at my mother's face and try to see it, what it

was, what was happening, and my mother would say, "Don't look at me like that. I'm not going anywhere just yet." And I'd try not to, but it was a hard thing to do, trying not to see what was right there in front of me.

3.

The next night at Ruby's Room I offered Rex up excuses, though he was leaving the country in a matter of days and it wasn't necessary. He didn't think a woman like me, whom he called smart and daring, should be alone. "Why are you still single?" he asked.

"My mom has been sick for four years and she needs all of me," I said. What I should have said was, My mom has been sick for four years and I need all of her.

"Come on."

"It's true. I can't think about anyone but her, about what she's in, and everyone else is small compared to that."

"What about when you're at work?"

"When I'm writing, it's all about her, and when I'm teaching—well, I try to be there for them."

"What about when you're in bed with someone?"

"It's probably about her too." I looked at his face, tried to gauge how far I could go. "That's when I'm most aware of what's happening to her, to both of us."

"You're going to need someone when she goes." He stopped. "I'm sorry," he said.

"It's okay."

"It's not my place . . ."

I lifted the cider to my lips, then looked away from him,

toward the bar. I recognized one of my best students, Ella Bloom, sitting with a young man in a white lab coat. She was stirring a short drink and shaking her head no. She looked angry. The young man was leaning toward Ella, his hand on her knee.

"She's a good writer," I said, gesturing toward the bar with my chin.

"Oh, yeah?"

"I mean, she's a student now, my student, but her poems are strange and wonderful. She writes about young girls a lot. This last poem was about bats, though."

Rex shuddered. "My least favorite creatures on the planet," he said.

I wanted to kiss him then, wanted to tell him I liked him, wanted to promise to always protect him from bats, but we weren't there yet, and I didn't know if we were even on our way. "Remember her name—Ella Bloom," I told him. "Maybe one day you'll be coming back here to interview her." I looked at Rex and wondered how many times he'd visit California.

"It's possible."

"She's newly married. I guess that's her husband there. You think he's a doctor?"

"Too young."

"You're probably right." When I turned to look at them again, Ella and her husband had risen from their stools and were making their way toward us. The anger seemed to have disappeared from her face. "Jack, Dr. Spark. Dr. Spark, Jack," she said, smiling.

"Hi, Jack," I said. "I'm Rachel. And this is Rex. He's visiting from London."

"*Outside* London. I live on a farm in Hampshire," Rex corrected me, leaning over to shake hands with Jack.

"I was just telling Rex here about your poems, Ella. That last one floored me." I turned to Rex. "The one about bats."

Rex grimaced so that only I could see.

Ella's husband looked at her. "You don't show me those poems," he said.

Ella shrugged. "They're not finished yet," she told him.

"They're *my* bats," Jack said. "I study them, I mean."

"Awful," Rex said.

"What was that?" Jack leaned closer to Rex.

"Awesome. I said that's *awesome*." Rex winked at me. There was a long pause.

"Why don't you join us?" I finally said.

Ella's husband shook his head. "I've got to be at the lab early tomorrow. And then after work we've got Christmas shopping to do, right, Ella?"

Ella nodded.

"Your bats are waiting," Rex said.

"That's right, waiting. You could say that." Jack was smiling, sly, like he had a secret.

"Jack works with dead bats," Ella offered.

"Alive or dead, bats freak me out," Rex confessed.

"They've got a bad rap," Jack said. "They're actually quite docile—nothing to be afraid of. They're more afraid of you than you should be of them."

"Rabies is pretty fuckin' scary," Rex said. "Where I'm from, there's lots of . . ."

The cider was hitting me hard, and though I didn't want to be impolite, I really had to pee, so I stood up. "You guys talk," I said. "I'll be right back, okay?" Rex squeezed my hand, mouthed okay, and I told Ella and her husband that it was good to see them and excused myself. I made my way across one room and into the other. I stepped around a dancing circle of young women and the gawking men surrounding them. I spotted Adam, a former boyfriend, standing at the pool table, chalking his stick, so I picked up my pace. I had safely reached the bathroom door when I was surprised to hear Ella's voice in my ear. She was shouting above the music, something bluesy I didn't know the name of. "I like your class," she said.

"You scared me," I said. "I didn't know you were behind me." My bladder was pounding as I held the doorknob.

"I'm not following you," she said, and then laughed. "Well, I guess I am. I mean, I guess I did. I wanted to tell you that your class is everything to me."

"Good. I'm happy you're in there." I glanced over at Adam, who was leaning down now, moving the stick back and forth between his fingers. I heard him break, the triangle of balls rolling apart. "Look, Ella, why don't you two stay and have a drink with us—I've really got to pee, though. Wait right here."

She shook her head. "We're in a fight."

"I'm sorry."

"He's *sorry*," she said.

"Oh," I said, feeling bad for Ella, but also wanting to avoid Adam's seeing me there, and more, feeling as if I was about to burst. I didn't know what to say next, but it didn't matter because her eyes had welled up and she cut me off.

"I've got to go. We've got to go," she said, her eyes spilling over.

"Wait," I said, reaching out to grab her hand, but she'd already turned around and was rushing away from me.

When I returned from the bathroom, Rex was alone at the booth, talking into his recorder. He clicked it off, stuck it in his bag, and made room for me. There were two shots at the table, one in front of my glass and one in front of his. "What's this?" I asked, sitting down.

"A treat." He was grinning. I knew we'd both be drunk very soon. And what the hell. I thought of poor Ella's teary eyes and lifted the shot to my mouth. Rex did the same. "They seem like good people, your student and her boyfriend, but they left rather quickly," he said after we'd downed them.

"*Husband*," I said.

"A little young for that."

"For what?"

"For making up their minds already, don't you think?"

"I don't know."

"It's a big decision."

"Either way," I said, "I don't like him."

"You just met him, Rachel." He was surprised and maybe a little defensive. I got a sense of what our arguments might be like if he lived here and we fell in love. "You're right," I said.

"You can't judge a guy in a couple minutes," he continued.

"You're right," I said again. And then I couldn't stop myself, "Come on, Rex, didn't the bat-guy freak you out?"

He shook his head.

"Just a little bit? Just a tiny little bit?" I held two barely separated fingers between our faces.

He held my fingers, my whole hand, and brought it down to the table, leaving his hand on top of mine. "It's not the people who work with bats or who study them, it's the bats themselves that scare all fuck out of me."

"It's charming," I said, "that you're afraid of them and unafraid to let me know you're afraid. I like that." I was feeling the shot already and letting the words tumble from my mouth.

"Listen, Rachel," he said. "I felt like we were on a first date yesterday." His voice was soft. "I haven't felt like that, inter-viewing poets. It's work, you know. You ask them questions; they tell you what you want to hear. It wasn't like that with you."

"I didn't tell you what you wanted to hear?"

He smiled.

"What part didn't you like?"

"You know what I mean."

I finished the cider with one long swallow and set the glass down. I smiled back at him. Rex looked at my smile, my mouth, then at the glass. "I'm still thirsty," he said. "You?"

"Didn't you say earlier that I was daring?"

He returned from the bar with cider and dark beer and wanted to talk. There were parts of his life back home he wanted me to know about. He mentioned his new girlfriend, his fourteen-year-old daughter who was just now beginning to hate him, who brooded and got tattoos, who pierced her lip and chin and forehead; and his baby boy, Blake—what words he knew, how the boy clung to Rex's shoulder when it rained. He talked about the farm, how he met his new girlfriend, how she was their nearest neighbor, acres and acres away, what fate was, how he didn't know she was a redhead until she removed her funny hat.

I was the kind of woman a man could do that with; he could be honest about whom he loved, that he didn't love me, and still I might let him in. Rex was perceptive. He knew this, I could tell—it was in his gestures. While he talked about his life there, his farm, his girlfriend, he leaned closer and closer to me, hand on my knee, on my thigh. And while he talked about his life there, I listened and moved closer to him as well, letting his hand move up my leg. Still, I pictured the baby, Blake, with horribly pink skin, riding a fat gray pig like a horse. I pictured the girlfriend's red hair spilling out over her thin shoulders when she removed that silly hat, and said, "I'm not capable of much."

He stared into his black beer, the blackest beer I'd ever seen. He smiled with a closed mouth. I looked away and spotted Adam, whom I'd almost forgotten about, leaving by the back door with a woman, and was relieved. Things became blurry then, and I was scooting one of my fingers into the thigh holes Rex had made in his Levi's. "They're bloody expensive where I'm from. I need to buy some while I'm here," he said, and I wanted to nibble those jeans right off of him, right there in the booth, with Brenda Lee or a voice just like hers coming from the speakers behind us, with smoke and dust and cinnamon wafting toward us from the bar, and hot little Christmas lights that kept falling off the edge of the booth, making a tangled mess in my hair.

There was an old woman, a grumpy regular I recognized, leaning against the jukebox. She stumbled over and sat down on the stool Ella had been sitting on. I thought about young Ella and her young husband and wondered if they'd patch things up tonight or if what was happening between them was bigger than just one evening. I wondered if she'd write poems about her troubles or if she'd come by my office to tell me more.

"Check her out," Rex said. The grumpy regular wore a lopsided wig and too much blush, a bitter orange smeared across her lips. She was screaming that her drink wasn't strong enough. "I can't fucking feel it," she said, tugging at the wig with both hands. "I need to feel *something,* damn it. Easy on the orange this time, hard on the rum." She pounded her fist on the bar. "Give a girl what she wants, would you?" she said, loud enough for us to hear.

"It doesn't matter how much she drinks, she'll never feel it," Rex said, leaning into me, gently beginning to untangle the lights from my hair. "She's immune to it. And her wig doesn't fit."

I wanted to tell him about my mother, how she owned a dozen wigs. Red and brown and blonde and black. An unusually thick wig. One made of human hair that didn't wear well, that fell in thin strands across her face after a day outside. I wanted to tell Rex about the synthetic ones, how superior they are, about the two my mother bought in Hollywood on Sunset Boulevard that promised to make her look famous, like Cher or Dolly Parton, and the one that hung down her back, and another that framed her cheeks and fell just below her chin. I wanted to tell him how sometimes, if my mom was in a rush or being picky, trying to match her hair with her dress, she'd scatter the wigs around the apartment. First I'd see several naked Styrofoam heads in my mother's room, on a pillow or on her desk, maybe a couple of heads in the living room, on the coffee table, or face down on the couch. And then, throughout the day, I'd find them—a wig on top of the television, another on a bookshelf, smashed between the dictionary and antique clock, one hanging from a hook next to the spare keys.

I wanted to tell him how one late night I accidentally sat on the Dolly Parton, how I pulled it from behind my back, screaming. I wanted to tell him how funny my mother thought this was, how she fell into my arms laughing.

I wanted to tell him how in the right light an unexpected wig looks like a little dog, asleep.

I wanted to tell him, but I knew from past experience that stories about my mother's illness, even ones meant to amuse, made people cringe and move away from me. So I let him talk about the farm, the miles and miles of dirt and feed, the wide-open spaces, all that air. He was telling me that the clouds at home were thick and heavy and black, how sometimes he was convinced that standing on just the right chair or ladder he would be able to touch one. He lifted the beer to his mouth and finished it off. He licked those lips of his again. He gave up on the lights a moment, set them on the ledge behind my head, so that they were still with me, but not as intricately. I could move, but still with an irritating sense of being attached to something.

"Do you like animals?" he asked, picking up the lights again.

I was trying not to panic, but the lights were warm against my scalp and the fake holly was sharp. "No," I said. "I don't."

"That's too bad," he told me. "They're wonderful. *She* needs a pet." He jutted his chin in the old woman's direction, since now both hands were occupied, busy in my hair.

"She comes here all the time. And she has a pet," I continued. "Her moody poodle is probably outside right now chained to a streetlight."

"Moody poodle, huh?"

"Yes, the dog's moody."

"That's great," he said. "I like that. Moody poodle," he repeated.

"That dog's a beast," I told him. "It snaps at anything that breathes. I hate that damn dog."

"Most people like animals," he said.

"Maybe some of them are just pretending."

"Why would they do that?"

"They want to communicate compassion," I said.

He shook his head.

"It's true—think about a girl leaning down to pet a kitten and what that gesture does to your heart. Maybe it's the heart people are after."

"She likes the kitten," he disagreed.

"Maybe the girl wants you to notice her heart, so she's pretending to have something inside it."

"Sometimes gestures are genuine."

"*Sometimes,*" I said.

"I don't want you to think that because I have a girlfriend at home, I don't like you," he said, suddenly.

"What?"

"Even though I got a girlfriend—" he began.

"A girlfriend isn't a wife. She's not your wife, right?"

"She's not my wife."

"That's fine," I said.

"I like her, though. I want you to know that. I don't want to lie to you, Rachel."

"You don't even live here."

"I know. I'm just saying that even though I have a woman at home, my gestures here with you are genuine. I like you and—"

"Look, Rex," I interrupted, "I'm not thinking about it, about her."

"Because sometimes you accept your lot in life, that's all I'm saying."

"Good," I said, not knowing exactly what it was he meant. "Whatever, Rex. I'm not thinking about your lot."

"And sometimes you're lucky enough . . ." He stopped then, was quiet a moment, working hard at the lights. "There," he said finally, "you're free."

"Great." I was exasperated. I tossed my hair because I could.

He kissed me then, his tongue inside my mouth. He tasted bitter from the beer, sweet and spicy from the schnapps, and my lips began to tingle. When the kiss ended, he took my face in his hands. "What happened when she followed you to the bathroom? Did the bat-guy hurt your student?" he wanted to know.

"She left me there," I said. "She was crying and I didn't go after her. I should have gone after her," I told him, leaning into him, leaning in for one more kiss.

4.

Yes, a condom might have saved my life, but latex over a particular penis made it any penis, and the act of wearing one was, at this particular time, like pantyhose over a face, every pore or wrinkle or distinct characteristic smoothed over until he was anyone or everyone—pizza man or Southerner, any man who came before him.

I fucked Rex once without protection because of flesh.

I fucked him without concern for my cycle or eggs or safety.

It was the night as much as anything. It was the particular darkness, my mother's heavy breath in the next room, the damn waves again and again, the sea moving into my bedroom and sheets, and it was Rex and all I wanted to see and feel that was his.

I risked everything—pregnancy and illness—because of skin.

"Let's not wake her," I said.

"You're over thirty and you live with your mum." It was a statement, not a question.

"She's sick," I reminded him. "Piece by piece."

"Piece by piece, what's that mean?"

"Like a turkey." I made a carving motion with an extended index finger.

"That's gruesome." He shook his head.

"Leg, thigh, breast."

"Stop it, Rachel."

"Neck," I continued.

"Don't," he pleaded.

"Hip," I said, quietly, almost to myself.

"You shouldn't talk about it, about her, like that. Are you drunk? Is that what's wrong with you?"

I laughed. "There's plenty wrong with me."

"Like what?"

"The list is long."

"Anything I can catch?"

"No," I told him. "I'm drunk, that's what's wrong with me, Rex. Too much cider, no dinner."

"I'm sorry about your mum. Come here." He was sitting on the edge of the bed in just his white briefs. He had a decent body, a natural body, the body of a man that didn't exercise—a bit of belly fell over the elastic. He curled his finger. "Come here," he said again.

I moved toward him.

"Let's not talk." He put his hands out. "Let me touch those hips of yours. Let's not say a word," he said.

Neither of us mentioned a condom. It was the first time I'd been unsafe in years; it was the first time I didn't insist. I could have blamed it on the cider, but I'd been drunk and naked plenty of times and still pulled one from my bag or bra or drawer. I could have blamed it on his accent or the fact that they'd recently found a chunk of cancer in my mother's shoulder, but several of my men had accents, and they'd been finding gray chunk after gray chunk for the last two years, yet I'd always been cautious.

Lately I was bold, keeping a handful of condoms in a candy dish on my nightstand. And I was slick and skillful too, positioning myself on top of whoever he was, and while he was busy with my breasts, I'd reach down and pluck one up. When he was really going, mouth and hands at once, I'd lift the foil package to my mouth and rip it open with my teeth. "Here," I'd say then, "if you want me, dress it up." And he'd be surprised, but hard already and agreeable, and what was most amazing to me was that he wouldn't even have noticed my preparation. He wouldn't even have seen me. He'd be staring at the condom as if it was magic, as if it appeared out of nowhere, as if I pulled it from behind his ear or out of a hat, so focused he'd have been with his whole face, every bit of him, mashed against my torso.

One of them was stubborn and did refuse. I'd met him at Angela's birthday party in September. I was sitting with my friend Claire at the dining room table when he walked up. He introduced himself as Johnny. He was from Argentina or Colombia—I couldn't remember which—and mispronounced my name, butchered it, in fact, like he did the sloppy hogs back home. His English wasn't perfect, but early in the evening he'd tried hard, wanting to communicate. He looked determined, face scrunched up, lips tight, fingers rubbing together, reaching for words.

Angela winked at me, pulled on Claire's sleeve, and when that didn't work, bent down and whispered something in Claire's ear. "Oh," Claire said, springing from her chair, leaving the two of us alone at the table.

I looked down at my lap and caught myself twiddling my thumbs. It was ridiculous, something I didn't know I did. I stopped myself mid-twiddle and made a plan in my head about how I might hold my body in the future. I thought about deliberate movement, gesture. I crossed my legs. I looked into Johnny's eyes for several tense seconds before turning away.

He leaned forward, elbows on his knees, and rubbed his palms together; he was struggling with nouns and verbs and adjectives, and I was charmed or horny or drunk on champagne, leaning forward myself, nodding, patient.

Meat was important for his family's survival, Johnny wanted me to know. He killed those animals without guilt or shame, in front of his two small nieces, younger brother, and sometimes in front of their friends. He didn't understand what he called California "vegenarians"—people who didn't eat meat. Was I one of them? he wanted to know.

I pointed at the chicken wing that sat in front of me on a paper plate. "No," I told him.

Angela's half-eaten birthday cake sat in the middle of the table, as did a dozen empty beer bottles, several unopened bottles of wine, and messy plates. Standing on one of the plates was a plastic fork, balanced on its end in the thick, creamy frosting, its lipstick-stained prongs straight up, nearly pointing at my face.

"Is that yours?" he said, looking at the fork.

"No."

"Are you sure?"

"Why would I stick my fork—" I began.

He pointed at the lipstick on the prongs, then at my own lips.

"Not even close." I backed up, smiling.

"I think yes."

"That's bright pink," I insisted. "I'm not wearing pink. I never wear pink. Do I look like a woman who would wear bright pink?" I said, catching myself, immediately regretting the coy question.

He looked at me closely, examined my hair and nails. He pulled on his chin, then refilled my glass. "Paint is paint," he said.

I stuck the creamy end of one of Angela's birthday candles into my mouth. It was sweet, horribly so. I pulled the candle from my lips, providing proof, a ring of my own dark shade on the waxy stick. "See," I said, "wrong color."

Later, in bed, he was calling me Rapel. Each time I corrected him, his pronunciation got worse. "That's like *repellent*," I said, "when two things, when two people, oh never mind," I said. "My name is Rachel," I told him, still drunk, thinking that maybe I *was* repellent or he was or we both were. I wanted to be a different woman, a woman who made better choices, and yet there I was on his bed, slipping off my shoes.

"Rapel," he repeated, pulling at my skirt.

I twisted around, faced him. "Listen, it's Rachel." I said my name slowly, deliberately, three damn times. I isolated the sounds in the middle of my name and looked at him, making those sounds again and again, because suddenly, sitting in his dusty, closet-sized studio, my skirt half on and half off, my blouse in a silk pile at my bare feet, one bra strap over my shoulder, it was terribly important that he pronounce my name correctly.

"Rasel," he tried.

"No." I pulled the bra strap up and tightened it. It snapped against my shoulder and made a sound.

"Rapel," he said for the last time, his face in my hair, and he said it firmly, definitively, in a tone that suggested that *he* was correcting *me*.

"It's my name. I know what my name is," I told him, giving up.

He wore all silk: black silk pants, a red silk shirt, even a silk band holding his hair back in a ponytail. It made me uncomfortable, all that silk on a man. He left the shirt on while we kissed, and I tried to hold onto his back, then shoulder, but the shirt slipped from between my fingers. His black hair spilled out, rested on the red collar.

When I went to unbutton the shirt, he pulled his chest away. "Hair doesn't bother me," I said. "Don't be shy," I told him, letting my hand fall from the bed, reaching into my purse. "Hairy or smooth, it's all the same to me." I handed him the condom then, and he shook his head.

"No," he said, grimacing.

"Yes."

"I don't like costumes."

"Costumes?"

"I won't cover it up."

I closed my legs like a pair of scissors. "Forget it, then."

He positioned himself on top of me, still in that gory shirt, and pushed my breasts together like an accordion. He propped his long, oddly thin, uncircumcised penis between them. I'd been with other uncircumcised men before, but Johnny had more foreskin than I'd ever seen. His penis looked like a skinny man with a hat on, all that extra skin like a stock-

48

ing cap, I thought—a bony boy bundled up as if he was heading into the snow.

Johnny was mesmerized, no longer interested in my thighs or neck but with my breasts alone, as if the two of them were detached from my body, something separate, as if they weren't quite mine and I wasn't quite me—the me he'd grown tired of already, the me who insisted on costumes, the me who twiddled her thumbs, the me who didn't know her own damn name.

He moved and moved, grunting, making friction, that hooded penis burning my skin. He went on and on, full of stamina and liquor, determined as he had been earlier about words, communication. It seemed it would never end. It seemed I would spend the rest of my life in just that position. He talked to me in low tones, in a language I didn't recognize. The act didn't make sense, and while he moved and groaned, I remember thinking: *Do you know you're not inside anyone?*

I read somewhere that when a man comes he gives up only one teaspoon of semen. With Rex I thought of sugar, the amount I dropped in a cup of tea. I wondered if my perception was off, or maybe, because it had been so long since I allowed it, my memories about quantity were skewed, or maybe the article I remembered reading was wrong.

Whatever it was, it seemed to me that Rex had come and come and come, wouldn't stop coming, kissed my ears and cheek, filling me up with cups and cups of himself. I wondered how he could have kept so much of anything inside him. Afterwards, I wondered how he could move and toss and breathe like he was fine, not suddenly missing something.

Immediately, I wanted him to leave—not because I didn't

like him, but because I did. And it was inevitable, his leaving. I wanted it over with now, the ridiculous kiss good-bye, the stiff wave, the back of his denim jacket. I was stuffed, my insides hot and full, and thought I might explode, right there, in my sheets, with a man I might have known if I'd had time, a chance, and since I didn't have either, I wished he'd just vanish. "Shit," I said. "What did we do?"

"What did we *do?*" He touched my shoulder, pulled me to him, so that my back rested against his chest. "I'll tell you what we did," he whispered.

His breath was hot on my neck. I wished he lived here.

"That's okay," I said. "I remember," I told him.

In the morning, we sat on the balcony, drinking coffee, looking out at the patio below, where handymen were setting up lounge chairs and tables, two guys in the corner putting together a gas grill. "I witnessed a suicide a few years ago," I said. "I was sitting right here and a girl fell from the sky."

Rex shuddered. "You saw her hit the ground?"

I nodded.

"Poor you," he said.

"Poor *her*," I said.

He put the cup down on the table, leaned forward, and reached for the sheet still wrapped around my body. I shook his hand away and we were quiet for several minutes. Finally, I asked about his farm. He told me about his favorite cows, how every one of them had a name: Bess and Bob and Tina and Janet, Buddy and Sid and Sally. He described their pretty spots, touching his own torso like a map. Here and here and here, he said. He wanted me to see. Cows weren't dumb. It was a myth, a lie, something said to make butchers feel better.

Anyone that raised cows knew they weren't dumb. I would love them, he was sure, Buddy and Sid, their antics. Those two would change my mind about animals. I'd love his farm, his baby boy, the black sky that framed his home. I'd even love her, his new girlfriend. She was a redhead, did he tell me that earlier? I was nodding, pretending to listen, but thinking about my mother.

"What's wrong?" he said.

"Nothing."

"Come on."

I leaned closer to him and touched his arm.

"What's on your mind?"

"You," I said, smiling. But really, I wasn't thinking about him at all. I had said my good-byes to him inside my head and was now thinking about my mother, how she often headed to Fabric King after a trip to the drugstore, how she was probably standing there now, touching assorted fabrics, deciding.

After the mastectomy, as soon as her arm was working again, my mother started making dresses. Without a machine, without a pattern—by hand. She went to the fabric store once a week at least, and bought yards and yards of various prints. And black, she brought back plenty of black for me.

The only thing my mom had to do was take a good, long look at my friends' asses and she knew exactly what sizes they were. She said, "Honey, both of your best friends are small, but their asses aren't. The three of you are *shapely*," she told me. And then she laid the fabric over her bed and cut a dress out in the shape of one of them. "It's healthy," she told me, "your shapely asses." She said their names out loud: Angela and Claire. "You'll never be alone," she said.

She sat either in the chair by the window or on the couch,

with or without a wig, and opened the sewing box. Then she sewed. She watched *Jeopardy,* then *Seinfeld,* and kept sewing.

She didn't do buttons or zippers, so she was limited in style and fabric texture. "It has to be durable, flexible," she explained, pulling the needle from her mouth. "The body is in charge," she told me.

Last weekend I opened my mother's closet, and there wasn't one store-bought piece of clothing. She'd given it all away. The closet was full, hundreds of her dresses hanging up—stripes and plaids and dots and flowers, summer pastels and earth tones, winter greens and dark browns.

On Sunday my mother stood in the hallway, pulling a bright red number over her bald head, working the stretchy fabric over her shoulders. And she was beautiful, at the edge of everything, standing on that cliff in our hallway, working the vivid dress over her still-sexy thighs.

I wanted to tell Rex about my mother's thighs, about where she was now, Fabric King, but more than that, I wanted to be sitting at the table with a man who knew me well enough to understand all of it. I wanted to tell him, but I was looking at his face and hands, and his hands were reaching for a second time between my legs, and the sheet was falling, and I didn't think he wanted to hear anything like that just then.

5.

At night in bed, I listened for her. I fought sleep, waiting until my mother's breathing was audible before I let myself fall.

I went backwards in time, remembering when my mother was healthy, busy with men of her own, busy with travel and plans. I'd just moved into my apartment on Belmont Street, and the bookshelves were built-in and the ceilings were high. My mother was in her late forties, with a new boyfriend, new hair color, and a fancy pair of sandals. It was 1990, and she was standing in my living room but couldn't stay long. She refused to put down her purse, a black leather bag that swung from her hip with each turn. She moved down the hall. She moved into this room, into that room, into the tiny kitchen that smelled of ammonia and flowers, and finally into the bedroom, where I wouldn't love any one of them, where the mattress, still in plastic, leaned like a crutch against the wall.

My mother was a woman who couldn't stay long, but she knew how to love a man. "I can't stay long. Did I tell you that?"

I nodded.

"Look, new shoes, did I show you my new shoes?"

"Nice," I said.

"Russell loves my feet. Do you like Russell?"

"He's fine, Mom."

"Do you think Russell is good for me?"

I couldn't tell the truth about anything, and it would take me months to unpack. There would be skirts and sweaters and dishes that I'd ignore, and there would be men and boys piling like dust into the corners of that new apartment, and then later, much later, there would be her lump and denial, and more denial, and then finally a diagnosis.

I wanted every minute with my busy mother, a woman who couldn't sit still with me. She wasn't looking at my built-in bookcases or high ceilings, couldn't focus on anything but the man who would soon be waiting for her at Disneyland. Dr. Russell Bell would be standing in front of the Haunted Mansion and had promised her a horse-drawn streetcar ride.

Did I think he'd like her sandals? she wanted to know, pointing one pretty foot my way.

Sometimes I skipped ahead and my mother was gone. I was living alone in her apartment. I was on the couch with a glass of wine, telling some man without a face all about her. He was bored, reaching for his gin and tonic. He scratched his arm. He nodded. *Sorry,* he said, unconvincingly. *A dozen wigs?* he said. *Handmade dresses? No pattern? You're kidding me, right?* He put his drink on the coffee table, a hand on my thigh. *Didn't know cancer could wrap around a person's heart— you making this shit up?* he wanted to know.

In bed I thought about the men who'd passed through me. I thought about the most recent one first, and then tried to remember the others. I tried to see their faces, their skin and teeth, but it was impossible, their features blurring into something vague. They became what they did for a living: artist, pizza man, teacher, baseball player.

Just before sleep, that moment when I wasn't sure what was real and what wasn't, they became their uniforms or props, suspended in the air above my head, twirling around like a baby's mobile: brush and oil paints, a chef's hat, a bat and mitt, an eraser.

Sometimes I imagined my own breasts were lost and I was searching for them. I knew them then for what they were: sneaky, independent, two pale liars.

People told me that when a loved one dies, he or she is never forgotten. Other people said that forgetting what a dead person's face looked like was part of the healing process. Some said that my life would never be the same, while others insisted that eventually, after a thousand cups of coffee and days at work, I would wake up one morning and not feel pulled into the carpet.

It was one A.M. when I got up out of bed and went to her room. I looked at my mother, her nose and lips. Her face was shaped like a perfect heart. I watched her body fall and rise. I listened. I leaned down and touched her skull, the fuzz there like a boy's new chin.

"Is he here again?" she asked, her eyes still closed.

"Who?"

"The man you were with last week."

"No," I told her.

"Rex, right?"

"Yes," I said.

"Rex," she repeated. "Where is he?"

"He's gone."

"He can stay here," she mumbled, "if you like him."

"I like him."

"Where is he?" she said again.

"He's on a farm now, with a redhead."

"Farms are dirty," she told me. "You don't want to be on a farm, honey." My mother turned on her side then, away from me, so that I no longer saw her face. She pulled the blanket around her body, up and over her head so that I saw none of her, not the smallest piece of flesh.

Ella Bloom

1999–2000

The Clinic That Ella Built

1.

This was where Ella talked to the girls who came to her, itching and burning and foul. This was where they stood, thirteen and pregnant, twelve and misinformed, thirty and oh so sorry.

She was a hand attached to a clipboard coming at Georgia Carter from inside a tiny window. Ella was nails and cuticles, knuckles and a white gold wedding band. This was where Georgia signed her name on a dotted line, so quickly that the signature could have been anyone's. From behind the glass Ella looked at the girl's messy, flippant cursive and shook her head.

"What?" Georgia said, sliding the clipboard Ella's way. There was a pen connected to it on a chain and a sticky note she'd placed on the paper. "Something wrong?" Georgia wanted to know.

The note said: *Make sure it's you, Ella. You know what I mean.*

Ella knew what she meant. She meant she would not answer questions for the others. It meant it better be Ella inquiring, sitting on the stool across from her, or Georgia was out of there.

Ella put the note into the pocket of her white jacket and slid the window closed. She nodded yes to Georgia's request, but still the girl stood there looking at the window and at Ella's face behind it as if she wanted more, as if Ella had something else to give her. Georgia's expression was one of expectation and disappointment, and on the days she visited, Ella couldn't help wondering about the girl's life, about what went on when she was somewhere else. Finally, Georgia was shrugging and turning her back, walking toward the plastic couches and coffee tables, the magazines and mute TVs.

Georgia was famous at the clinic, returning month after month with various problems. Syphilis in February, condyloma in April, and then, in August, the first of three unwanted pregnancies. The first one was immaculate, she explained. "I haven't been with a boy in months," she said, straight-faced, looking right at Ella.

"Then it's a miracle," Ella said.

"It *is*," she said, adamant, her voice rising.

"Hasn't happened since Mary," Ella continued.

"Mary?"

"The Virgin."

Georgia shrugged.

"A miracle," Ella repeated.

"You wouldn't know a miracle if it kicked your ass."

"You've got that saying wrong."

"So what?"

"It's '*bit you* in the ass,' Georgia. You wouldn't know a miracle if it *bit you* in the ass."

"Whatever," she said.

This was the stool where Georgia sat and squirmed, where

she smacked her minty gum, where she sighed and swore and rolled her eyes. This was the cubicle where Ella leaned in and asked Georgia questions about boys, about precaution, about recklessness and sandals, about movies, instinct, and regret. This was where Ella leaned back and took notes. This was where she tapped her pen on her knee and stared right back at the girl.

And here in the front of the clinic was where Ella's husband of six months waited for her to finish up. These were the afternoons when Jack's research for the day was complete, when his boss sent him away from the laboratory. "Go," his boss said, "you've just gotten married."

Jack was a scientist who studied bats: the Fruit, Long-tongued, and Ghost-faced. He spent mornings just inches from their hairy faces, pinning their leathery wings to corkboards. He attached tiny clips to their eyes to keep them open. "That's gruesome," Ella told him. "They're dead," he reminded her.

Ella believed that while Jack sat on the couch in the clinic waiting room, flipping through the magazines he settled for— *People* and *Glamour, Modern Teen* and *Bride*—the bats were still on his mind.

This was Ella's coworker, Sarah, who was good with numbers, who was tall and lean and busty, who walked with a swish. This was where she stood at closing: behind the counter, just feet from Ella's husband. This was the adding machine on a low table in front of her, perfectly level with her crotch. And this was Sarah punching those numbers with manicured nails, tallying those numbers, while Ella, a matriculating English major with a disdain for math, stood in the back of the clinic, her designated space, in yellow gloves and ridiculous rubber jacket, dunking the day's speculums into the hottest water, water so hot that the steam lifting from it had, on more than one occasion, melted her mascara—her eyes stuck shut then.

Sometimes, at closing, Sarah wore her white jacket, but more often than not the jacket hung on a chair beside her. Then, with her cocky posture and attitude, her full, high breasts would make themselves known in a sweater or T-shirt or low-cut blouse. Often the little radio to her right was turned down low, blues or jazz coming from it. Sometimes, she ate peanuts from a glass dish. Sometimes, a candy bar, still in its wrapper, half eaten, sat by her side. Maybe a can of soda.

Ella wanted to believe that her husband, at least those first few afternoons, deliberately avoided the view; she saw him in her mind's eye holding the magazine in front of his face for protection. She told herself that from across the room he couldn't hear the music and that the smell of peanuts wafting from Sarah's space must have turned him off. Unfortunately, this vision of a reluctant, loyal Jack was most likely optimism on Ella's part. More likely the blues or jazz crooning from the little radio and the sight of Sarah working and lifting things to her mouth was immediately too much for him, and the clinic filled with tension and innuendo. Most likely Jack peered over the pages of that magazine, rapt.

Ella imagined that every so often Sarah looked up at her husband from the day's business and smiled. She imagined that Jack returned the smile and did a little something with his eyes. She understood that a man and a woman smiling like that through September and October and November were probably making mutual plans, plans that ripened with every grin.

This was the clinic hallway. This was the dirty floor, which would later be mopped with the harshest cleanser. To the left was the locked cabinet full of blood. Vials lined up like spices, needles and cotton balls, ointment and swabs. On the wall hung a stethoscope, a clipboard, and a bad picture of a sunflower. On the counter a roll of condoms and a rubber breast. It was one of Ella's many jobs to teach the girls to find the cancer. It's like a little stone, a tiny rock, it's like a pea made out of lead. "Here, right here," she said, letting the pads of her fingertips point out what one day might threaten them both.

This was where Ella took off the yellow gloves and let them drop into a bin before moving, hip first, through the double doors. This was the first Monday in December, the day she found peanuts on the floor, the radio full of static, the day she found Jack and Sarah kissing. Sarah, her coworker, who was supposed to be punching numbers, placing her hand inside her husband's black jeans and counting, Ella was sure, his balls. And this was Sarah becoming the number-two woman in Jack's life and inching her way toward number one, and even Ella understood that simple subtraction.

2.

"We're young," Jack said later. They were sitting in his car outside the clinic, and Ella was crying into her hands. It was ninety degrees outside, and though they were standing still, going nowhere, Jack had the engine running and the air-conditioning on. "Turn it off," Ella said, rolling down the window.

"I'm hot," he said weakly.

She looked at the clinic's awning above them. "We're in

the shade, Jack," she said. "Roll down your window and turn off the car."

"Okay," he said.

Two teenagers, a girl and a boy, entered the fast food restaurant to their left, her first, him sheepishly behind. The girl was scowling, throwing up her hands in apparent frustration. "Come on," the boy said. "Wait up," he begged.

It seemed to Ella that everyone was fighting.

"We're twenty-five," Jack said, stating the obvious. "We're young," he said softly.

"How many times has this happened?" she wanted to know.

"This is the first."

"Must be exciting."

"No."

"Tell the truth, Jack. It's exciting and you know it. You're at the beginning of something—imagine the possibilities."

"Ella, please."

"If this isn't exciting, what the hell is? Is marriage exciting? Is sitting and staring at the same woman every single morning for the rest of your life exciting? What were we thinking, getting married like that?"

"About love, I guess."

"You guess?"

"We were thinking about love, Ella."

"I should have figured this out," she said. "Who listens to Billie Holiday while they add up the day's Pap numbers? Who listens to *that* while she's figuring out how much money the day's herpes cases brought in?"

Jack shook his head.

"Her posture and tits—what an idiot I am," she continued. "You've been picking me up for months now, flipping through magazines you don't give a damn about, waiting when you hate to wait."

"I wait."

"You don't wait *well*."

"What's waiting well?"

"Someone who sits or stands patiently. Someone who doesn't have to be occupied or entertained. He doesn't stare at the bitch in the white coat—or without her white coat—that's someone who waits well."

"Stop it, Ella."

She picked up her purse from the floor and searched for tissue. She blew her nose, then stuffed the tissue in the tiny ashtray, which she knew would irritate him. It bloomed out like a white flower. "When do you wait, Jack? Huh? Huh? Answer me." She slapped her thighs with her palms. "When?" she said again.

He stared at the tissue, reached over to stuff it farther inside or pull it out, but seeing her face, changed his mind mid-reach. She stared at his hand, full of indecision, hanging in the air a second before returning to his side. She wondered how much indecision, if any, he'd felt that afternoon before rising from the couch and making his way to Sarah.

"At the movies," he said. "I wait in lines."

"You fidget and squirm and cuss under your breath— that's not waiting."

"At the grocery store," he continued.

"How long does it take you to decide which line is the shortest? How long do you stand there staring, watching the checkers to see which one works the fastest before you decide which line is the best bet?"

"Okay," he said.

"You stand and stare, surveying the situation like a grocery store critic or something."

"Point taken," he said.

But she wasn't finished. "You don't wait well," she said, "and you were trying to fuck some goddamn stranger."

"Ella, no—"

"Let me ask you this," she said, "who made the first move? Did Sarah ask you to come up to the front to help her with something? Did she act helpless or pretend she couldn't add? Because that's her thing, adding. She never read a book in her life, I'm sure, but she's got that adding thing down." She looked at him hard. "What I want to know, Jack, is why you got up from that couch. And what those steps were like for you."

"There was a problem with the calculator and I—"

"What a joke," she said.

"I helped her—"

"You helped her, that's right."

"It was a mistake," he said.

"Why didn't you just stay at the lab with your bats?"

"I wanted to be there when you finished."

"September, October, and November." Ella counted the months on her fingers and shook her head.

"I wanted to give you a ride home," he said.

She looked him up and down, and suddenly he was all evidence. His hair, always short, had grown out, and she noticed the blond curls resting on his collar. The green shirt was new, too, a different look for him, and it matched his green eyes, making them stand out in his face. And the black jeans—he'd lost two inches in his waist, gone from 36s to 34s in the last three months. What was she thinking when she'd asked the salesclerk to ring those up? That he was slimming down for *her?*

He tapped his knuckles on the steering wheel. He squirmed in the seat. "Don't stare at me," he said. "I feel badly enough as it is."

"Bad," she said. "You should feel *bad.*" Still, she kept staring. His new goatee did little to cover his weak chin, and she was glad about that. Let him keep that shit on his face forever, she thought.

They sat without saying anything for a good five minutes. "When I was a kid," he said finally, "I always fought with my dad in the car, my mom too. We'd be taking a road trip or even going to the corner store for milk, and boom, a nasty argument. Now I know why."

Ella didn't respond. She turned away from him and stared out the window at the parking lot, at the black asphalt, not saying a word. She wondered how hot the asphalt was, if it was hot enough to fry an egg. She imagined what it would be like to walk on the asphalt in bare feet, wondered how long she could take it.

"Because there's nowhere to go," he continued.

"You're trapped, Jack," she said to the window.

"That's not what I mean."

She turned and looked at him.

"I don't know what I mean, Ella."

"I know what you mean. You mean that one person is sitting right beside another person, in close proximity, and there's not a lot you can do about it. But that's only when the car's moving, Jack. That's about speed, the freeway, danger."

"Maybe," he said.

"And we're not on the freeway. We're not even on our way to the corner store for milk. Go ahead, unlock the door. Step outside, Jack. We're sitting still," she reminded him.

"I'm not going anywhere."

"Go," she repeated.

"I don't want to."

"The goatee looks stupid, you know? You don't look like a guy who'd have a goatee."

"I'll shave it for you," he said.

"Not for me—don't do anything for me."

"If you don't like it . . ."

"It doesn't look right on your face."

"Okay—it's gone. Tonight I'll get rid of it."

"Suit yourself," she said, reaching for the door handle. "I'm going to take the bus home," she told him.

He leaned toward her. He wrapped his hand around hers and around the handle too, and they stayed there like that, his body almost horizontal, at an angle in front of her, for a good few minutes. Finally, he pried her hand away and placed it, with his, in her lap. "No," he said softly.

She didn't move or struggle. Instead, she let his hand rest on her hand—and she let both of them rest in her lap.

The teenagers, arm in arm now, came out of the restaurant. The boy was smiling, holding a fat, white bag of food. There was a ridiculous skip in his step.

"We're young," Jack said again.

"And married," she said.

"Yes," he said, "that too."

3.

The Monday before she caught Jack and Sarah kissing, Ella spent the evening with her husband watching a documentary he brought home from his work about the Livingstone's Fruit bat. The film was meant to awaken her curiosity. He wanted to entice her into coming to his lab for a visit. It was something she avoided, seeing him with the bats, up close in that environment. *I'm too tired,* she'd say. *Another day,* she'd insist. *I've got an exam to study for, all this paperwork from the clinic to look over.*

It was dusk, and Jack was crouched down on the living room rug in front of the TV and VCR in just his boxers, rewinding the tape. His back was broad and smooth and tan. "I want you to come to the lab this week," he said over his shoulder. "I want you to pick a day and give me one hour. Just one hour, Ella."

"It's a busy week. I've got a final on Thursday," she said.

"I've been there a year already."

"Has it been that long?"

"I want you to meet people—and the bats too," he said, turning, smiling at her.

"They're dead, Jack."

He scowled playfully, then returned to the tape. "I want you to meet the dead bats, then," he said.

"We'll see."

"I've been to *your* work." He pushed the start button, then jumped up and moved to the couch. They sat side by side with a bowl of popcorn between them, watching the film. The lights were off. A vanilla candle was burning on the coffee table. Because there was only one beer left in the refrigerator, they passed the bottle back and forth.

Ella avoided the lab itself, but she loved the facts and was learning them: the bats were endangered, they were mostly black with spots of golden fur, their wingspans could reach up to five or six feet. Males and females looked alike.

As their name implied, they liked fruit—no blood for them, just papaya, pineapple, figs, and avocados. It made them seem nicer somehow, more considerate than other bat species that were out in the night sucking on sleeping goats and cows.

The Livingstone's wings were actually five distinct fingers covered by thin skin. There was a thumb, which had a finger-nail and was used mainly to grip branches, leaves, and fruit. Jack swore to Ella that the bats used their thumbs to hold on to their loved ones. Ella looked down at her own hands, her own fingers, and thought about knuckles, fingertips, and nail polish. She twisted her wedding ring and moved closer to her husband.

"Bats are shy," he said. "And sweet. The rumors aren't true. These here, they don't even want blood."

"I still don't think I can love them," Ella said.

"You don't have to love them," he said. "It would be nice if you were just more interested in what I do."

"I *am* interested," she said.

"You want to learn things from far away," he said. "You don't want to see them for yourself."

"That's not true," she said. "I work at a family planning clinic. I see things up close all the time. Ever see gonorrhea on a slide?"

"No," he said, "but I like to have faces to go with the names you talk about."

"You work with bats, Jack—not people."

"I wish you'd take more of an interest in my work, that's all."

"I know," she said. "And I'm trying. I'm watching this film with you, aren't I?"

He reached into the bowl for a handful of popcorn. "If you want, I'll bring home the film about the Hammerheads in Africa. They're like bar whores."

Ella smiled.

"They're wild," Jack said, chewing and talking at once. "The horny males come from miles around to one specific place, looking for females."

"Like going to Ruby's Room," she said.

Jack nodded. "Then the males do a little wing dance," he said, doing a shimmy and shake on the couch himself.

She laughed. "What about the females?" she wanted to know.

"They fly around, checking out the dudes. When the female finds a guy whose dancing turns her on, the two of them *make friends.*"

"Like Ruby's Room," she said again.

"Then the females go off alone to have their babies."

"Like the girls at the clinic."

He kissed her quickly on the lips before turning back to the screen, where a Livingstone's was spreading out his wings. "Look at that," Jack said. "Would you look at that?"

"I'm looking," she said.

"Amazing," Jack said. "Just look at his thumb."

In bed later, Ella wanted to talk about Georgia Carter. "What's with you and this girl?" Jack wanted to know.

Ella shrugged.

"She gets to you—I can see it in your face," he said.

"You smell like butter and beer," she said, teasing. "That goatee of yours sops up everything."

"You like it though, right? You think it looks good, don't you?" Jack tugged on the goatee and looked at her for approval.

"It looks fine, Jack, but I do sort of miss your face."

"My face is right here," he said.

"Your *whole* face."

He propped a couple pillows against the headboard and leaned back. He folded his hands on his bare stomach. "What's with Georgia now?" Jack asked, giving in.

"She's pregnant," Ella said. "And says it's immaculate."

He laughed.

"It's not funny," she said.

"It's sort of funny, Ella," he said.

"It's not—she looks right at me and says the most ridiculous things."

"She doesn't expect you to believe that."

"I think she might believe it herself."

"Then she's crazy."

"She's not crazy."

"Well, she's a liar, then."

"How can I help her if she lies to me?"

"You can't."

"How can I tell her how to protect herself if she denies that there's a partner?"

"Or *partners.*"

She put her cheek on his chest, and then her palm. She touched the few dark hairs and one tiny mole.

"You can't help all of them," he said, stroking her hair.

"Her mother left—moved to another state. Her brother's

off at college. And there's something wrong with her father," she said.

"You think he touches her?"

"No, no, it's not that," Ella said. "He has some sort of brain injury or illness, like early Alzheimer's."

"How old is she?"

"Sixteen, almost seventeen."

"Old enough to know what she's doing."

Ella shook her head into Jack's chest. "I wish I'd met her years ago. When she was twelve or thirteen, I could have helped her."

"Who knows," he said.

"I could have," she insisted. "Girls like that have to begin somewhere, Jack. Maybe she loved a boy at school, gave it up to him, and he dumped her. Maybe he didn't like her at all, just wanted to get into her pants."

"So she moved on to the whole football team?" His voice was sarcastic.

"Yes, Jack—so she moved on."

"Maybe this Georgia's a free spirit—or plain horny. Some girls are just hornier than others," he said. "You suggest she play safe. That's all you can do."

"There's something about her."

"There's something about *you*," he said, lifting Ella's chin, his lips coming down to meet hers.

4.

Ella had been working at the clinic for nearly five years. She'd seen other counselors and two doctors come and go. She'd watched girls turn into women, and grown women lose so much weight that they turned back into girls. There were unexplained bruises and swollen faces. She listened to what were obviously lies and also to what was so horribly the truth. There were timid girls who were afraid of the boys they left in the waiting room, and there were cocky girls leaning in to confide in Ella about pregnancies: *He thinks it's his, but I don't fucking know whose it is.*

There were forgettable girls clustered together in the waiting room. Girls wanting the pill, tossing their hair or applying lip gloss in unison. Girls who were excited, almost giddy, starting out and wanting to be safe, and there were others who seemed tired already at fifteen, weary, heads bowed, eyes to the floor. Some were shy, while others were bold, brazen, with their cigarettes still glowing at their lips. "Put that out," Ella would scold from behind the window. "Where do you think you are? What are you thinking?" she'd say.

Ella had been hired as a counselor but performed minor medical tasks as well. She took blood pressure, weighed them, and also took blood from their fingers. She'd smear a few drops on a tiny slide and print the girl's name underneath it with a special pen. She'd hold a jerking finger still with two of her own and prick it with a lancet.

"Are you a doctor?" one exceptionally nervous girl asked.

"No." Ella held the tiny razorblade and aimed.

"What are you then?"

"I'm an English major."

"A *what?*" The girl was horrified, trying to pull her finger from Ella's grip.

"I write poems." Ella held tight.

"Poems? Are you kidding?"

"Nope," Ella said, bringing the lancet down, jabbing at the pink pad of the girl's finger.

A week after she was caught kissing Jack, Sarah cornered Ella outside examining room number 2 and said that she'd be leaving the clinic by spring. She'd sworn that she was back with her longtime boyfriend, Eddie, and that he'd asked her to marry him—they'd even set a date. "I have work to do," Ella said, walking away from her.

Their schedules only overlapped on Thursdays, and even then Ella did her best to stay at the opposite end of the clinic— if Sarah was with clients, Ella did inventory. If Sarah was in the counselor's lounge, Ella ate her lunch in the back room. Still, the clinic was small, and it was impossible to avoid her completely.

On a Thursday morning Ella was sitting on the couch in the counselors' lounge, looking at a new girl's chart. Dahona Strickland was thirteen and her complaints were numerous: fever, body aches, weight loss, and a vaginal rash that had spread to her thighs. Ella closed the folder and stood up. She held the chart under her arm and began walking down the hall toward the waiting room. She was wondering about Dahona, thinking about the horrible diseases and their beautiful names: chlamydia, gonorrhea, and condyloma. How melodic the words themselves were, how if she didn't know what they looked like on a slide, they might sound like perfect names for a girl. She was thinking about the next poem she'd write for Rachel's class when Sarah turned the corner. She met Sarah's eyes for the briefest second and Ella decided that she'd call her new poem "Sarah," and she'd use the worst case of herpes she'd ever seen, use that poor Amy Duncan—whose sores were so ripe and so plentiful that she refused to urinate—to describe Sarah's condition. "I'm getting married, Ella. It was a mistake," Sarah said, but Ella was already halfway down the hall, on her way to Dahona Strickland, and pretending not to hear her.

After the incident with Sarah, Jack had started dropping new words into their conversations: *experience, loyalty, monogamy,* and *repetition.* Ella thought of drowning again and again and again, as if you could go underwater and stop breathing more than once. She thought of the girls with swelling bellies who came to the clinic so full of boys who did not love them, so full of boys they couldn't possibly love—or perhaps they could. She thought about Georgia's repetition, one boy and then another, one disease and then a month later its filthy cousin.

Ella had seen girls like Georgia who came to the clinic repeatedly, whose habitual visits remained with her long after they turned their backs and swayed away. And she'd seen girls like Amy Duncan and women like Rachel Spark, who showed up only once and never came back, but were memorable still. They made indelible impressions, and their missed follow-up appointments left black holes in her days.

To the left of the clinic's front door was a bench meant for patients, but often Ella spotted protesters sitting there. Sometimes, Born Again Paula sat for hours at a time. Paula in too much blush and pink lipstick. Paula with a seemingly cheerful ponytail that bounced when she moved or came in too close, talking about Jesus or maybe *to* him, screaming about the innocent unborn. Paula with one shoe on and one shoe off, white pump on the bench beside her. Paula rubbing her bare foot, her blisters and yellow sole.

Paula's favorite poster would be upside-down beside her, leaning against the bench—the stick she held for hours a day, pointing toward the sky, the bloody fetus breach now, upside-down like one of Jack's sleeping bats.

In the mornings Ella scooted past Paula and the others, sipping her coffee and trying not to look at them. More than once Paula called Ella by name, saying, "Ella-the-devil, you're going to hell," and Ella wondered which girl had given her up, betrayed her, and told the woman her name.

The protesters left their Styrofoam coffee cups on the concrete. They left their pamphlets and prayer books on the bench, where the patients could not rest because they, the protesters, were tired of standing and holding their posters high, were tired after hours and hours of saying, "Look at this, think about what you're doing. Who are you off to kill?"

And on that Monday twelve-year-old Amy Duncan, with her fierce case of herpes, pushed past Born Again Paula and knocked her down. A twelve-year-old girl, thin and pale in her blue sweater and long, floral skirt, knocked big Paula to her knees with just one shove and became the clinic's skinny heroine of the day. Amy stood expressionless in front of Ella. She refused Ella's smile and congratulations, and refused the stool Ella offered her, choosing to stand instead.

Hers was a pregnancy Ella could only guess about and the worst case of herpes the clinic had ever seen. Hers was an adamant silence—a girl Ella suspected was mute until she said, finally, clearly, one loud resounding *No,* as in, *No, I will not talk to you, I will not answer any questions.*

"Will you nod at me yes or shake your head?" Ella said.

She nodded.

As the interview went on, Ella ignored the questions on the sheet in front of her that called for multiworded responses, explanations, or declarations, and the girl nodded or shook her head. Ella wanted to say, *Who touched you and gave you a disease? Who made you pregnant? Whom did you let in or whom did you refuse?* But instead she said, "Do you want the pill, Amy?"

And the girl shook her head no.

"Do you itch or burn?"

She nodded once, and then again.

"Let me help you, Amy."

"No," she said—her second audible no of the day.

It was her skin Ella remembered later, the blue veins running up the sides of her cheeks to her ears, and the shove she mustered up for Born Again Paula that sent a grown woman to her knees, and that *No*, that resounding, unswayable *No*.

5.

At the kitchen table, Jack asked to be forgiven. "Please, Ella," he said. "Please. I'm begging."

She stood at the window with her coffee cup, threatening to leave. "There are places I could go," she said.

"It was just the one time." His voice cracked.

"San Francisco or Santa Barbara. My cousin's in Santa Barbara, you know. I could go there."

"You've got school, your job," he tried.

"And there's not a school in Santa Barbara?" she said sarcastically.

"It was just a kiss."

"A kiss is a very big deal, Jack. It might hurt less if you were really drunk and fucked someone." She talked without looking at him. She moved the shade to one side and watched the twin boys across the street leave their house. They kissed their mother at the door, first one and then the other standing on his toes to meet her lips. It was eight A.M., a weekday, and the boys were obviously on their way to school. Matching backpacks and little blue jeans.

"Look at me, Ella," Jack said.

"She touched your dick, maybe your balls," Ella said, not turning from the window.

"Look how sorry I am."

"I can't tell these boys apart," she said.

"Please stop this," Jack said.

"Tim and Tom, who's who?"

"It was just a kiss," he said again.

"Just a kiss," Ella mocked. She turned from the window and went to her husband. She put the coffee cup down. She pulled out a chair and sat at the table across from him. She looked at Jack's face, rested her eyes on his lips. He was tan. He'd shaved, but looked even more ridiculous to her now because the area where the goatee had been was pinkish and pasty, chafed. "You need some lotion for your face," she said.

"It's itchy," he said, reaching up to scratch it.

"Don't," she said, stopping him.

"I am so damn *sorry*," he said.

"I'm glad we don't have kids. It's a good thing we didn't do that," she said.

6.

Eventually, Georgia Carter told Ella the truth about her pregnancies, and Ella believed it was a sort of progress, them communicating, the girl's honesty. "He's just a guy I met up with at the 7-Eleven, my brother's friend," Georgia confessed about number one, the miracle. "He's just a guy I hooked up with after detention," she admitted about number two. "He's just a guy I met at a rave," she said about number three.

"Aren't you tired, Georgia?" Ella said.

"Of what?"

"Boys."

She shook her head.

"Aren't you tired of surgery, then?"

"Fuck, yes," she said.

All the counseling cubicles were taken, so they were in the video room. Ella passed that room all day long but had been inside it only twice. It was the room where men and boys were invited to watch short, dated films on vasectomies or sexually transmitted diseases. It was where the clinic lured them with the promise that information and education would offer them a smoother future, where the clinic bribed them with hot coffee or chocolate, tiny muffins and doughnut holes. If the door was left open and Ella was coming down the hall, she would smell the sweet cakes and coffee. She heard the booming voice-over describing the ease of transmission or the finality of the procedure, and was reminded of junior high sex-education class. More than once she turned around and caught a glimpse of a man's body, his vasectomy on the screen or a herpes sore blown up to the size of a planet.

"The *worse*-half room," Georgia said as Ella led her down the hall. "We're going to the worse-half room."

"The what?"

"You know, the worse half. Idiots always introduce their husbands or wives like that. Here's my *better half*," Georgia said, mocking.

"I get it."

"It just takes you a while," she said, smiling.

"Men aren't always the worse half, you know."

"Of course not—don't forget it's my mom who up and left my sick dad and me," she said.

The television was off. There was a bowl of fruit drops in the middle of the coffee table. "You guys should really get the individually wrapped candies," Georgia said.

"Why?"

"Germs," she said, pointing at the candy. "Each piece probably has piss on it, or worse."

"I doubt it," Ella said.

"I'm serious," she said. "I saw it on *60 Minutes*."

"*You,* Georgia Carter, are worried about germs?"

"Yeah, I am," she said.

"There are more dangerous things, bigger risks to one's safety than eating fruit drops, don't you think?"

"Isn't it too early for one of your lectures?"

"It's never too early," Ella said, smiling.

"Obviously not," she said.

There was a pink box open on the counter against the wall that Georgia had already explored. A little napkin with three doughnut holes sat in front of her. Every so often she pulled a piece of coconut from one of them and put it in her mouth.

Ella stared at Georgia's bitten nails. Georgia caught her and placed her hands in her lap. She curled her fingers, made fists so that there was nothing for Ella to see. "Don't stare at my hands," she said.

"Sorry," Ella said.

There were posters on the walls, one advertising the pill, which Ella made a mental note to discuss with her boss, and another for condoms, which made more sense, considering who was usually sitting on that couch.

"You clinic people are so transparent," Georgia said, looking at the posters.

"We're on your side," Ella said. "I don't know why you can't see it."

"I can see it," she said, unconvincingly.

"How's your job going?" Ella tried. "How's the yogurt business?"

"Mrs. Yates is pretty cool. I had to miss a few days last week on account of my dad, and she didn't even freak out. I think she feels sorry for me."

"I know it's tough, Georgia. I wish you'd—"

"Let's talk about something else, okay?" the girl said, interrupting.

Just then Sarah popped her head in through the door's crack and began talking to Ella in that sweet voice she'd been using since she'd been caught with her tongue in Jack's mouth. "We've got more girls out here," Sarah said meekly. "Should I call Dana and ask her to come in?"

Ella looked at her watch. "We'll just be a few more minutes," she said. "We're finishing up."

"Are you sure?" Sarah said. "Because Dana owes me a favor. I covered for her last week. It's no trouble, Ella. I can call her."

"We're just wrapping up," she said again.

Sarah stood holding the door, staring at the two of them.

"Don't bother Dana, okay?"

"Okay, okay," Sarah said, nervous, closing the door.

Ella looked at Georgia, who had placed the backpack in her lap and was shielding herself with it against anything Ella might be preparing to say. "You lost some weight," she said. "You're down to a hundred and ten, Georgia."

"So?"

"I'm wondering how low you plan to go. You're tall."

"I eat," she said. "It's not like I don't eat, okay?"

Ella nodded.

"What's that chick's name?" Georgia wanted to know.

"Who?"

"The one that was just here."

"Sarah."

"She bugs me."

"She's okay," Ella said.

"She's a bitch," Georgia said.

"Not nice."

"I'm just saying, I know a bitch when I see a bitch, and that girl who was just here, that's a bitch."

"She's okay," Ella said again.

"Bullshit," Georgia said. "You hate her too. I can tell. I bet something happened between her and Jack."

"What?" Ella was surprised.

"He used to wait for you. I'd see him sitting on the couch. I haven't seen him in weeks." Georgia paused. "She's just the type."

Ella tried not to smirk, but then gave in to it—what her mouth and eyes were doing. "Let's talk about you," she said.

"Whatever," Georgia said, reaching down and picking up a doughnut hole. "These are pretty stale, you know? If I was going to eat something, I wouldn't eat these." She tapped at it with her finger.

Ella smiled.

"You people could at least get fresh doughnuts. If you're going to have candy with piss on it, at least get us fresh—"

"They're not really for you," Ella interrupted.

"Who are they for, then?"

"Other visitors."

"Figures," she said.

"Listen, Georgia," Ella said, changing the subject, "what about the pill?"

"Remember how sick it made me?" She took a small bite, then put the doughnut hole back on the napkin.

"That's right."

"I was sick and fat."

"I remember."

"You remember I was *fat?*" she said, worried, looking down at her flat stomach.

"I remember you were *sick*. You weren't fat—you were never fat. If you think you're fat, we need to talk about it."

"I'm not one of those girls who sees a fatty in the mirror. I know I'm not fat, Ella. Don't make something out of nothing."

"I'm just saying—"

Georgia cut her off. "*I'm* just saying that when I was on the pill, my tits were huge. Did you notice how huge they were?"

"No," Ella said, "but you told me."

Georgia flipped out her palm and looked at Ella. "Give me some of those condoms," she said.

7.

They took a gondola ride at dusk. Their gondolier, a red-cheeked boy Ella recognized from school, helped her into the little boat. "Ladies first," he said. "My name is Daniel," he told them. Jack's palm, held up like a stop sign, refused the gondolier's help, and he stepped into the boat on his own.

There were wool blankets. There was a lantern, a bottle of red wine, cheese and salami, a basket of sourdough bread. Jack had his arm around Ella's shoulder. He gave her a sweet kiss on the cheek and yet another apology in her ear. *I wasn't thinking, I only love you, I'm sorry, I'm sorry*—twice before the boat even left the dock.

They sat with their backs to the gondolier, whose chest, Ella noticed, was strong and memorable in his black-and-white striped shirt. He wore a red scarf around his neck, a beret—the whole gondolier getup, but despite the charming costume, Daniel looked and sounded like the California surfer boy he most likely was.

A spray of water splashed into the boat when he reached down to pick up the long oar for the first time, and it was Daniel's muscled arms she noticed then. He said, "If you two want me to sing, let me know. I do Italian ballads. I'd be happy to sing to you both."

"Thank you, but no," Jack answered without turning around. He reached into the basket and pulled a piece of bread from the loaf. It seemed to Ella that her husband was tearing the bread harder than necessary, with a gusto that seemed strained and overdone.

The houses along the canal were unique, no two of them alike. One with pillars. One with an outdoor spiral staircase. A redbrick beauty to Ella's right, and to her left a modern structure made up primarily of windows. There were Victorians and A-frames, a three-story magnificent construction beside a humble duplex. There were lights going on in kitchens and dining rooms, people sitting down to dinner with family. Daniel slowed down at a particular house, a two-story Victorian with a large doll propped up in the second-story window. The doll, which at first Ella had mistaken for a little girl, must have been over three feet tall. "When I was a kid, dolls like that scared me," she said to Jack.

"She's a doll?"

"Look how still she is. Look at her blank face."

"I recognize you from the University," Daniel said.

"Yes," Ella said. "I've seen you around. You an English major?"

"Double major, English and marketing."

"Smart," she said. "Someone literate who might also get a good job." Ella pulled the blanket over her knees and leaned into Jack, who was leaning in the opposite direction, moving toward the wine. Their shoulders gently collided, and then he was leaning forward and she was leaning back into the spot where his body had been. Jack uncorked the bottle, set two glasses on the ledge in front of them, and began pouring. He handed Ella the fuller glass of the two. "Merlot," he said, "your favorite."

"Thanks," she said, taking a sip. "I recognize you too," she said to Daniel, half turning around.

"You're Ella Bloom, right?"

"That's right."

"The poet," Daniel said.

"I don't know about that," Ella said.

Jack leaned into her, and she felt his whole body stiffen, go rigid beside her. "I'm Mr. Bloom," he said, over his shoulder.

"What's wrong?" she said.

"Nothing," he said, reaching into the basket once more for a slice of salami. "He called you the poet. He knows your name," Jack said quietly.

"How do you know my name?" she asked.

"I get around."

Ella laughed. "I'm sure," she said, "but I don't."

The gondolier laughed with her. "You've got Rachel Spark for poetry."

Now she turned around completely. Daniel's lips were red

like his cheeks. His dark hair was wavy, hanging out from under the beret. He noticed her looking and reached up to adjust the hat. "Are you in that class?" she asked him.

"Just transferred out. A business class I had to make up was only offered on Monday nights. Barely missed the deadline."

"Too bad," she said. "Rachel is great."

"I've had other classes with her. I'm going to take her again, too."

"You should."

"I sat in the middle row, behind you. I saw the back of you," Daniel said, "so this is a view I recognize."

Jack turned around abruptly and looked at the gondolier. "Look, Danny," he said.

"Name's Daniel."

"Look, Daniel, how long have you been doing this?" Jack asked.

"Three months, Mr. Bloom."

"Yes, well," Jack said. "Sometimes people want to be alone, you know?"

"Okay."

"It's supposed to be romantic," Jack said.

"I get it."

"Come on," Ella said to Jack. "Relax. He's just being friendly."

"Friendly, huh?"

"Yes—he's being polite, that's all. Let the guy sing, Jack. I wouldn't mind hearing a song," she said.

"How about one of those songs?" Jack said to Daniel. "And don't sing too loudly, please. I want to be with my wife here, you know what I mean? We're married. This poet here is my wife."

"Maybe later," the gondolier said. "I don't feel like singing now."

"Don't sing then," Jack snapped.

"I won't," Daniel said.

The sky was orange and pink and gray, the sun falling between two fat clouds. Seagulls shrieked above them. A man and his small son stood by the rocks, holding hands. The boy had a kite shaped like a spider under one arm. "Hey Jerry, hey Ray," Daniel said.

"How's it going, Daniel?" the man said.

"Been better," the gondolier answered.

Ella nudged Jack. "Be nice," she said. "It's embarrassing."

"What did I do?" Jack whispered. "It's Danny who's rude."

"Isn't this boat ride supposed to be for me? I thought you were sorry," she said.

"One thing doesn't have to do with the other," he said.

"I think it does," she said.

Daniel, who had refused to sing, was now humming instead, and his humming and the wine and the water and the sound of the oar hitting it was, despite Jack and the gondolier's testy interaction, lulling Ella, calming her down. She was feeling the wine and she was feeling noticed, her whole body going slack against Jack's tension.

A pair of black ducks followed the gondola and came up beside her. She tossed them chunks of bread. "Aren't you sweeties," she said to the ducks. "Aren't you little midnight sweeties?"

Twenty minutes into the ride and Daniel hadn't said a word to them since Jack shushed him. Ella's husband tried to kiss her under every bridge. Her cheek was what she gave him when he came in for the first few kisses, but finally, under bridge number four, she gave him her lips. The bottle was empty at their feet. She tasted the salami on Jack's lips. She felt his regret. She believed he was sorry, that he loved her. They were drunk.

"I wonder if couples ever fight out here?" Ella said to Jack.

"We almost did," Jack said.

"I mean *really* fight—have a rotten time. Do you think it's possible?" she said, snuggling into him.

"Ask Daniel," Jack said, finally loosening up. "If you want to know, ask him."

"No," she said.

"Daniel," Jack said, "you still mad at me?"

"I'm not mad at you," Daniel said. "If you don't want to talk to me, you don't have to. We don't have to be friends."

"Let's be friends," Jack said. "You want to be friends with us?"

"I've got friends."

"Can I ask you a question anyway?"

"It's your ride," the boy said.

"Ella's wondering if you've ever seen a couple fight out here?"

"Once."

"What happened?" Ella asked.

"An older guy was opening a bottle of champagne and accidentally hit his wife in the face with the cork. The wife was pissed, screaming and shouting, calling him an asshole."

"Did he hit her in the eye?" Ella wanted to know.

"The cheek."

"It must have hurt," she said.

"The wife wanted me to turn the boat around and give them their money back. I think it was their tenth anniversary or something."

"She just flipped out, obviously," Jack said.

"*Please*," Ella said.

"I felt sorry for the guy, but for her too. Her face was all blotchy—it looked like he hit her."

"Maybe they had other problems too," Jack said.

"Maybe so," Daniel said. Apparently the boy wanted to talk, now that the dock was in sight. It was dark and the birds were quiet, lights on in every home and window they passed. "Once, a couple did the opposite."

"What's the opposite?" Jack said.

"They were kissing under the bridges, like you're supposed to, like you two have been doing, and then we came out the other side and the guy's head was gone."

"Was he going down on her?" Jack wanted to know.

"At first I thought he lost something, his wallet or his keys, and was searching the floor. Then I saw his head move under the blanket. It was pretty raunchy."

"Enough about cunnilingus," Ella said, both annoyed and flushed.

"*Cunna* what?" the gondolier said.

"Hey," Jack said, "I thought you went to college, Danny. Don't you go to college?"

"I go to college," the gondolier said, steering into the dock. "And the name's Daniel."

8.

When Ella's poetry teacher, Rachel Spark, showed up at the clinic, Ella hid her face behind a clipboard, mouthing at Sarah, "That one is yours."

"Where?" she said. "Who?"

"That one over there," Ella said, pointing.

"The young girl?"

"No, the woman beside her. Dark hair, black blouse."

"Oh, the lady."

"The woman," Ella said. "No one says 'lady' anymore, Sarah. A woman, okay? And I know her."

"Sorry," she said, "but I'm off. My shift is over." Sarah took off the white jacket, placed it over her arm, and gave Ella a mousy look. "Sorry," she said again. "I've got to go," she said.

"Fine. Whatever," Ella said, sounding more like Georgia Carter than herself. She turned her back on Sarah and reluctantly slid the little window open. She paused a moment before popping her head out. "Rachel," Ella called, "I've got some paperwork for you."

Rachel rose from the couch and straightened her skirt. She picked up her purse, swung it over her shoulder, and came up to the window. She looked at Ella's face and her eyes widened. "You didn't tell me you work here," she snapped.

"You didn't ask, Dr. Spark."

"I'm not a doctor. How many times do I have to tell you that I'm not a doctor?" She leaned toward the window, whispering harshly.

"I'm sorry," Ella said.

"I'm sorry too."

"Whatever goes on here is confidential. I'm a profession-al," Ella continued.

"I want to go to sleep," Rachel said.

"What?"

"For the procedure, I want to be put out."

"Of course," Ella said. "And it's confidential," she repeated.

"Good," Rachel said. "Give me whatever it is that you want me to sign."

9.

It was Friday night, and moments earlier a woman was hit by a car in front of their apartment building. Jack told Ella that at first he thought the woman was pushing a baby in a stroller, but when the baby popped out of the stroller and landed in the bushes, yelping, he realized it was a little dog. "It's a dog," Jack said, excited. "It flew out of there like popcorn." The dog was blond and fluffy. He looked well taken care of, Jack told her.

On the balcony in his bathrobe, Jack watched the scene and reported it to Ella. She was sitting on the couch in her nightgown and slippers, drinking a cup of tea and reading Diane Ackerman's *A Natural History of Love*. Although she didn't mind hearing Jack's rendition of the scene outside, Ella didn't want to witness the mess first hand.

"She's not that bad," Jack said. "She's standing up. She's gesturing to the police." Jack waved his arms around, imitating the woman.

"I want to finish this chapter on cheaters," Ella said.

"Cheaters?"

"Adulterers."

"Great," he said, sarcastically.

Moments later Jack had quieted down, which made Ella feel left out; she wanted to know what was happening. She thought about getting up off the couch and joining him but decided against it. "What's going on now?" she asked.

"The woman is scratched up," he told her. "A gash on her cheek, and her shoulder looks fucked up too."

"Is she old?"

"At least fifty—maybe older."

"Did you know," Ella said, "that seventy-two percent of American men say they've been unfaithful and fifty-four percent of American women?"

"Put down the book, Ella—come outside."

"That number seems pretty high. Don't you think that's a pretty high number?"

"What do you want me to do?" he said.

"You're not alone. That's all I'm saying. Most people behave like you behave."

"Stop it," he said. "Come out here with me."

"It's not exactly a romantic scene. Wait until they take the woman away and clean up the mess."

"What mess? There's no mess. Come out here," he said again.

"Let me finish this."

"She's up and walking," he said. "She's talking. They're helping her onto a stretcher."

They lived on the second floor of a high-rise. The building was on the ocean. If Ella went down into the garage and walked out the door to her left, she'd be on the sand. People who paid more rent had balconies that faced the sea. Their balcony faced the street.

It was a busy boulevard, with cars and trucks, apartment buildings and old houses too, with palm trees and crazy black birds that flew from ledge to porch to branch. Sometimes those birds appeared out of nowhere, moving abruptly in flocks. Ella would be on the balcony writing a poem or watering the ferns, and the sound of their many wings going all at once would startle her.

In the two years they'd lived there, three women were hit by cars—not one man that they knew of or had heard about. There had been over a dozen small accidents. Once, making love, they were interrupted by the sudden sound of screeching tires and metal crashing into metal, and Jack had jumped up to look, which is something she wouldn't forget.

"The woman is gone now," Jack said. "Listen to the sirens. They're taking her away."

"I want to finish this chapter," Ella said.

"They're checking to see if the driver is drunk. Don't you want to watch him try to touch his nose? It'll be fun," Jack said.

Ella put down the book and picked up her robe. She hung the robe over her shoulders without putting it on and joined Jack on the balcony. "Did you know that the average man's ejaculate contains only five calories and is mainly protein?" she asked.

"I knew about it being protein."

Ella wanted to be outside with Jack but didn't want to get too close. She brushed off a chair with her hand and sat down. "I always thought it had more calories than that," she said.

"What else are you learning in that book?"

"There's two hundred million sperm in one orgasm. And a guy's come shoots out at twenty-eight miles per hour."

Jack looked out at the street. "Just about the speed limit here," he said. They were quiet for a moment. "Don't you want to put on your robe? It's cold," Jack finally said.

Ella shook her head. "My teacher came to the clinic this week," she told him.

"Which one?" Jack rested his elbow on the railing and turned to her.

"Rachel Spark."

"The poetry teacher?"

"Yeah."

"Did she come for herself or with someone else?"

"Herself," she said. "She was pregnant."

"Was?"

"Actually, she still is."

"She's going through with it?"

"No—Dr. Wheeler tried to give her an abortion, but it didn't work. He was afraid her pregnancy might be tubal. We sent her to another clinic."

He turned back to the street. "That must have been weird for her, seeing you there."

"She wasn't happy."

"Come closer, Ella. Stand up. That chair is dirty." He motioned to it and made a face.

"I'm okay."

"Let me help you put the robe on."

"I'm okay," she said again.

"I want to be near you. I want to keep you warm."

"I know," she said, "but I'm fine. Comfortable. I'll sit here and you tell me what's happening in the street."

"I thought you were going to try," he said.

"I'm out here, aren't I?"

Jack sighed. "What else does it say in that book? What about marriage?"

"The first marriages happened by capture. When a man saw a woman he wanted, he took her by force. Sometimes he got a buddy to help him."

"The best man."

"Do you feel captured?"

He shook his head no. "I captured you," he said. "I might

have behaved like that seventy-two percent, but that's because I was weak, not because I don't love you."

Ella stood up and walked toward him. She let him help her into the robe and stood beside him by the railing, looking out. The streetlights were orange—the one directly in front of them blinked on and off, obviously ready to give up completely. It cast a glowing circle on the sidewalk, and then the circle disappeared. Several couples and a small group of people were gathered, watching the man try to touch his nose. A woman stood by a fire hydrant with three big dogs on leashes.

"Those dogs must outweigh her," Jack said.

"You didn't capture me," Ella said.

He shrugged, gave her a small smile, and they stood there a moment, looking at the man. He was walking a perfect line. "Look," Jack said, "the guy's not drunk. He's just a bad driver."

10.

Ella had been trying to make things work with Jack for four months when Georgia came to her with condyloma. It was April and raining, the fat drops pounding the roof of the clinic.

Earlier, driving to work, Ella almost hit a pair of schoolgirls. They were holding hands, stepping off the curb and into the street, shiny lunch pails at their sides. They were walking against the light, and Ella wondered where their mothers were, why they weren't taking these girls to school. Ella swerved and one girl dropped her lunch pail, which Ella heard crunch under her tires.

She pulled over to the curb, stopped the car and got out. The girl was crying, staring into the street at her smashed lunch pail and sandwich. Her apple had rolled into the gutter. "Here," Ella said, opening her wallet, "here's some money." She'd planned to give the child a five but could only find a twenty, so she gave the girl that. "Buy yourself lunch," she said. "Don't cry. Look, here's twenty dollars."

The girl stared at her palm, at the money Ella offered her. She sniffled. She wiped her nose with the back of her hand. Her friend nudged her. "Take the money," the friend said.

So when Georgia, who'd recently been diagnosed with HPV, came into the cubicle, dripping wet, pulling off her jacket and shaking off her umbrella, Ella was in no mood. The umbrella was broken, one metal bar twisted, like an injured leg, or like the bat's wings she'd been dreaming about, Jack had been talking about, the metal bar like one of their covered fingers. "Your umbrella's broken," Ella said.

"It's a windy fucking day," Georgia said.

"Sit down."

"My jacket is soaked. Can you hang it up somewhere?" She held the dripping jacket in the air between them.

Ella noticed that Georgia had filled out a bit. Her face was fuller. "You look good," she said.

Georgia mumbled something under her breath. She dropped the jacket in Ella's lap, leaving a wet stain on her lab coat.

"Damn it, Georgia."

"Sorry," she said.

Ella stood and put the jacket over her arm. She walked down the hall to the closet, huffing so that Georgia could hear. When she sat back down, she stared hard at the girl and shook her head.

"I'm up to one-twenty. Are you happy now?" Georgia said.

"The question is, are *you* happy?"

"What's that supposed to mean?"

And Ella did what she'd been trained not to do: she raised her voice. "How does a girl like you *begin,* Georgia? I mean, how does it start? What were you like at twelve or thirteen?"

"A girl like me?"

"Yes, how does it begin for you. That's what I want to know."

"What are you talking about?"

"Can't you find yourself one boy? And be safe with him?" Ella said. "Or how about keeping your legs closed? There's an idea."

Georgia leaned back on the stool. She shook her head. "I could get you fired for that," she said.

"Go ahead," Ella said.

Georgia glared at her.

"Go tell my boss I'm a horrible counselor. I'm certainly horrible with you—haven't made one bit of difference in your life, your behavior," Ella said.

"*My behavior,*" she said.

"It's useless, the time we spend together. You're never going to stop."

"It's not your *job* to stop me. Just do your *job,*" the girl said.

"I obviously can't," Ella said.

Georgia looked at her. She leaned forward and spoke. "You think finding *one boy* is the big answer? You think marriage is some great thing? I wouldn't want *one boy* if that one boy was Jack Bloom."

"Stop it," Ella said.

"I'm just saying—"

"I know what you're saying, Georgia, and you're sixteen years old. Don't talk to me about my life."

"I know how old I am."

"I don't think you do. You don't know what it means to be sixteen—how many times you should, should . . ."

"Should what?"

"Should be saying no, Georgia—you should tell those damn boys no."

"Something's wrong with you," Georgia said.

"Look," Ella said, "right now, this minute, something's wrong with *you*. Your health. Condyloma needs to be watched. You've got to take care of yourself."

"Yeah, yeah," Georgia said, flippantly.

"It's not enough to just look at a boy—you can't see condyloma, at least not in the dark," Ella continued, knowing her words were futile. "It's difficult to spot, that's what I'm saying. You've got to be more careful."

Georgia nodded.

Ella told her that the virus, HPV, could be dangerous. She told her that if it went to her cervix, it could cause cancer. There could be changes in her Pap results. Abnormalities.

Georgia leaned forward. "Hey," she said, "what's it doing now?"

Ella looked at her.

"Do I have cancer *now?*"

Ella had the girl's test results right there in her lap, and though she'd already read them and knew that Georgia was okay, she opened the folder for dramatic effect and pretended to be reading from it. She slapped the folder closed and said nothing.

"What's it say?"

"You're fine right now, Georgia."

"I knew it," she said. "I feel great. Nothing's wrong with me." And then she was rummaging through her purse. "Fuck, no gum," she said. "I need a mint or something."

"I'm telling you to be careful with this one. You'll be treated, the symptoms disappear, everything's fine, and then it can come back. I'm not saying that it will, but it can—it's possible. If it goes to your cervix, you won't even know. You've got to watch out, take care of yourself. Don't miss appointments."

"You should leave him first, Ella. You should pack your bags and go. It's your marriage, right?"

"Don't assume things." Ella shook her head, pissed. "Your imagination astounds me," she lied.

Georgia shrugged.

"Besides, I'm not going to take relationship advice from *you*. Come on, Georgia. Think about it."

"Do you have any gum?" Georgia asked. "How about a mint?"

"Nothing."

"What about a piece of candy?"

Ella patted her pockets for proof. "Nothing," she said again.

"Damn," Georgia said.

"Look, Georgia, you're okay now, but I want you to be vigilant."

"I heard you."

"I want you to stay on top of this—don't miss even one Pap."

"Right," she said. "Okay. I wish I had a mint," she said.

11.

There were a half dozen ten-story buildings all in a row. There were palm trees and short green hills, ecology scholars and technical engineers, bat lovers and defenders of poisonous snakes. He'd been spending more and more evenings here, thinking things through, he said. He felt more at home at work, especially these last few weeks, he told Ella.

They went to building number 3 and took the elevator to the fifth floor. Jack punched in his code, and the glass doors opened for them.

And there, pinned to corkboards, were the bats he studied and loved.

Jack took her by the hand and led her around, introducing her. She knew he'd given the bats names. He'd spoken about them, calling them Candy and Rudy and Maggie at home, but it was different standing there, watching him coo, watching him talk to the dead bats as if they could hear. She thought about this and let go of his hand.

"Here we are—finally," he said, pulling up a stool for her to sit on. He opened his arms out wide and looked around. "What do you think?" he asked her.

"It's intense," she said.

"Let me get us some coffee. Let's have some coffee and talk about things."

Jack left the room to make coffee, and after a few seconds alone with the bats, Ella was aware of her heart and lungs. She left the lab too and stood in the hall, waiting. She was thinking about the documentary he brought home months ago. The Livingstone's bat that was born in the Los Angeles Zoo a year earlier and had been rejected by his mother. The bat had to be nurtured by a human. Michael, the zookeeper, cared for the orphan bat. He named him Oliver. The bat had to be fed almost constantly, so Michael kept him in his bedroom. Ella imagined Michael feeding Oliver pears and peaches and tiny chunks of apple.

When Jack found her in the hall, he kissed her cheek. "I'm sorry I left you there," he said. "I should have—"

"It's okay," she said, cutting him off.

Jack carried only one cup of coffee. "I can't find the extra cups. We can share, right?"

"Okay," she said, taking the cup from him, bringing it to her lips and taking a sip. The coffee was hot and perfect, with just the right amount of cream. They stood in the hall a moment and looked at each other before moving back into the lab.

Jack pulled out two stools and they sat down next to each other. It was a lot like sitting side by side in a bar, except that instead of rows of bottles above their heads there were bats behind glass cases. Jack picked up her hand. "Can you trust me, Ella?" Jack said. "Can you at least make an effort?"

When he said effort, Ella thought of high school math tests. She thought of gym class and running an extra lap. She thought of trying not to cuss or giving up caffeine. She thought of Sarah's lips on Jack's lips. She remembered Sarah's hand making its way into her husband's jeans. Ella remembered that the zookeeper Michael taught Oliver to fly. *How did that work?* she was wondering. *How did a man without wings teach a bat to use his own?*

"I'll make an effort," she said, and it sounded silly, like a lie, like something she could not possibly make.

Jack clapped his hands together like a kid and jumped up from the stool. "Good," he said. "Let me introduce you to Carmen." For a minute she thought he had a secretary, a dark-haired beauty that he hadn't mentioned, but he took her hand for the second time that day and pulled her to the back of the lab, where Carmen, pinned like the others, hung behind a glass case.

"Livingstone's Fruit," Jack said.

"So this is Carmen," she said, relieved.

"Isn't she wonderful?"

And Carmen was wonderful, Ella agreed, especially her wings, spread out like a blanket, like a huge black fan.

12.

They stuck their brown lunch bags on a shelf in the refrigerator, right next to the samples that were waiting to go to the lab, the brown bags of gonorrhea and syphilis. In the common room they ate their sandwiches, sipped soft drinks, and discussed the girls of the day—this one raped by a quiet neighbor, this one left in a gutter by a boy she still loved, a boy Ella *better not* be looking at, she said, and this one, Georgia Carter, with an object stuck inside of her, way up high, so high that no amount of pull or tug or yank could release it.

It had been several months since Ella had seen Georgia, months since her condyloma had been diagnosed and treated, months since they'd had that argument about Georgia's behavior and Ella's marriage, and now Georgia sat there, looking at Ella as if she were any one of the counselors up front; it was a look she might have given Sarah, whom she obviously didn't like or want to know. "I think about you," Ella said meekly.

"Yes, well," Georgia said. She shifted on the metal stool, obviously unhappy behind their inadequate curtain. "Can't a girl get some privacy?" she said, sighing. She pulled a piece of gum from her blouse's little pocket. She popped it between her lips and chewed without inhibition; Ella could see the white stick bending and folding in her mouth.

She leaned forward and spoke to Georgia softly. "Can you tell me what the object is?" she asked her.

Georgia shook her head no.

Her weight hadn't changed since she'd last been to the clinic, so perhaps Ella didn't need to worry there. She'd cut her bangs, and they framed her face now. She looked funny to Ella, like an overgrown baby. Georgia noticed her looking and brushed the bangs with her hand. "I'm sorry about last time," Ella said.

"Whatever."

"I am, Georgia. It was wrong of me. I should have called you to apologize. I picked up the phone, in fact, I . . ."

"Stop it," she said.

"Okay," Ella said, leaning forward.

"It would have been *unprofessional* to call. You're only unprofessional to a point."

"I'm sorry," she said again.

Georgia muttered something under her breath that Ella could not make out. She sneered. Ella asked if she were here alone.

"I've got a boyfriend now."

"Good," Ella said, not sure if she believed her.

"His name is Jim. He's tall, seventeen. We've got the same birthday," she said.

"Is Jim here?"

"He sells shoes—makes a lot of commission. He wants to take me away."

"Where?"

"The mountains."

"Is Jim here?" Ella repeated.

"Say what you mean—you want to know if he's okay with

this, with the fact that I've got something stuck up there." She motioned to her pelvis. "Right?"

Ella shook her head.

"What you want to know is *does he still love me.*"

"No," Ella said, "I'm not talking about love."

And Georgia looked at her hard and said, "Of course you're not."

13.

At closing Ella gathered the speculums up like silverware, and after dipping them into the steaming water, stuck them in an oven to bake. Later, she'd bake sweet bread for a man she thought she knew, and even later, he would leave her, but not before giving her a germ or two of her own.

Years from now, he would stand with a new wife at the mouth of Bracken Cave. Inside the cave twenty million free-tailed bats would be hanging by their toes. At dusk these bats, pouring from the cave, would swirl and loop in search of blood.

Years from now, Georgia's condyloma would spread to her cervix, causing a cancer they would not find until it had eaten everything.

Georgia had a banana inside of her. Dr. Wheeler shook his head and smirked as he confided to them in the common room. It was lunchtime. Just moments earlier, Ella, so anxious to hear Georgia's verdict, grabbed the wrong bag from the refrigerator shelf. She sat peeking inside at the sample of gonorrhea on her lap. She quickly folded it closed and feigned fullness.

"It was months ago," Sarah whispered into her ear. "I'm sorry," she said.

Ella nodded.

"I told you it wouldn't happen again and it hasn't. It's okay if he picks you up from work. I'll stay away from him, I promise."

Ella nodded again.

"I'm sorry," Sarah repeated.

"I heard you the first time," Ella said.

"He's just, he's just . . ." she stammered.

"He's *just* my husband," Ella said, louder than she had intended.

Dr. Wheeler looked at her. "What, Ella? Did you say something about your husband?"

"No," she said. "It's nothing."

"It was a banana," Dr. Wheeler said. "A banana," he repeated, looking at them. "Can you imagine a girl wanting something so badly?"

Rachel Spark

1997–1998

Creatures

1.

I knew there were women who were proud of their mastectomies. I had a *DoubleTake* magazine open on my nightstand, left there purposely with the hopes that my mother would find it. A pencil ran the length of the magazine's spine, saving the page. Even though I knew photographs weren't going to affect my mother's decision, I wanted her to see these beautiful tattooed women—one with a colorful snake where her right breast had been, one with halos of red and yellow flowers circling both puckered scars.

My mom had started talking about reconstructive surgery, dropping comments about balance and symmetry into our conversations. It was summer, just over a couple of years since the mastectomy, just six months before her first recurrence, two years before I met Dirk or Rex, and my mother wanted her body back, she said—as if it, her body, had taken a trip or been stolen from her, and breast reconstruction would return it to its rightful place. I wanted my mother to wait until she'd been healthy for at least three years before deciding because I knew that the disease was most likely to recur within that window. I wanted her strong when or if it showed up, not recouping—but she wanted to get on with things. I believed that these things my mother wanted to get on with included meeting a new man, and I worried that her self-image was wrapped up in what was no longer hers—breasts, abundance, and probable health.

It was morning, a Saturday, and she stood in front of her bedroom mirror in a black one-piece bathing suit, white shorts, and tennis shoes, complaining, saying, "I'm out of whack, Rachel. I feel like I'm about to tip over." The two of us had planned to have our coffee downstairs, sit outside on the sand, and play a game of Scrabble before it got too hot.

I stood in the doorway, towel over one shoulder, holding the game under my arm.

"Look at this," my mom said, pulling at the black fabric where it dipped and wrinkled. She held the rubber breast in the other hand. The problem, she said, was that her remaining breast seemed bigger and was cumbersome without its match. "Look at it," she said. "Look at me."

I was looking. I did look. I looked all the time—when my mother was dressing or undressing, when she was stepping out of the tub, when she was sleeping. I had looked the night before, as my mother stood in the kitchen, ready for bed, saying goodnight. She held a steaming cup of chocolate. She blew into the cup and the vapor rose. I smelled the milk and sugar. Her hair, as they had promised, had come back in curls. When she leaned forward to kiss my cheek, I noticed the blue gown, the way it fell over her healthy breast, the way the silk wrinkled and dipped where her left breast had been, how it behaved like the black fabric my mother was now pulling on.

Unlike her, I wasn't thinking about aesthetics or symmetry, but time—the days and weeks and months out of her life that the reconstruction would certainly steal. "Think how stressful the surgery would be on your body," I said. "Are you ready for that sort of stress? Is your body ready?"

"Where are the beach chairs?" she said, irritated, changing the subject. "Are they in the front closet?"

"What did the doctor say—that it could take you up to six months to recover?"

"That's the worst-case scenario, Rachel. Why must you always think like that? How did I raise such a negative daughter?" She put the rubber breast down on her dresser and sat on the bed. "I need you with me."

"Where else am I going to go?"

"No—I need you to support my decision. I mean, *if* I make that decision. I haven't decided yet," she insisted.

"Yes you have."

My mom sighed. She shook her head, looked at me. "You ever drink too much and not know where to put your feet?"

"Maybe."

"Well, that's how I feel. I'm out of whack." She picked the breast up from the dresser and placed it inside her bathing suit, filling the space. She stared at herself in the mirror a moment. "Let's go," she said, turning, looking at the game under my arm. "I'm going to win," she said.

2.

I went with my mother to Dr. Morgan's office for a consultation. The waiting room was plush, ridiculously so, I thought. I sat on the overstuffed velvet couch, my mother on a matching chair. The two of us looked at each other and said nothing. My mother gave me half a smile.

On one wall hung a framed montage, letters from happy patients, complete with pictures of body parts: a wallet-size photo of a man's profile, a five-by-seven of a blonde woman's taut stomach, and another five-by-seven of what looked like a teenage girl, bent over—all I could see was her navy blue bikini bottoms, her good thighs, and half of her face as she twisted herself at the waist and neck to smile at the camera. Her position looked painful, and I wondered how long she had to hold it, to bend like that, before someone snapped the picture.

A marble coffee table sat in the center of the room. Several unlit candles in exotic holders were scattered about. In one corner stood a lavish fountain with water pouring from a cherub's outstretched palm. A framed sign on the coffee table read: *These candles are decorative. Please do not light them.* A candle without the possibility of light, I thought, is a trick, like a breast that's really a stomach, misplaced fat and skin.

Next to the cherub was a magazine rack that stretched the length of the wall. I got up from the couch and went to the rack. Every magazine I'd ever heard of was there, as well as several unknown to me. I picked up *Cosmetic Surgeon* and flipped through it, pausing at an article titled "What's Looking Good Worth to Los Angeles?" I continued flipping and found one that interested me: "At Risk, In Need." The piece was about American surgeons who dedicated time to third world countries. Mostly, they fixed cleft palates.

I sat on the couch with the magazine open across my lap. I glanced at my mother, who was reaching inside her bag, searching for something, then looked back down at the magazine. Several pictures of children with serious eyes and deformed mouths stared up at me from the pages. One small boy appeared shaken, his dark eyes huge and surprised, as if he'd looked in the mirror and couldn't believe it himself. I was thinking about the boy, his cleft palate. I was thinking about my mother, how her boyfriend, a man she'd liked from school for years and had just started sleeping with right before she was diagnosed, abruptly stopped seeing her. I was imagining my mother tipping over at the grocery store, her body out of balance as she said, a shoulder falling into the canned pears or peaches. I was moving my tongue along the roof of my own mouth, thinking about that.

My mom pulled some dark green fabric from her bag. She held a needle up to the light and aimed. She threaded the needle and began to sew. It would be a dress or a skirt, that wrinkled pile of green that was in her lap, and I would forever remember her—making something pretty out of nothing.

I had just closed the magazine when an unnaturally happy and buxom brunette came into the waiting room, holding a clipboard, and calling my mother's name. "Elizabeth," she said, "Dr. Morgan is ready for you now." I put the magazine on the table and looked at my mother, who was folding the fabric and putting it back in her bag. She stood up, held the bag at her side, and asked the woman if I could join her.

"Sure," the nurse said.

"Come with me," my mother whispered.

"You want me in there?" I was surprised.

"Yes."

"You sure?"

"I said yes—but I want you to behave yourself."

"I'm an adult," I reminded her.

"Adults misbehave," my mother said under her breath.

"I'll stay here," I said.

"Come with me," she said again.

The two of us sat quietly while Dr. Morgan prepared his slide show. I looked at the doctor's pockmarked face, wondering why he of all people didn't pretty himself up. Why didn't he skip one game of golf or elaborate luncheon and have that imperfect skin scraped away?

He showed us a slide: a woman whose face I couldn't see, just the thin, bland line of her mouth and hesitant chin—a woman with poor posture, a wrinkled belly, and two thick scars where her breasts had been. The surface was strangely flat; it appeared scooped out and hollow. I would have thought that to go in that far, to dig that deep, they would have damaged the woman's heart. It amazed me that the concave area could house any organ at all.

"This is the *Before* picture, obviously," Dr. Morgan said, pointing at the woman.

In the *After* picture the woman stood up straight with her new breasts. The breasts were big and full, standing up like a teenage girl's, which only magnified the rest of her, all creases and folds. Again, I saw the thin line of her mouth, this time with lipstick, this time smiling.

"How fresh were the scars in the previous slide?" I asked the doctor.

"*Rachel,*" my mother said.

"I'm just asking," I said. "You don't mind if I ask, do you?"

"Fresh?" he said.

"Yes," I continued. "How long had it been since the woman's mastectomy?"

"Double," he said.

"I noticed that. How long had it been?" I repeated.

"Six months."

"Wouldn't it have been a good idea to wait?"

"For what?"

My mom sighed.

"For what?" Dr. Morgan repeated.

"Until the area heals," I said, though that wasn't what I wanted to say at all. What I wanted to say was: *My mother had a huge tumor in her breast two years ago and she's probably still sick. Under that handmade dress, she's probably dying, you greedy ass.* "Until the woman feels better," I said quietly.

"That woman right there feels fine," Dr. Morgan said, pointing again. "Sometimes we team up with the cancer surgeon and take care of aesthetics immediately. As soon as the doctor removes one, I'm there sculpting another."

"Like art," my mom said.

"Exactly."

"How's it done?" she asked. "And don't get too graphic, please. I don't need to know everything." My mother smoothed her dress out across her legs and let out a little laugh. "I'm not my daughter, that's for sure—please, Dr. Morgan, keep the details to yourself."

He talked about the latest procedure, taking fat and muscle from a woman's stomach. He jutted his chin at the screen, at the woman. "Here," he said, "and here too. I take fat from here and make a breast there." He pointed his pen at the woman's torso, first at her puffy belly, then at her sunken chest.

"Amazing," my mom said.

Dr. Morgan smiled. "It's like getting a free tummy tuck."

"A bargain," I said, flatly.

"I could use one of those. Imagine how good my dresses will look then, Rachel." She smiled at the two of us and patted her small stomach.

"I'm imagining."

"Maybe I'll have to take them in, do some alterations."

"What about the nipple? How do you do that?" I asked.

"Well, we either take a bit of skin from inside the labia or—"

"*Oh, my,*" my mother said.

"Or what?" I said.

"Or do without one," he said.

"And how about pain?" I wanted to know.

"Demerol works well. You don't have to worry because your mother would be medicated those first few days—"

"So it's painful, then? It sure sounds painful. Skin from your labia, huh?" I looked at my mother and raised my eyebrows.

"Well, she'll be uncomfortable."

"Sounds *very* uncomfortable. I had a dentist talk to me once about discomfort," I said. "Do you remember that dentist, Mom?"

My mom nodded.

I looked at the doctor. "I had an abscessed molar—he hit a nerve. Nothing *uncomfortable* about it."

"We've got effective drugs," Dr. Morgan said.

I shook my head.

"And remember," he continued, "your mother has already been through a mastectomy, through chemotherapy and radiation."

"Nausea, lethargy, pain," I added.

"Yes, yes," he said, as if we were agreeing.

"No," I said.

"No, what?" he wanted to know.

"Nothing," I said, realizing that we'd been talking about my mother as though she wasn't in the room, as though she was a small girl without an opinion. But she didn't seem to mind. By now she'd risen from the chair and walked over to the screen. She stood in the slide machine's yellow glare, her back, shoulders, head and neck partially illuminated. She was bent over, intent, and so close to the woman's breasts that if she'd opened her mouth, she could have taken a bite.

3.

In the car on the way home, I was angry. "What irritates me is that he knows how painful the surgery is. He said it himself: days of Demerol. That's being in a stupor for days. And the bit about carving up your labia? That's butchering one area—and a rather important area, I might add—to pretty up another," I said.

"That's optional. He said that I could opt out of that one. I'm sure the breast would look nicer *with* a nipple, though."

"I'd certainly opt out. I'd opt out of the whole damn thing."

"Did you see the woman's breasts?" she asked.

"Yes."

"Couldn't even see the scars."

"They were there," I said, stopping at a red light on Sunset Boulevard. I twisted in the seat and faced my mother. "You know they were there, right?"

"No," she said, turning away from me. "I don't know that. I got up close—you saw me. There wasn't one sign of Dr. Morgan's good work. He's a brilliant man, an artist. You shouldn't be so hard on him, Rachel. You're full of judgment. I don't judge people the way you do. Where did you learn that?"

"I'm not going to pretend that I don't have opinions."

"Opinions are one thing, but judgment is another. You were sitting there asking him smart questions, but not looking at the woman. Where's your empathy?"

I shook my head. "I'm just saying there were scars there, even if you couldn't see them."

"I'm the one who got right up next to the woman, and *I* didn't see any scars." She was defiant, crossing her arms across her chest.

"He had to sew something to something, didn't he? It's not like he used glue. There's sewing going on—he had to use stitches."

But my mother was busy then, looking out the window at a pair of transvestites or transsexuals, a brunette and a blonde, in matching shorts and halter tops. They sat at a bus stop just feet away, arm in arm. "What pretty girls," my mother said.

"They're not girls."

"Well, whatever they are, they're pretty."

The light turned green but I didn't move. Horns honked. A man hung out his car window and called me a bitch as he sped away in a silver convertible. "I hate Los Angeles," I said, accelerating too hard. We lurched forward and I quickly shot my arm across my mother's chest to keep her from hitting the dashboard. "I'm sorry," I said.

"It's fine—I'm fine," she said, obviously still mad.

"Why can't you get your treatment at Memorial? Beach Memorial has a great reputation. They've got a Woman's Center."

"You know why not."

"Is it really because of the movie stars here?"

"They get better treatment. They stay alive longer because the doctors are very good up here."

"It seems to me that a movie star is dropping dead every

week, Mom. It's on the news. They die just like the rest of us."

"I trust these doctors," she said.

"The scars were there, you know that, don't you?"

"Look," she said. "I just want to get undressed one night and not have to remember the whole thing. I want to forget."

"I understand that," I said. I twisted my neck, making sure my blind spot was clear, and moved lane by lane into the fast lane. It made sense, my mother's desire to forget. I wished I could forget, too, but there were things about my mother's breast cancer that I knew and couldn't stop knowing—the tumor's size, the lymph node involvement.

Still, there were moments when even I almost forgot. I'd be laughing with Angela at a bar or coffee shop, talking to my students about their stories or poems, and the tumor would be far away from me. Later, I'd be sitting with my mother, playing Scrabble, or maybe I'd be watching her from across the room, sewing a new skirt, and the tumor would appear behind my eyes. I'd be at the movies, reaching into a bag of popcorn or riding my bike on the beach, and it would show up—a fat, sneaky thing, a stalker the size of a plum.

4.

From the lobby window, I could see Angela sitting in the car, waiting, the cigarette's red cap rising to her lips. I had one hand in the mailbox and waved with the other, motioned to my friend with one finger that I'd just be a minute.

In the car, I opened the package addressed to my mother from The Beauty Club. It was something we shared—makeup and tips, brow pencils and powder. I thought there might be a lipstick I would like. I had planned to put the lipstick on and show up at my mother's dinner table, and maybe I'd ask her if I could keep the new lipstick or maybe my mother would just offer it up to me the way she offered everything else.

Inside the brown envelope was a lipstick, yes, a tube of dark mascara, and a rosy blush—all toys we could share—but on the bottom of the envelope, way down deep where I had to dig my hand in and feel around, was something cylinder shaped and hard, no cosmetic that I recognized.

We were almost downtown, stopped at a red light, and I was telling Angela that I thought I'd die when my mother died, and I didn't mean it figuratively. I meant I thought I'd stop breathing and my heart would quit, and Angela was listing reasons to stay alive. "Lemon drops," she said. "Tacos. You like movies and books," she said.

"Not enough to stay alive for them," I said.

"Music," she tried.

I shook my head.

"Red wine. Orgasms." She paused. "A good night's sleep."

"That's sort of like being dead, though, isn't it?"

"Maybe."

"To see how it all turns out."

"What turns out?"

"All of it," she said.

I was shaking my head no when I pulled the vibrator from the envelope. I thought about shoving it back inside quickly without telling Angela what it was, but she had already turned to me when she heard me gasp. It wasn't just the vibrator and thinking of my mother masturbating that upset me, but also that my mother's boyfriend had stopped sleeping with her, and that no amount of love I gave her could equal what was in my hand.

It was impossible not to imagine my mother, alone and flushed, using it, her quaking thighs and one heaving breast, her body so incredibly hers then, most aware of itself dying or coming, and I understood that she was a woman who wouldn't submit passively to one fate without, in that participatory way, remembering the other.

"How about Mexican food?" Angela said. "Let's get some of those tacos that make life worth living."

"Tacos sound good," I answered, putting the vibrator back inside the envelope and folding it closed.

"It's good that your mother is still concerned about these things."

"What things?"

"You know, pleasure."

"I'm hungry," I said. "Can we talk about food?"

"We are," Angela said.

5.

My mom had made her decision. She returned from the doctor's office, beaming, excited. She put her purse down on the dining room table. She set down her sunglasses and keys, cleared her throat. I was sitting on the couch, reading a student's short story. Daniel Gilb's piece was about a quadriplegic teenage boy who loved and hated his father. It wasn't bad. Daniel was a good writer, bright and passionate, and I was enjoying it. My mother cleared her throat again. "Rachel," she said. I put down my pen and looked at her. I folded my hands across one knee. I rocked back and forth like a toy horse. "What?" I said. "You made up your mind, right?"

She nodded.

"I knew it."

"I'm cancer free—"

"*Now,*" I interrupted.

"Yes, now."

I rocked again, harder. I stopped myself.

"It's not about vanity or even beauty. I know you think so, but it's not. It's more about poise."

"Poise?"

"If I'd been small breasted to begin with, who knows what I'd do now. I'd probably just live this way. Maybe I'd get a tattoo like those women in the book you left out," she said.

"It's not a book, Mom, it's a magazine."

"Whatever it is, I am not one of those women. Cheers to them, that's what I say—but that's not me."

"Okay."

"Don't try to change your mother, Rachel. You always say that I want to change you, but—"

"I just wanted you to see them."

"I saw them." She paused, then continued. "It's terrible having a D cup on one side and nothing on the other." She walked toward me, stood in front of the couch, holding her remaining breast in her palm like an offering.

"I'm sure it is," I said.

"I feel like I'm going to tip over sometimes—literally, fall down."

"You're not."

"But I feel like I could."

"You say that, and it doesn't make sense. Tipping over? That's about vertigo or something. Maybe you've got vertigo." I paused. I picked up the pen and began tapping it on the coffee table. "I wish you'd just wait," I said again.

"For what?" She sat down on the opposite end of the couch and faced me.

I was silent.

"I know what you're thinking," my mother said. "You're a pessimist. You've always been one. I don't know where you get that—all that negative thinking, all that worrying."

"You've never worried about anything."

"I guess not."

"That's why we're in this—" I began, and then stopped myself.

"Go ahead," she responded. "Say it."

"I'm not saying anything."

"Then I will. That's why *we're in this mess.* That's why the tumor got so big, because I didn't worry." She nodded. She clicked her tongue. "It was my tumor, Rachel. And it's gone now. You worry enough for both of us, don't you think?" She scooted closer to me. Our shoulders were touching. "If all that worry added one tiny thing to your life, just one, it would make sense. As it is, I don't see the point of it," she said.

"Worry doesn't need a point."

"Maybe it does."

"There's no point," I admitted.

She looked at the papers in my lap. "How's the story? Is that Daniel's new story?" she asked.

"Yeah."

"You like that boy, don't you?"

"He's my student."

"I know that, but if you like him, you like him. I don't believe in those rules."

"I do."

"If he's special, he's special. He's been taking your classes for years. He lives here and he likes you," she said.

"He's young."

"You're young. I think you should give him a chance. Get to know him, at least. He's not flying in and flying off—he lives here," she said again.

"I'm not *that* young."

"How's the writing?"

"It's good." I picked up the pages and looked at Daniel's words, one bold syllable after another.

"What's the story about?"

"He's always writing pieces about boys without legs or without use of them—teenagers who can't move."

"I like a more cheerful story myself, but you're the teacher."

"The reconstructive surgery scares me," I said.

"It's good *you're* not having it, then." She patted my knee and stood up.

"You know what I mean."

"I'm glad you're here, Rachel."

"You told me that this morning."

"I'm telling you again."

I looked down at Daniel's story and pretended to go back to work. "You got a package yesterday," I told my mother.

"From The Beauty Club?"

"It's on your bed," I said.

"Great," my mother said. "I've been waiting for that. There's a lipstick in there I think you might like."

I didn't look at her, but stared at the boy's words. "I opened it up, didn't see anything interesting."

"Did you try on the lipstick?"

"Wrong shade," I said.

6.

The surgery took six hours and went as expected. Dr. Morgan emerged from the double doors noticeably exhausted. He stood, damp-faced, in front of me and removed his paper hat, using it to mop the perspiration from his forehead. He crinkled the hat in his fist the way another type of man might have smashed a beer can. He stuck the hat in the pocket of his white jacket and looked at me. "She's fine," he said.

"Can I see her?"

"You can see her, sure, but she's out of it."

And my mother *was* out of it, so out of it that I sat for three hours watching her sleep. Every so often she'd moan and try to turn, but her torso was wrapped up in gauze, inches and inches of gauze, so that movement was impossible. She was huge, big and round, like a very pregnant woman or globe under the sheet.

I sat in a chair by the window, writing in my journal. Sometimes I looked out and watched families coming or going—one person in a wheelchair the focus, and the relatives or friends circling the wheelchair—the whole scrum moving toward the parking lot or hospital doors.

The drugs made her mean. At one point she woke up, called me a bitch, and told me to leave. "I don't need you," she said.

The tone of my mother's voice startled me, and I dropped the journal and pen to the floor. I got up and went to her bedside, curled my fingers around the metal rail. "You'll be home in less than a week," I told her.

"Get out of here," she said.

"You don't know what you're saying," I tried.

"Go away—I don't need you," she repeated. "I want to be alone. Leave," she said angrily.

From her bedside I could see the hospital hallway. A young woman dressed like a candy cane pushed a cart of magazines, books, and flowers toward the elevator. Two little girls in matching denim skirts and white blouses played a board game in the middle of the hallway, just outside the room across the way. I wondered why a nurse didn't ask them to move.

I returned to the chair by the window, sat there until I heard my mother's heavy breaths, and then I stood up. I got on my hands and knees to search for the pen. It was a special pen, my favorite, one that my mother had given to me for my twenty-fifth birthday. It was engraved with my name. I crawled under the bed and imagined staying there, sleeping, spending the entire night with the dust and the springs, my mother's body above me, parallel with my own, the two of us, finally, in perfect agreement. But the tile was cold and hard. I spotted the pen and picked it up. I crawled out.

"Where did you come from?" my mother said.

"I dropped my pen."

"I hurt," she said, whimpering.

I touched her hand, but she sneered and pulled away from me. She tried to lift her head, but couldn't. Her curls fanned out against the white pillow. "I don't need you," she said again, dry lips sticking to her teeth.

"You're thirsty. I know you're thirsty," I said, putting the pen on her nightstand and reaching for the plastic pitcher and cup. "Let me give you some water, Mom."

She tried to lift her head again and when she couldn't,

allowed me to support her. "Here," I said, slipping my hand behind her neck. "Let me help you."

She took a long drink of the water, then pulled her head and neck from my grip. "Go home," she said again.

I snatched the pen from the nightstand before turning to my jacket and bag. "You'll like me again in the morning," I said, before leaving her there.

At the elevator I pushed the button and waited. Out of the corner of my eye I watched the little girls who'd been playing the board game, now being scolded. A man stood above them, shaking his finger in one small face and then the other. "She's sick," he said, his voice loud enough for me to hear. "She's very, very sick." The girls looked up at him, matching faces blank as the hallway itself. The elevator doors opened and I stepped inside. "You need to behave. You need to be good girls," I heard the man saying as the doors closed.

I drove down Wilshire Boulevard, through Beverly Hills, where the white, clean streets depressed me further. Those were the stores where people looked at what was on your feet to determine your worth. You needed fine clothes and perfect breasts, two of them, in stores like that. As much as I wanted a cup of coffee, I refused to stop until I was in Hollywood. Once there, I pulled into a Denny's parking lot, turned off the ignition, and sat for a full ten minutes before getting out of the car.

Inside the restaurant I sat down at the counter and waited. An older waitress was placing the check in front of the customer to her right. She was picking up the gentleman's plate, smiling over at me. The waitress swung around, saying, "I'll just be a minute," and I could smell the leftover food, the greasy bacon and eggs, wafting from the woman's arms. It was unpleasant and I thought about leaving the diner, but decided to stay.

By the time the waitress made it over to me with the steaming pot of coffee, I was crying. "Can I get a cup to go?" I said.

The woman had silvery blue hair piled high on top of her head. "Sure, honey," she said, turning away.

She returned with a Styrofoam cup and a small white bag. She leaned toward me and winked. "Got you a blueberry muffin on the house," she whispered.

"Thank you," I said, sniffling. It was embarrassing, crying in public, like being caught at Safeway with my eggs and bread and milk, weeping in the checkout line. "I don't know what's wrong with me," I lied.

"Is it a man that's got you so upset?" the woman said.

I shook my head.

"Not a day goes by without me remembering those who left me. I'm still mad," she said, "at *all* of them."

I looked at the woman and tried to smile. "It's not that," I said. "I'm, I'm—" I stammered, realizing I didn't know what I was or how I felt.

"One thing I know: whatever's got you so upset, you'll live through it—that's the amazing thing." The woman's lips and cheeks were too pink, a bright, unnatural color. She wore blue eye shadow and huge fake eyelashes, the kind I remembered on my mother's eyes in the late sixties. Over the woman's right eye, where the glue had come loose, the lashes were half on and half off. I thought about spiders. I thought about my mother's rubber breast and the body glue she used as adhesive. I felt guilty for leaving my mother, despite her insistence, in that hospital room alone.

"Your eyelash," I said, pointing.

"Thank you, honey," she said, reaching up to make it right.

7.

My mother told me that the doctor had stood at her bedside late that night, only hours after the surgery, and gave her a limited list of options. She said it was surreal, the Demerol, how the only light coming from the hallway haloed him in yellow.

I imagined Dr. Morgan was delicate at first, careful with what he was about to suggest. Perhaps he was coaxing, kind and smooth, like a boy in the beginning. I imagined him flipping through my mother's chart, shaking his head sympathetically. *It sounds worse than it is, this therapy, these leeches,* he said. Perhaps she was squirming, moving in the white sheets like a worm herself. *I don't know,* she said. *Bugs? Living things?*

Yes.

Creatures?

That's right.

I don't know, she said again.

Maybe he said her name twice. *Elizabeth, Elizabeth.*

Oh God, she said. *It's a nightmare, you coming in here so late, suggesting this . . .*

We use them on noses, on digits, too.

Digits?

Fingers and toes.

Say what you mean, doctor—or what I can understand this late, my God.

Okay, he said.

Digits, what kind of a word is that?

It's a word we use.

We?

Doctors.

You're a good doctor, she said, her voice softening.

Then it's a go? he said.

I didn't say that.

Perhaps Dr. Morgan had a limited amount of patience. This was the middle of the night, remember, and I was sure he would have rather been home with his wife and family than standing at my mother's bedside. Maybe he had people on the floor to attend to that were terribly sick. People with failing limbs, with fingers and toes that could not breathe. Perhaps Dr. Morgan's jaw set then, the muscles in his neck and back tensed; perhaps his manner changed. And perhaps like a boy with a reluctant girl, a hard boy in the backseat of his father's car talking about his balls, he said, *Blue, the breast is turning blue.*

Blue? she said.

It won't last.

What now?

The breast needs help.

My mother thought this was curious, the way he talked about *the breast* as if it were not, after all, a part of her, and maybe he was right. Perhaps it was more his than hers. The breast, at least at that moment, wasn't *her breast,* but something completely separate from the rest of her body, so estranged and alienated, it was dying on its own. She moaned and mumbled something.

You decide.

A nightmare, she said again.

It's your call. We could always remove it—which is such a waste—all that work, and your courage.

I don't want to see them, she said.

Not them, he said.

What?

We use one leech at a time.

No details, please—remember, I don't like details.

I remember, he said. *You won't feel a thing. Good decision,* he said.

8.

After he went to my mother and suggested leech therapy, Dr. Morgan called me at home to let me know what was happening. It was eleven P.M. and I was sitting in the living room with Angela and Claire. They had convinced me that a late night drink at Ruby's Room might take my mind off of my mother's surgery and the subsequent drug-induced hostility she'd aimed at me. I was trying not to think about my mother. I was drinking a beer, painting clear nail polish on a potential run in my black tights, trying to let it all go, when the phone rang.

The doctor explained that my mother's body was rejecting the new breast. "The area isn't responding," he said. "The transplanted tissue isn't getting what it needs."

"Which is what? What does the tissue need?" I wanted to know. Angela and Claire looked at me. I put my hand over the receiver. "It's my mom's doctor," I whispered.

"Blood," he said, matter-of-factly.

Angela looked at her watch. "What's going on?"

"Wait," I said.

"You want me to wait?" the doctor said.

"I'm sorry," I said. "I've got friends here."

"It's good you've got friends with you. You've been through a lot," he said.

"My mother has been through a lot," I corrected him.

"Both of you have."

"Yes, well." I lifted the beer to my lips and finished it off, then pointed at the empty bottle, gesturing to my friends that I wanted another one. Angela stood up and headed into the kitchen.

"You seem like a team to me."

"Can you help her?"

"I've suggested leech therapy to your mother."

"Jesus."

"It's not as bad as it sounds," he said.

"They're alive?"

"Think of it like this, Rachel—we've reattached a part of her body that was damaged, let's say bitten off by a dog. Let's say a dog bit off your mother's nose and someone quick on his feet saved the nose and put it on ice." Dr. Morgan paused.

"Go on," I said, taking the bottle from Angela and twisting off the top. I took a big sip quickly, feeling the cold beer in my mouth and throat. I was imagining my mother without a nose, imagining some quick-thinking man putting the nose, like a bottle of wine, on ice.

"Let's say I reattached the nose—did a good job, minimal scarring, all of that—"

"Please, Dr. Morgan. It's late. I'm a nervous wreck here."

"I understand," he said. "I'm sorry. I know this is hard for you." He explained the two options: either he could remove the starving tissue, leaving her with a dramatic tummy tuck and nothing else, or he could attach leeches to the area and depend on them to get the blood flowing. He was confident they'd do the trick.

The leeches themselves were clean, medicinal. They'd been starved for months prior, with just this feast in mind. They'd be determined enough, hungry enough, he hoped, to stimulate the blood, to bring it up through her body and into that makeshift breast—which, by the way, was beautiful, perfect, it would be a shame to waste a breast like that.

"She agreed to this?" I said.

"Yes."

"She's okay with this?"

"As okay as can be expected," he said.

"God."

"I'm on my way in there now to begin the therapy—but wanted to let you know."

"You're going in there with bugs *now?*" I said, horrified. My friends' eyes widened, their mouths dropped.

"It's one bug, actually. One leech at a time."

"Can I see her?"

"I'd let her sleep through this first treatment. She's fine," he said. "They're medicinal," he repeated.

It was midnight, and Ruby's Room wasn't crowded. The three of us sat in a booth, drinking our third beers of the night. A group of men sent over shots of tequila. One man, an unlit cigar hanging from his cracked lips, delivered them to our table. His face was red, especially his nose. There were visible cracks, fissures, in the corners of his mouth. I thought that perhaps he worked outside, on a boat. Perhaps he made buildings. Perhaps he fished leaves, dead flowers, and insects from swimming pools.

The man set the tequila directly in front of Angela, as if all three shots were for her. He looked into her eyes. Angela stared back.

Claire shot me a look.

Finally, I interrupted the tension, saying, "Thanks, thank you, *thanks.*"

He looked at me, pointed out his buddies with a nod. "Thank *them,*" he said, the cigar bouncing. I looked over at the men, who were sitting in a booth across the way. I couldn't make out one face. From where I sat, they were a sea of beards and caps and grins.

"I heard your big laugh," the man said to Angela. "And, well, I had to meet you. A girl with a laugh like that is some kind of fun, and I mean that sincerely," he said.

"Some kind of fun, huh?" she repeated.

"I'm buying whatever you want next—for you and your friends here." He wagged his cigar good-bye before turning back to his buddies.

Usually, I didn't drink tequila, but now there I was with an empty shot glass in front of me, a slice of lime sucked dry, and that distinct taste still on my lips. After the cigar guy left, Claire scooted her tequila in Angela's direction, and now Angela was stacking the two empty shot glasses on top of each other. "I'd forgotten what this stuff tastes like," she said.

"I don't want to remember," Claire said.

Angela was telling me that she'd have opted for the reconstruction herself. "I think it's important to stay whole," she said.

"Even with the leeches?" I asked her.

"Yes."

"Not me," Claire said.

"I saw a television show recently where a man lost his ear," Angela began. "And this beautiful doctor—my, he was gorgeous, a prince—anyway, this doctor put the ear on ice—or was it already on ice? Either way," she said, "they saved the ear like you'd save a trout or something. Then he sewed it back on. It's amazing what they can do these days."

"I missed that one," I said.

"Well, it was like what's happening with your mom," Angela continued. "They used leeches to get the blood going. They're hungry fuckers, that's for sure. They starve them to get them ready. I read about it in *Time*."

"It's cruel," Claire said, shaking her head. "We're all the goddess's creatures."

Angela rolled her eyes. "Creatures?"

"Yes, and we all have a place in this world."

"Right now, *their place* is at my mother's breast."

"We're talking about leeches, here, Claire," Angela said. She pulled my empty shot glass her way and balanced it on top of the others, making a precarious ladder.

Claire, huffing and sighing, removed the shot glass. She looked at Angela, who was then smiling and waving across the bar at the cigar guy. I picked up my beer and took a big swallow.

"What do they do with them once they're fed?" Claire asked.

"I think they toss them into a bin to die, or they die on their own. I don't remember that part of the article." Angela paused. She looked around the bar. "Not even one attractive man in here."

"What about the cigar guy?" I asked.

"He's not attractive," Angela said.

"Well, then, why—"

"Because he likes me, Rachel—because he likes what he sees, at least."

Claire shuddered. "I'd hate those leeches on me," she said,

changing the subject or not changing it at all. "I'd hate—" she began, but Angela cut her off.

"I'd do what your mom did," Angela said. "I'd choose surgery, even with the leeches. I mean, what's the alternative—walking around without a nose or ear or breast?"

"For my nose or ear, yes," Claire said. "For my finger, of course, but for a breast, no way."

"What's the difference?" Angela wanted to know.

"If a body part that's basically just flesh and fat turns on you, if it's sick, who wants it?"

"You can say that now," Angela said, "because you're a lesbian."

"I'm not a lesbian. I have a girlfriend, but I'm not a lesbian," Claire said.

"In my book, you're a lesbian, Claire. You can call yourself bi or whatever, but to me—"

Claire interrupted her. "What does my sexual preference have to do with any of this anyway?"

"Back in high school, you would have chosen the reconstruction—when you were straight or pretending to be."

"I wasn't pretending."

"Come on you two, don't fight," I said.

"We're not fighting, we're discussing," Angela said.

"It's okay, Rachel," Claire said.

"Now that you're with women, Claire, you don't have to look as good. You don't have to worry about pleasing men," Angela said.

I laughed.

"That's ridiculous," Claire said, looking at me.

I stopped laughing. I wasn't about to get in the middle of this.

"It's not ridiculous," Angela argued. "Listen, men get

pleasure visually, from seeing. Everyone knows this—you know this, Claire. And you'd admit it if you were honest."

"Claire's honest," I tried.

"I'm honest," Claire said. "And lesbians want to look good for their partners. You don't know anything about it."

"I thought you said you weren't a lesbian," Angela said.

Claire shook her head.

"It's not about vanity, it's about a man's judgment. It's why you lesbians get to be fat, it's why gay men live at the gym. Not that you're fat, Claire, you're fine. I'm talking about a majority here. Think of your new girlfriend. What's her name—Leona, Lora?"

"Lora," I said. "She's very nice."

"That's right, Lora. I'm sure she is nice, sweet as can be, heart of gold and all of that, but I bet little Lora's ass is as big as mine—and I bet she doesn't have to worry about her ass because she's *nice,* because you, Claire, don't care one way or another about her ass. If it spread from one end of this bar to the other, I bet you wouldn't complain." Angela picked up her beer and finished it off. She exhaled heavily. "I want another," she said. "You, Rachel?"

"Just water."

Angela swung her legs out of the booth and stood. "What if I bring you one last beer and you nurse it for the rest of the night?"

"Okay," I said.

Angela turned, leaving us alone. "She's nuts," Claire said. "I can't believe what comes out of her mouth."

"She likes to talk."

Claire leaned across the booth. "I wouldn't have the reconstruction even if I was straight. I'm not judging your mother or anything, I just wouldn't have it myself."

"Who knows, Claire. I wanted my mom to wait another year because I'm afraid of the cancer coming back."

"I'm not judging her," she said again.

"I want my breasts," I said. "I'm scared of them, but I'd want them back if they took them from me. I don't know what I would do—what choices I'd make."

"You'd get on with things, Rachel, that's what you'd do. You wouldn't worry about the cosmetic side of all of this when your survival was at stake. I know you, Rachel." She paused. She looked around the bar. "Did you see that guy's lips, those cracks?"

I nodded.

"He freaked me out."

"I know."

"I mean, is the size of someone's ass so important?"

"My mom thinks all three of our asses are big."

"Your ass isn't big," Claire said. "You're in proportion." She was quiet a minute. "Wait, your mom said *my* ass was big?"

I nodded.

"I'm a size five—what's she talking about?"

"She says that our asses are big compared to the rest of us. She calls us shapely."

Claire smiled. "Your mom's a funny one," she said. "And anyway, you don't have to kiss someone's ass. You kiss their lips. And Angela's new friend, his lips are gross. Lora's lips are soft."

"Good point," I said, laughing.

"That guy had skin hanging from his lips, and he thought he was okay, just fine, and it was—Angela doesn't care what his lips look like. She's just happy that he likes the way she looks. He's a dry-lipped beast," Claire said, laughing, and then the two of us were laughing, drunk and silly, and couldn't stop.

I pointed over at Angela, who had just turned from the cigar guy's table and was heading back to the booth with drinks. Claire caught her breath. "She's right, you know. Angela's right. I hate it when she's right," she said.

"Who's right?" Angela said, putting the beers in the middle of the table, two more shots of tequila, and a napkinful of lime.

Claire was quiet.

"Let's drink," Angela said. She climbed into the booth, and then raised the shot glass in the air. "Let's toast."

I reached for mine.

"Don't be mad at me, Claire." Angela was talking to the back of Claire's head because Claire had twisted around and was now facing the bar. "You like that bartender? Her name is Stephanie. She likes men and women. Mostly women, I think. I could introduce you to her. Want me to?"

Claire ignored her.

"Okay, be mad at me, but be mad later. Let's cheers to Rachel," Angela said, bringing the shot glass to her mouth.

I joined her.

"To Elizabeth," Angela said. "To Rachel's mother, mother of us all, mother of all God's creatures, and, and—"

"And?" I said.

"And to her breast-saving leeches," she continued.

I nodded.

"And mostly, certainly, always, to survival—to whatever the fuck it takes," Angela concluded, smiling.

Claire picked up her beer.

The three of us toasted, glasses clinking, then leaned our heads back and swallowed.

9.

Angela had offered to spend the night at my mother's apartment so I wouldn't wake up alone. Moments ago, she had slipped out of Ruby's Room's back door with my spare key, a naughty smile on her face, and the man with the dry lips on her arm. I told her to go ahead and take my room, that I'd sleep in my mother's bed. Claire, after a ridiculous amount of reassurance, after I had promised to take a cab and ignore last call, finally called Lora to pick her up.

I left the booth and moved to the bar. Now, it *was* last call and I didn't ignore it but ordered one more beer. It was one-thirty bar time, which gave me twenty minutes or so. Adam Anderson, whom I hadn't seen in years and hadn't missed, was sitting next to me, drinking a cup of coffee.

In the late eighties, when I was a student, he taught anatomy and biology part-time at the university. He wasn't my instructor. I didn't meet him in a class, but at a poetry reading—one of his own. Ten years ago it was his abortion I'd had when the two of us didn't like each other enough to chance the combination of genes. Now he was full-time, a professor, he said. He was surprised that I was teaching on campus myself now, in the building right next to his—and even more surprised that I hadn't stopped by to say hello.

"You work there, right across the way," he said, grabbing his chin. "I remember when you—"

"Don't remember, Adam," I said.

He laughed, nervously. "Okay," he said.

"It's not a good idea," I said.

"Well, anyway, you look good, Rachel. You're a better-looking woman than you were a girl."

"And that's a compliment?"

"Yes," he said. "You grew into your looks, your face."

I looked at him, puzzled.

"You grew into your features, that's what I'm saying."

"Features, huh?"

"That's right. You look good, okay? I like the way you look now. You've grown up, and I—"

"We never liked each other," I interrupted. I didn't look at him, but stared straight ahead at the wall. It was blank, the wall, and I remembered when pictures of huge-breasted women hung on Ruby's walls, creamy women, naked against black felt. I wondered who convinced the owner, Mac, to change his décor. I wondered if Mac had found someone, fallen in love. I wondered what Adam would do if I moved back to the booth, if he'd follow me or let me go.

"No," he said, "maybe we didn't." He picked up his cocktail napkin and began ripping it into tiny pieces.

I stayed on the barstool. I shook my head. "I thought I liked you," I said, "but I didn't know anything."

"You knew some things," he said.

"I didn't know—"

"Do you like me now?" he interrupted.

I finished my beer in one long swallow. "I don't think so."

"We're different, that's all."

"No," I said, feeling the beer, feeling bold. "You were a real fucker, that's what it was." I turned on the stool and faced him.

"Damn," he said.

"And I didn't know how to be—" I began, and then stopped myself, realizing I didn't know how to finish the sentence.

"Be *what?*" He let out an awkward laugh. He paused. He lifted the coffee cup and looked inside. "There's no cream. Goddamn, she forgot the cream. I can't drink this shit black," he said. "Stephanie," he called. "Hey, Steph."

"*What?*" the bartender turned from two men she'd been serving or flirting with. She set the bottle of vodka down. I heard it smack the counter. She wiped her hands on her apron and looked at Adam, then at me. I thought I saw Stephanie wink my way, but couldn't be sure; anything at all could have been happening. "What now, Adam?" she said.

"I need some fat in this coffee," he said.

"Fine," she said, reaching behind the bar. She was pouring the cream into Adam's cup and he was still talking. "Make it white, Steph," he said. "You know I like it white," he said.

The bar lights did their late night flashing, and patrons began to grumble and gather their jackets. Adam was smiling, and I was still trying to finish that sentence in my head. I looked at his dark, thick eyebrows, his green or blue eyes, and was trying to finish that impossible sentence.

"You want a ride home?" he asked.

10.

Fellatio was one part of a whole, I believed—a piece of a more complicated act, one scene from a full-length play that required two energetic thespians. I'd never been generous or gracious or confident or stupid enough to give a man a blow job in a car or empty movie theater, to give him *just that* on a freeway, to offer up my mouth—the way Angela claimed to—at a stop sign or before breakfast. A hand was one thing, I'd decided long ago, but a mouth was something else altogether.

Still, years ago, in a parking garage outside a Huntington Beach nightclub, in Adam's car, I did just that. He'd wanted to take me home, his or mine, it didn't matter, he said. Neither of us knew then that I was pregnant, that he'd drop me off in front of a clinic in two week's time, that he'd stuff crumpled dollar bills into my hand for a cab home before speeding away, and that the check he'd mail to me for the procedure would bounce. Neither of us knew, and I looked good, really good, he'd said. Had I lost weight? Did I like his new car? Was I letting my hair grow out?

"Out of what?" I asked.

"It was a bob, wasn't it?"

"It wasn't a bob."

"Yes, it was," he said, emphatically. "Few weeks ago it was all one length, to your chin." He cut into his own chin with the side of his hand, demonstrating.

"It was someone else, Adam. I haven't changed my hair," I said.

"Hair grows. It's growing, that's all."

"Okay," I said, giving up.

"You look good," he said again.

I was surprised at myself, and he was more so, when I unzipped his pants and held him in my hand, right there, in the car, in the garage. "Tinted windows," I said. "A showy man like you with tinted windows—why? You hiding something?"

When he started to answer, I stopped him with a finger to my lips. "Shh," I said. "Don't talk, Adam. We've said enough. We say too much. A pair like us should shut the hell up," I whispered.

He was nodding and breathing heavily. With my free hand I released the emergency brake. I put my chin in his lap and didn't even flinch when I heard shoes outside clip the concrete, a woman's laugh, a man's voice, a car door just feet away opening and closing, the engine turning over, again and again, until finally, the car screeched off. I had this to do, only this. I was determined, eager; it was as if I'd been born or starved with just that meal in mind. I held my lips inches from him, touched him until he stood right up. *All that blood,* I remember thinking, *he's jammed now, stuffed with it.*

11.

Moments earlier at Ruby's Room I felt okay or thought I did, but now in Adam's car my head spun. I was quiet until he turned down my street. I believed his red leather interior only added to my queasiness. "It's red in here," I said. "Everything, Adam—the seats, the steering wheel. It's garish. What were you thinking? When you bought this car, what was on your mind?"

"Not you," he said, obviously insulted.

I laughed. "Apparently not."

I asked him to drop me off in front of my mother's building. He wanted to come up. He wanted to talk. "I feel sick," I told him. "When I'm sick like this, it's hard to be polite. I'm sorry about your car, the way it looks—I mean, I'm sorry about what I said." I opened the door and stepped out.

He asked for my number, but I didn't think he wanted it and I didn't want to give it to him. Not tonight. Not ever. At one time I would have written my number, somewhere, anywhere—on the back of his hand if he'd allowed it. I would have written down my number before he even asked. "No, Adam," I said, closing the door, leaning down to see him one last time. He looked stunned, mouth hanging open.

"I thought I remembered you," he said.

I shrugged. "Sorry," I said.

He leaned toward the passenger window. "We're old friends. What's wrong with having a conversation with an old friend? Can't I get your number?"

"We're not friends," I said.

"Not even a number, Rachel?" he tried again.

"No," I said, "not even that."

12.

I found Angela's tights in the hall. I poked my head in and saw her bra hanging on a lampshade, one black cup visible, the other hidden, wrapped over the lightbulb, dimming the room. I knew Angela thought it was exciting, a night like this, that in the morning over toast, she'd be full of animated details, but now she was alone in my bed, a woman wrapped in a sheet, a woman who'd been touched and left—in less than two hours.

I went to my friend and covered her with the blanket. Angela's cheeks were moist. She was glistening. I could almost feel it. His scent—that cigar he'd been holding between his lips at Ruby's—was still there, clinging to Angela's skin. "I'll smoke this puppy when I get out of here," he had said. "I'm a man with patience," he told the three of us. I thought about that man, generous with the shots of tequila and compliments. He'd liked Angela's profile, her teeth, her dark hair and eyes, her laugh. He'd introduced himself as "Big Brad, the sober one—ten years this July," but still the shots kept coming. I remembered his puffy face and dry lips, his red nose, his grin as he sat across the bar from us, lifting his glass of water in the air. I remembered him pointing that unlit cigar in Angela's direction and winking.

Here it was just three A.M. and Big Brad was gone, the sober one was tucked under his own sheets or his girlfriend's or his wife's. His harsh kisses, however, were still there, in the bedroom—three hickies on Angela's neck turning from pink to red to purple.

13.

While my mother slept that first night, leech number one escaped, wiggled out from under the gauze and traveled her body, from breast to neck as a lover might have. It twisted by her shoulder blade, pausing at her collarbone, and rested at her neck, where it sucked and sucked and sucked.

In the morning, I opened the heavy door to her hospital room and found the leech there, fat and full—the size of a big man's thumb. I stood with my hands over my mouth, not making a sound. My mother was still asleep or doped up, but what I believed to be reflex or intuition or simply an itch brought her hand to her neck. She opened her eyes, touched it, and screamed. I held my breath.

Two nurses burst through the door, an older nurse followed by a much younger nurse. The older nurse joined my mother, matching my mother's screams with her own equally horrified gasps. The young nurse, a stern woman with a mouth like a cut, glared at the older nurse. She narrowed her eyes and grumbled something I could not make out. She pointed at the door. "Stop it, Donna," she said, "or get out."

The older nurse composed herself. She straightened her white pants, adjusted her polyester jacket. She fiddled with the stethoscope that hung around her neck.

I was biting the inside of my cheek. Madly. I tasted blood. My hands shook.

The stern nurse shot a nasty look in my direction.

"Help her," I said. "Do something."

The nurse went to my mother's bedside. She twisted my mother's head to one side, and with a gloved hand, slowly, deliberately, peeled the plump creature from her neck.

"Goddamn," she said to all of us. "Grow up."

14.

My mother spent a week in the hospital recuperating, and when I wasn't visiting her or teaching, I found myself researching leeches on the Internet. I was gathering facts—perhaps I'd write a series of poems or maybe a story. As was discovered the morning after my mother's therapy began, one problem with leeches is that they migrate, moving from the needy area of the body to other areas, private areas. In the nineteenth century, leeches were reported to have disappeared inside a woman's rectum, attached themselves in the upper airway, and ascended into her uterus.

The Hirudo leech has three jaws and three hundred teeth, and is the leech most doctors, including Dr. Morgan, prefer.

The leech uses its own anesthetic, so its bite is painless—my mother later attested to that.

When the leech was placed on my mother's breast, it injected an anticoagulant serum to prevent blood clotting, which was, after all, the point—why the leech ended up there in the first place—that anticoagulant, that thinning, flowing blood, which fed not only the larcenist worm itself, but the tissue it pinched and visited.

The leech ate and ate, gorged itself until it had ingested enough blood to equal five times its body weight. In the end, before it was dropped into a bin with its satiated cousins to die, it was a bloated, fed thing; it was a body plump with mother.

The whole thing was a vile contradiction, and though I had done the research and tried to think about it rationally, I still had nightmares and a growing distaste for snails and ants and even cats—anything that crawled or pilfered.

Now, mid-December, six weeks after reconstruction and the medicinal leech therapy that followed, the two of us were at Dr. Morgan's office, waiting for the bandages to come off. My mother sat on the table in a blue gown, excited, swinging her legs like a girl. Dr. Morgan had just joined us, and I'd moved from my mother's side to the far corner of the room to give them space.

While I watched the doctor talk to my mother, I remembered that the word *leech* might have been derived from the old English word *laece*, or *physician*. The first written record of the therapy was found in the *Corpus Hippocraticum*. Hippocrates believed that disease, all disease, was caused by imbalance of the four humors: blood, phlegm, black bile, and yellow bile. He thought that the medicinal use of leeches could play a central part in restoring balance. I thought about my mother tipping over in the grocery store, reaching for the frozen peas and falling into the freezer. I stared at Dr. Morgan's back, the tilt of his head, and wondered if, when the bandages were removed, my mother would finally feel balanced, restored, if those matching breasts she'd longed for would be enough.

Christmas music played throughout the office. It seemed to me that something was wrong with the speakers because the music was louder, more intense, than it had been only moments earlier. I was staring at the speakers, wondering what was up—was the volume intentional?

"Forgive us," Dr. Morgan said. "They're broken. Someone is coming later this afternoon to fix them."

"Is it like this in every room?" I wanted to know.

"Just this one."

"Lucky us."

"Rachel," my mother said. "Be nice."

"I could ask the girls up front to turn it off, if you like."

"Oh, no," my mother said. "Let's not punish everyone. It's not that loud—right, honey?"

I didn't answer her.

Christmas music was just one of the things about the holidays that annoyed me—the inability to escape those songs, the same songs every year, and there I was in the doctor's office with "Silent Night" something more than background music.

A miniature stuffed Santa Claus sat on a chair of his own. I was right under the speakers, near the stuffed Santa, and near the sharp instruments that sat on a paper cloth. There were bottles of blue liquid lined up, cotton balls, flesh-colored tape, and oversized Q-tips. The scissors were huge, no scissors that I recognized. They looked like two carving knives held together in the middle by a small band of metal, the kind of knives the doctor and his family probably reserved for holidays, for the big roasts his family ate just a couple times a year.

Dr. Morgan picked up the scissors and snipped at my mother. He unwrapped the bandages from her torso with anticipation, as if she were a gift, and I imagined him on Christmas morning, untying the ribbon on a present from his wife and kids with the same expectant look on his face. The gauze came away from my mother's skin, up and over her shoulder and head. Each sheet was pinker than the one before it, and the last one was more than red, stained and maroon and sticking to her flesh. He pulled at it slowly, carefully, but still my mom winced.

When she was half naked before us, Dr. Morgan actually said, "*Ta-da,*" almost sang those two little words, revealing to us what he gave her: a new breast, which was really a fat thing without a nipple from what I could see, red scars like bloody highways surrounding it.

"Beautiful," he said. "Happy holidays," he said.

And I nodded in agreement because it was, after all, an improvement over the hollowed-out space that was there before. I thought a moment about valleys and vacuities and holes, teeth that hurt, cavities, and the ditch that had been my mother's chest, and then I thought about mountains and islands and trees, protrusions and tumors, too.

"Beautiful," my mother said, looking down.

"Yes, beautiful," I agreed.

Georgia Carter

1996–1997

Cream

1.

At thirteen, these things scared Georgia Carter: other kids with IQs as high as hers, clowns, cartoons, and the flowers outside her bedroom window before they opened. She liked to understand things, especially her own fears. About the clowns, it was easy. It was the paint and puffed-up clothing; it was not knowing what was underneath or whom. And cartoons—well, they were just violent. But the other smart kids and the flowers outside her window, she didn't understand. Especially the flowers. They just sat there, closed up and full of fragrance. What was there to be afraid of?

One Friday afternoon, while her father was teaching math, while her mother was at the office, while her brother, Kevin, was working at The Fish Joint, dropping chunks of cod into hot oil, Georgia offered up her virginity to her brother's best friend, Craig. She presented her virginity to Craig on the hand-painted clown plate. There were chocolate cookies on the plate as well, ones with white cream oozing from the middle. The more cookies Craig ate, the more of the clown she saw, parts of him at a time. A painted eye here, half of those exaggerated lips, until finally, all of him, his whole scary face revealed. The clown looked up at the two of them from the plate, black crumbs dotting his cheeks like fine hairs you'd never find on a clown.

Georgia was thinking about those hairs as the boy opened her thighs. She was thinking about how a girl like her could be reading, doing English homework one minute, making plans for college, then offering a boy her sandwich cookies and virginity the next. The whole half hour that he was down there she heard him, saw him, pulling things apart—like the cookies, how he split them in two, then scraped away their creamy middles with one swift sweep of his bottom teeth.

In her sheets with a boy three years older, she made herself into someone new and tall. She planned a spicy wardrobe in her head, tight jeans and short shirts that would show her belly button. She watched the top of Craig's head, his dark curls swirling about like the tongue itself, and she saw her whole life opening up or closing. She started thinking that she could crack his pretty skull in half if her thighs were stronger. But they weren't—and neither was she, really.

A boy like Craig would never do what she really wanted of him, which was stand with her under the sun, holding her hand in front of her third period gym class. Just stand with her. Lean against the wire fence, touching her pink knuckles with his fingertips.

Now he stood at the foot of her bed with sweat on his face. He wiggled into his Levis and almost scowled. Yes, it *was* a scowl—his lips, the same ones he kissed her with, now twisting into a grimace. It wasn't the face he made when he reached for her cookies. It wasn't the face he made when he reached for her breasts. She had the feeling that he won, though she wasn't sure what the game was called; she didn't even know she was playing it. If this afternoon were Monopoly, she'd have given him Park Place and Boardwalk, offered up her thimble, her pink and blue and yellow bills.

Still, at the front door, she was purring. "Will you meet me on Monday after third period?" she asked.

He moved about on his feet, shuffling in his tennis shoes, one behind the other, then he started talking about science class. "We're dissecting an animal on Monday," he began.

"Oh," she said.

"Yeah," he said, "a cat. I can't get to the Junior High in time."

"I guess not," she said.

"Besides, you're in the smart kid classes, aren't you?"

She shrugged. She thought about lying, telling him no, that was a rumor, but what sort of rumor would that have been?

"You're like a genius or something. No way," he told her.

"I'm not a genius," Georgia said.

"Whatever."

"I took some test and they stuck me in those classes. I don't even want to be there," she said.

"I've got to go," Craig said.

Georgia was sure he did have to go, and also sure that it was a momentous occasion for a boy like Craig to attend science class, to see those organs being scooped out of a cat, and even more momentous if he held the knife himself, did the cutting and the scooping. He'd be busy afterwards, she was certain, processing the whole valuable experience. Of course she understood. Of course she wasn't mad. Yes, certainly, she'd tell Kevin that Craig came by looking for him.

2.

Within weeks Georgia was famous. Her brother's friends came knocking when he wasn't home. She wore tight shirts, shorts, and sandals when she answered the door. Her mother's best perfume and the smallest bit of lipstick. The friends were obvious, coming without their surfboards or guitars, coming when they knew Kevin was away frying fish. One stood on the porch at eleven A.M., a Saturday, a fluorescent blue condom already in his fist. "Hey, Georgia," he said, "how's it going?"

"It's going," she said.

Usually she let them in, but this one with his plans in his fist was weird. His name was Harvard, but everyone called him Harvey. His front teeth hung over his bottom lip.

"Where's your mom and dad?" he said.

"Looking at new houses."

"What's wrong with this one?" He leaned forward, trying to get a look inside.

"Nothing, probably," Georgia said. "It's just something they do together on the weekends. A habit. We're not moving or anything. They just like to look."

"Can I come in and see it? The house, I mean."

"You've been here before, Harvey." She rolled her eyes, shook her head. "God," she said.

"Come on, Georgia."

"Why?"

"I don't know. We can watch cartoons or something. It's Saturday," he reminded her.

"I hate cartoons."

"Well, we can talk."

"Talk, huh?"

"Yeah, why not?" He lifted his hand over that mouth of his and yawned. The yawn was overly dramatic, fake, and came booming into the air between them. "I'm tired," Harvey said. "We can lie down. We can rest together."

"You want to talk *and* rest, huh?"

"Yeah," he said, bending toward her.

"What's that in your fist?" she asked.

And that's when he uncurled his fingers and the condom fell to the porch. He let out an embarrassed laugh and dropped to his knees. She left him there, like that, reaching for the blue condom, on the ground, like a knight about to propose.

3.

It was days later, late afternoon, and Georgia was sitting on the couch watching the news. Kevin was at work, but Georgia's parents were home—her father asleep, sprawled out on his chair in the den, her mother at the kitchen table, reading the paper.

When Georgia heard a car pull up to the curb, she parted the curtains and looked out the window. It was Josh, one more of Kevin's friends, turning off the engine and opening his car door, stepping into the street. It was Josh spraying something minty, she assumed, onto his tongue and looking toward their front door.

Georgia dropped the curtain and turned back to the television, already making a plan in her head about how she might avoid dinner with her parents. She could smell the night's roast baking in the oven, the garlic and rosemary, and though she was hungry and her mother's meal was tempting, she wanted to join this boy for a ride if he, as she suspected, asked her.

Josh was tall and muscular, popular and friendly—the best surfer in town—and Georgia had hoped he'd eventually come to her the way the others had. And now he was on the porch, knocking.

Moments earlier Georgia had been mesmerized by a particular news story, one in which a botched liposuction procedure had resulted in the death of a sixteen-year-old girl. At first Georgia assumed that the reporter was talking about malpractice, a doctor, but when she saw footage of two police officers steering a handcuffed teenager toward a police car, Georgia realized she had been mistaken.

The handcuffed girl had been a receptionist for Cosmetic Plus, a clinic on Fourth and Bower, and was a senior at Diamond High School in Seal Beach, which was just ten minutes away from Georgia's own school. Apparently, the handcuffed girl had tried liposuction on her best friend's thighs and accidentally killed her.

Georgia imagined the girls, playing doctor in the middle of the night. After hours, and the two of them sneaking inside the clinic, using the arrested girl's key. She imagined they were giggling and excited, planning to get something for nothing. They had a goal in mind: one of them would be more perfect in the morning. The receptionist had probably watched the procedure before, had stood in the hall, peering in, or maybe gawked at the doctor's side, holding a tray of equipment: a scalpel, a glass jar of cotton balls, a rubber hose. The reporter had shaken his head, his dark hair stiff and obedient. He'd

made a tsk-tsk sound with his mouth, apparently not under-
standing their motivation—why would two girls try such a
thing? Georgia was answering that question in her head when
she heard Josh's car door slam.

Now there was his knock and the doorbell ringing and
Georgia was getting up off the couch, straightening her skirt,
saying, "I'll get it."

"Who's that?" her mother said, pushing her glasses up on
her nose. "Georgia, who's there?"

"It's Rebecca," Georgia lied, closing the door on her knee,
putting her calf and ankle and foot between her and the boy
so as not to shut him out completely. "She wants to know if I
can go study."

"I'm making a roast," her mother said.

"I've got a geography test tomorrow, Mr. Rupert's class.
You know how much better Rebecca does when we study
together—remember last month? Remember how happy her
mother was?"

"It's nearly dinnertime, Georgia," her mother said, looking down at her watch.

"I'll eat later."

"I don't know."

"Save me a plate—please."

"All right," her mother said, giving in. "But be back by
eight. I want you home early."

"Eight?" Georgia whined.

"Not a minute after nine. It's a school night, Georgie," her
mother said.

Once in Josh's car, Georgia pretended he was her
boyfriend. She pretended she was on a date. She told herself
that he liked her. He was, after all, smiling and polite in a way
Craig was not. He had both hands on the wheel—therefore

nothing blue and glowing, no obvious plans in his fist—though anything at all could have been in his pocket. Georgia rolled down the window and started chatting. She told Josh about the news, about the girl from Diamond High School who was arrested. "She's in jail," Georgia said.

"It sounds like she's getting what she deserves," he said.

"It was an accident."

"She killed her friend."

"I know, but—" she tried.

"But what?" Josh said, shaking his head.

"Nothing," she said.

"They should hang her," he continued, his tone and mood changing now. "Or give her the chair."

"It was an accident," she said again.

"Let's talk about something else," Josh said. He turned right on Second, passing the stores and restaurants, heading toward Pacific Coast Highway and the beach.

Georgia looked out the window, at the palm trees, at the busy street, shoppers carrying bags, couples holding hands, young mothers or maids pushing strollers. Three girls she recognized from school stood at the stoplight on her right. They had Rollerblades swung over their shoulders, and were laughing so loudly that Georgia could hear them from where she sat. She stared at them hard, wishing they'd feel her stare, and look into the car. She wanted them to see her with Josh, but they didn't look, were obviously too busy with each other to care. Georgia turned to him. "What do you want to talk about?" she asked.

"Let's talk about Craig," Josh said, a sly smile on his face.

Georgia tried to smile herself, but the smile was weak and silly. She twisted in her seat. She shook her head no.

"Come on," he said.

"I don't know about this," she said.

The light turned green and Josh accelerated. "Do you like my car?" he asked, ignoring her last comment.

"Yeah."

"It was my mom's, but now it's mine," he said proudly.

"Pretty cool," she said.

"Damn straight. Not everyone gets a car at sixteen, but my mom feels like shit since she left us. She's so fucking guilty she'll give me whatever I ask for. School clothes, a bike, a new surfboard—top of the line."

Georgia almost said, "That's great," but stopped herself. She didn't know what to say, so she just nodded. He wasn't looking at her anyway, but up at the rearview mirror, trying to change lanes, watching the traffic. "Kevin has a car," she said finally.

"That thing?"

"It gets him where he needs to go," she said.

"It's a clunker," Josh said.

Georgia shrugged, but he still couldn't see her, didn't seem concerned with her response, because now he was pulling into the beach parking lot, turning off the car. "Relax," he said. "You want to be here, right?"

Georgia didn't answer him. She didn't know where she wanted to be, didn't understand why just a half hour earlier she'd jumped off the couch, excited, and now felt uncertain. She almost wished she were home, sitting down with her parents for that roast.

"What's wrong?" he asked her.

"Nothing," she said, biting her bottom lip, staring straight ahead at the windshield in front of her. "If you like the car, Josh, you should wash it. It's dirty."

"I know."

"It would look better, you'd like it even more, if it were clean. Don't you think so?"

"Probably."

"I could help you wash it this weekend," she offered.

"Not going to happen. I'm surfing with your brother this weekend."

"Oh," she said.

"Look at me," he said.

It was dusk, and the sun was fat and orange, falling into the ocean. She looked at Josh. He wore a striped T-shirt and a pair of shorts. In that light, his knees were pink, pinker than the rest of him. They sat in silence for several minutes before he put his hand on the seat between them. He inched the hand closer to Georgia, his fingertips brushing the hem of her skirt. He spread his fingers out so that his hand became a starfish.

4.

Georgia stood in 27 Flavors, trying to decide. Her friend Rebecca was twelve but looked eighteen, with huge breasts and full hips, with makeup on her face like art. "I want frozen yogurt," Georgia said, staring at the ice cream. "This stuff is fattening."

"Who cares?" Rebecca leaned over the counter, peering in. "It's delicious."

Earlier the two of them had stood outside Kevin's bedroom door, eavesdropping, while he talked to his friends— three of whom had seen Georgia naked: Craig and Josh and Anthony. Harvey was there too; Georgia recognized his whine. The girls put their ears to the door. Liz Phair was on the radio, and the boys were talking about chicks' voices and chicks' bodies. Kevin was saying, "What a guy really cares about is a girl's body. Fuck her face. And who cares if she can sing. Who cares about what her face looks like. It's the body you fuck. If she's fat, her pussy's fat."

And his friends said, "Yeah, that's right." Their voices sounded like one voice, and Georgia couldn't tell them apart. They could have been one boy, and she started thinking about how similar they were, even without their clothes, even inches from her face. She stood with her friend at the door, imagining all she'd done with the three of them, listening to their laughter. And then her brother mentioned paper bags, said he wanted to put one over an ugly girl's face while he fucked her titties. "Better than fucking a fat girl any day, though," he said. "Fat's the worst."

"Come on," Rebecca said now, "get some ice cream. You're skinny, Georgie. What do you have to worry about? It's me with these hips," she said, slapping her side.

"I don't know."

"I want that," Rebecca said, pointing at the tub of Chewy Chocolate.

The boy behind the counter wore a red-and-white uniform, a little square hat on his head. His pimply chin jutted out from the rest of his face, which was sunken in comparison. With a chin like that, the boy could have leaned over the counter, pointed himself in Georgia's direction, and tapped her on the shoulder with it. With a chin like that, he could have pushed her away.

Georgia looked down at the tubs of ice cream—pink and green and white, one with little chunks of creamy cookies, one with nuts, one with ribbons of fudge, another with bits of brightly colored bubble gum balls. She suddenly felt short of breath, and she tried to breathe, she thought about breathing, and it was a strange thing, having to think about what only moments earlier came naturally.

"What's wrong with you?" Rebecca said. She held her ice cream cone, and her tongue was going around and around in a circle.

"I'm going outside," Georgia told her.

"Why?"

"I need air."

Once outside, Georgia replayed those moments at her brother's bedroom door. She was thinking about those boys and their identical fingers. She tried to imagine their chins and noses, their individual voices, wanting to see each boy as distinct, but it was impossible. She was thinking about paper bags and breathing when Rebecca bounced out of 27 Flavors. "God," her friend said, "just leave me in there with zit face. I'm sure."

"Sorry, Becky. I don't—"

"I have a date with him this weekend," she interrupted, obviously excited.

"Who?"

"Zit face—the guy who served me." Rebecca turned what was left of her cone upside down and sucked out the rest of the chocolate.

"I didn't think you liked him," Georgia said.

"He's not so bad, actually. He goes to Diamond High and knows that girl who killed her friend. Did you hear about that, the girl who killed her friend?" she asked.

"No," Georgia lied.

"Well, I guess she was trying to suck the fat out of her friend and—"

"I heard about it," Georgia said, cutting her off.

"Why'd you lie? Sometimes, Georgie, you're so weird. I don't always get you," she said.

Georgia shrugged. She shook her head. "Becky," she said, cautiously, almost whispering. "What does 'fucked her titties' mean?"

"You don't know?"

"I have an idea. I kind of know."

"Well," Rebecca said, chomping on her last bite. "He sticks his dick in your nipple hole."

"Oh my God!"

"And then," she continued, "he moves it in and out. You'd be surprised how much that little hole stretches."

"No one's doing that to me," Georgia said.

"Why not? It feels *good*." Rebecca rolled her eyes. "Grow up, Georgie," she said. "Live a little. No ice cream, no titty fucking. What's wrong with you?"

5.

Other men and boys noticed Georgia. It was as if they saw straight up inside her, all that she had done. It was like a list had been written and they were privy to it. She understood that her body belonged to the whole damn street. Three of them looking related, like brothers or cousins, pulled up in a white truck. The bearded one leaned out the window, his head and neck, an arm, his big hand grabbing at the air around her, saying, "Let's go make a pretzel together." And Georgia misunderstood him or she understood him perfectly. "What?" she said. "What do you want?"

The next day after school Georgia was walking home

alone, passing a group of high school boys, and it took every
bit of nerve to put one foot in front of the other. She thought
about crossing the street or turning around, right there in the
middle of the block, hitting her forehead with her palm, pretending to have left something at school—a book, a pen. She
thought about that but kept walking.

"Georgia," one of them said.

She ignored him.

"Georgia?" he said. This time her name itself was a question.

She stopped, looked directly at the boys. "I'm not
Georgia," she said. "You've got the wrong girl," she told them.

6.

After a day at the beach, she sat with Rebecca on a bench in
Huntington. Pacific Coast Highway. The sun was coming
down on their tan shoulders. They sat with a Jack in the Box
bag between them, taking turns dipping their hands inside the
bag, pulling out fries. From a distance, if someone were to pull
up in the far lane and look at the girls, they might have
appeared older than they were.

"Let's play a game," Rebecca suggested.

"What do you want to play?"

"Count the Love."

"What's that?" Georgia asked, and as her friend answered,
she was certain that Rebecca was inventing the game as she
went along.

"Let's see," she began, "we count the number of guys who

notice us. And we can't leave this bench until we get to, uh . . . until we get to number sixty-nine."

"What if our bus comes?"

"We'll catch another bus," Rebecca said. "It'll be fun."

"Okay," Georgia said.

And the two of them sat there, waving their bus by five times. They counted them: those leaning out their truck windows, those who sprayed them with kisses from dark jeeps, those who shouted "You're beautiful" or "I love you" or "Suck my big dick." Even if the light was green and the boys and men were zipping by, many of them still had something to say.

"That counts," Rebecca told Georgia, "even if we can't make out the words."

Georgia nodded, shoving the last of the fries into her mouth.

"When you're young like us," Rebecca said, "guys love you. But once you hit seventeen it's all downhill. You lose it."

"Lose what?"

"*This,*" Rebecca said, waving her hand in front of her like a game show model presenting a prize, a washing machine or shiny new boat. "All this *love.*"

"Love?" Georgia said, doubtful.

"Or whatever it is," Rebecca said.

7.

Georgia's mother was head paralegal at a law office in Manhattan Beach, and when she came home from work in the afternoons, often went to her bedroom and fell asleep.

Georgia herself couldn't nap—there was always too much on her mind—and she envied her mother's ability to sleep during the day.

This particular afternoon her mother stood in the living room, in front of the reclining chair that her father usually sat in. Though it was five, a half hour past his usual arrival, he wasn't home.

Georgia sat at the dining room table, studying. She looked up from her homework. "Where's Dad?"

"Work," Georgia's mother said flatly, in a tone that suggested she didn't want to talk about him. She leaned down, pulled off her black pumps, and then fell heavily into the chair. She rubbed her calves, first one and then the other. Her legs were long and slim, as beautiful as the rest of her. "I'm tired," she said. "Diane's got me doing four cases at once. That's too many, Georgie. Do you know how hard your parents work?"

"Yes."

"And do you know why?"

"Good food and pleasant shelter," Georgia said, having been through this conversation several times before.

Her mother smiled. "Honey, get your mom something cold to drink."

Georgia went to the kitchen and poured a glass of iced tea. When she returned to the living room, she handed the glass to her mother. She looked at the dining room table, thinking about the homework she'd left there, and decided it could wait. She sat down on the couch, across from her mom.

Georgia's mother lifted the glass to her mouth, ice cubes clinking, and looked at her daughter. "What are you staring at?" she said. "What's with you lately?"

"Nothing's with me." Georgia picked up a fashion magazine from the coffee table and began thoughtlessly flipping through the pages.

"Are you okay, sweetie?" her mother asked. She had her hand placed on top of Georgia's hand, stopping her daughter mid-flip.

"I want to read this, Mom."

"Okay, read," she said. "As long as you're fine," she told her.

"I'm good," Georgia said, unconvincingly.

Her mother nodded. "I'm glad you're good," she said. "It's a mother's job to worry, though. I know you and Kevin are doing what kids do, but your grades are fine and your teachers seem to like you. I should be happy that you're doing as well as you are." She sighed, relieved.

Georgia thought about Kevin's ugly girl with a paper bag over her head, getting titty fucked. She gave her mother a weak grin. "I have a question," she said, closing the magazine, holding her spot with one finger.

"Yes?"

"Is there a hole in my nipple?"

"A *what?*"

"A hole. Rebecca said that there's a hole there."

"That girl—so sweet when she was little, but she's growing up to be bad news. What happened to that girl?"

"Nothing happened to her." Georgia rolled her eyes. "Answer my question, please."

Her mother leaned back in the chair. "Yes, honey, there's a hole there," she said.

"Oh."

"When you have a baby, milk comes out of it." Her mother closed her eyes. She made circles at her temples with her fingertips. "Just the sound of a baby crying can bring on the milk. One time you ruined my very favorite blouse."

"Sorry."

"I'm tired," her mother said. "Let me rest now, Georgie."

"One more thing," she tried.

"Can't it wait? Don't you have some homework to do? Isn't that what you left at the table?"

Georgia looked at the table, then back at her mother. "But—" she began.

"Please, sweetie," her mother said, "give me just an hour of quiet time."

8.

"There's the kind of girl you fuck and the kind of girl you marry," Kevin said. He was standing at the refrigerator door in his fluorescent surfing shorts and socks, his body tilted forward so that his face and bare chest were nearly inside. Georgia stood in the kitchen doorway, holding a caddy filled with nail clippers and files, a half dozen bottles of her mother's nail polish. She stared at her brother's back, which was broad, with freckles and a million red pimples. Some of the pimples were white and ready.

"Where's the milk?" he said. "I can't find the goddamn milk." He was moving things around. "Shit," he said, taking ketchup, a bag of red cherries, and defrosted hamburger meat from a shelf and placing them on the counter. "Have you seen the milk?" he asked her.

"No," she said. "Maybe Dad—"

"Dad's been weird lately," Kevin interrupted. "Have you noticed?" He looked at her.

Georgia shook her head no.

"He's forgetting shit. He asks me a question, I answer it, and ten minutes later he's asking me the same damn thing."

"I haven't noticed," Georgia said, realizing she hadn't spent much time with her dad lately.

"I don't think they love each other anymore," Kevin said.

"Of course they love each other," Georgia said.

"I can't wait until I move out. No more running out of milk, chicks on the couch, music as loud as I want it."

"You're only sixteen," she reminded him.

"I'm older than you."

"So?"

"I swear, when I'm on my own, I'm having one big party—day and fucking night."

Georgia moved from the doorway to the kitchen table and sat down. She started looking through the bottles of polish. She picked one up, shook it, and held up the shiny red for her brother to see. "What do you think of this?" she asked him.

"I don't think about it," he said. "Guys don't think about those things—a chick's nails, come on, Georgie."

"What about our voices or our faces?"

"Huh?" he said, not really listening.

"If you move out, how do you plan to pay rent?" she asked, changing the subject, not wanting him to realize she'd been standing outside his bedroom with Rebecca at the door, eavesdropping.

"The Fish Joint pays me." He turned and glared at his sister. "It's just a matter of time. I'm saving money—or I'm going to start saving. This week, you watch, I'm going to put something away. You'll see," he said.

She looked at Kevin, doubtful.

"What?" he said.

"Nothing." Georgia opened the bottle and began painting

her nails. It was useless, really, because there was very little nail to paint. She bit them, her cuticles even, until they were raw and sore. She was hoping that if she painted them red, every time she lifted a finger to her mouth, she'd see a stop sign, that tiny red nail coming toward her. "So tell me about that theory of yours," she said.

"What theory?"

"There's the kind of girl you fuck and the kind of girl you marry, Kevin, huh?"

"That's right." He pulled the milk carton from the fridge.

"Don't you have sex with the girl you marry?"

"Yeah, you fuck her, but it's about love and having babies. Procreation. You'll understand when you like someone or when someone likes you—or when you do it." He opened the cupboard, took a glass from the shelf, and placed it on the counter. He held the carton closed and shook it, then poured the milk. He set the carton in front of Georgia, sat down at the table, and stared at his sister. "You haven't done it, have you?" he said.

"No," she lied, not looking up from her nails.

"You telling me the truth?" he said, leaning toward her.

"Yes," she said. "Don't be stupid," she told him.

"Because I'll kill the guy. You wait until you're married— or at least in high school," he said.

"I know, I know," she said.

"Even then, in high school, if I find out, he's dead meat. You wait until college. College is good."

"College is a long time away," she said.

"Exactly."

"You'll be gone by then, living in that party house of yours. How are you going to know what I do if you don't live here?"

"I'll know." He was full of bravado. "I mean it, Georgie—

172

I'll rip his legs off or his head," he said, grabbing, ripping at the air in front of him, pretending to do just that to Georgia's imaginary guy.

The two of them sat there, across from each other, and Georgia blew on her little nails.

"Just don't get fat," he warned. "Guys hate fat girls." She stared at the white ring the milk had left above his top lip, and thought about his ugly girl who was *not* fat, his penis shoved in her nipple.

"Kevin," Georgia said, surprising herself, "does titty fuck-ing hurt?"

"None of it hurts *us*," he said, "which is way cool."

"Way cool," she said, sarcastically.

"It's true," he said. "It's you guys who scream when you lose it."

"Yeah," Georgia said.

"*What?*" he said.

"I mean, I've heard that it hurts."

"You've heard, huh?"

"Yes."

"It's nothing you've done, right?"

"Of course not."

"I'm just saying, Georgie—"

She interrupted her brother. "Girls talk, you know. It's not like I don't have friends."

"Your friends shouldn't be doing it either."

She rolled her eyes at her brother, who was leaning back, balancing the chair on two legs. "What's the story with Rebecca?" he said.

"The story?"

"Yeah, what's with her?"

"She's seeing the guy from 27 Flavors."

"Zit face?"

She nodded.

"She's getting big anyways," he said, setting the chair upright. "Big girls are gross," he said, getting up from the chair and walking away from Georgia, whistling, down the hall.

She sat for several minutes, staring at her hands, trying not to move. Her mother told her that you needed to wait at least thirty minutes for your nails to dry. Georgia tried to stay still, but the more she thought about not moving, the more she had to do just that. She tapped her foot on the kitchen tile. She waved her hands in the air in an effort to speed the process. She blew once more on her nails. Finally, she lightly touched a thumbnail with a fingertip. It smeared a bit, but she couldn't help herself.

Georgia got up and put the milk away. On the counter, the hamburger meat was bleeding through the plastic. It was fatty—twenty percent, which meant her mother was planning tacos or spaghetti. She stared at the white chunks of fat nestled in the red meat and felt her stomach flip. A line of blood trailed the counter. Georgia wiped it up with a dishrag, then tossed the rag into the sink.

On her bed, she listened to Kevin still whistling in the next room and stared down at her nails, the polish smeared around her cuticles, a red and bright mess.

9.

At dinner Georgia's mother carried a roasted chicken on a silver platter. She wore a pale yellow blouse with an apron over it, her hair up in a shiny bun. "Who left the hamburger meat on the counter?" she asked. "I woke up from my nap and the whole kitchen smelled terrible."

Kevin was talking to his father about school, ignoring her. "I'm doing great in biology," he said. "It's cool when we dissect things."

"My boy," his father said, "smart, like his old man. Maybe you'll be a doctor. I could've been a doctor, you know."

Georgia wondered how her father went from "could've been a doctor" to a high school math teacher, but didn't say anything.

"Who left the meat on the counter?" her mother asked again, placing the platter in the middle of the table. "You know there's a window right there," she said, pointing to the kitchen. "And when that curtain is open, the sun comes in and cooks whatever's sitting there. Imagine the bacteria," she said, wiping her hands on the apron, looking at her family.

Georgia pointed at Kevin, who was busy demonstrating how Dr. Evans opened the cat and lifted out its organs.

"Not now, Kevin. Not at the dinner table," his mother said. "Eat up," she told Georgia. "You look skinny. Have you lost weight? You don't look right."

Georgia moved the chicken leg around on her plate with a fork. "Does Craig take biology?" she asked Kevin.

"Craig? No way. He's in the easy classes. He's even in home economics because he says there's free food and girls there. He'll do anything to get a chick."

"You should take more math classes is what you boys should do. And you too, Georgie. Math is fixed—it's made up its mind. No recipes with math, just calculation and answers," his father said.

"Eat something, Georgia," her mother said again. She took off her apron, went into the kitchen and left it there. When she came back, she carried a sauté pan with oily mushrooms and a serving spoon. She scooped generous servings onto their plates, stopping by Georgia, pausing, looking at her daughter. "I want you to eat," she said again.

"Okay," Georgia said.

Her mother pulled out a chair and sat down. She held a fork poised over her plate of food. "Go on, Georgie," she said, "take a bite."

"How are you doing in biology class?" Georgia's father asked her brother.

"I just told you," he said.

"Your father doesn't listen," her mother said. "I talk and talk and he doesn't hear a thing. It's getting worse, too."

"Biology class is okay, then?" her father continued, lifting up a chicken leg and taking a bite. Georgia watched his mouth and thought about her secrets—all of them. She held on to the table with clenched hands, not picking up her fork, and wondered what her father saw when he saw her. His chin and lips glistened, and she wondered what he'd think and remember of the girl she was becoming . . .

Rachel Spark

2000

If a Tree Falls

1.

It's Friday night, hours before my abortion, and I'm sitting in my mother's bedroom watching television—an old show called *Hazel*. It's set in the 1950s and every night about midnight, whether I've been sleeping earlier or not, I hear the TV click on, and I hear Hazel's grating voice coming from behind my mother's bedroom door. Hazel is a maid who watches over a doctor's family. The doctor and Hazel are good friends. She sacrifices herself to get him out of trouble. I know this because for the last two nights, despite my strong feelings about Hazel, and the doctor, too, I've sat in the big chair across from my mother's bed, eating crackers, drinking club soda, and watching the show with her.

I'm not eating or drinking anything now, though. No food, no water, nothing past midnight. I wonder if those orders mean I can't brush my teeth in the morning, and decide right now to do just that; when I wake up I'll rebel, break their rules. I had sex without a condom once, one damn time, and look at the result.

I feel my mother's suspicion. Every now and then she looks up from the set and twists her eyes my way, but only for a second; the look is a glance, as much as she can take of me right now. "People get in trouble all the time," she says, staring hard at the television.

"Yes," I say, staring hard at the idiot Hazel myself.

"What's that mean, yes?"

"Just that." I pull the blanket up over my bare feet, covering my toes and soles, the painted nails which seem garish in this light.

"I heard you throwing up earlier," my mother continues, still not looking at me.

"Yes."

"That's all you're going to say?"

"Yes," I say again.

"It's not the flu, I know that," she says.

"Isn't there enough in this room to think about? Don't we have enough to worry about?"

She turns around and readjusts her pillows, patting them, smoothing out the cases, and then propping them against the headboard once again. "You get sick in the late afternoon and evening—not like me, not like I was with you, and not like the rest of them."

"The rest of them?"

"Other women."

"Stop it," I say, and I say it in a low voice, a serious voice, which surprises even me. "You hear me, Mom?"

"Yes," she says.

"What's that mean, yes?" I say, and I am mocking her. She is dying and I am pregnant, and I am mocking her. "What's that mean, yes?" I say again.

2.

Weeks ago, my mother and I were at The Moroccan Inn on Second Street, sitting at a table outside, eating falafel, hummus, and pita, and I was wishing my period would start. I was four days late. I was thinking about Rex on his Hampshire farm with his redhead. I was imagining Rex milking one of those cows he loved. I saw him sitting on a short stool, bent over, hands pulling on udders, filling a bucket with thick milk.

"You okay?" my mother asked.

"Fine," I said, trying to look it.

"You listening?" she wanted to know.

I was nodding, tearing a piece of pita, and trying to look interested.

"You seem distracted," she said.

"No, no—I'm fine," I insisted.

My mother had recently met Gilbert Wolff, a six-year lung cancer survivor at the radiation clinic, and was giddy, eager to talk. His recurrence was aggressive, but his sense of humor was sharp. He was a tree surgeon, an educated man, a sick man with a healthy attitude, she told me.

It was a Sunday afternoon, warm and breezy, in Belmont Shore. The street was crowded with shoppers, couples, and families. A single man pushing a stroller stopped at the newspaper stand in front of us, and when he turned around with the paper under his arm, my mother smiled at him. "Can I see the baby?" she said.

He came closer to the table, stopped, and pulled the blanket from the baby's chin so that we could get a better look. The baby's cheeks were so fat that you couldn't be certain the child had eyes.

"What's his name?" my mother asked.

"Bruce—we call him Brucey," the man answered.

Brucey's cheeks were striped with a fine, downy hair that came down from both sides of his head. I thought of pork chops. I thought of rockabilly men in plaid shirts and cuffed jeans. Brucey didn't like being stared at or maybe he didn't like his blanket being messed with because he let out a fierce screech. "Adorable," my mother said.

"Thank you," the man said, smiling proudly. He covered screeching Brucey back up before strolling away.

"He was *not* adorable," I said.

"He will be," she said. "The hair will fall off that boy's cheeks and he'll be just as sweet as can be." My mother had on the Cher wig. Her nails and lips were a pretty pale red, and she wore one of her dresses—a blue-and-yellow floral print. I was looking at my mother's face, admiring her skin—where were the telltale signs, the dark circles and sunken cheeks?

"Tell me about Gilbert," I said.

"Tan, sixtyish, full head of gray hair, and a lump in his neck." She offered this last detail like it was just one more physical characteristic. Then added, "I want to love him."

"You want to *love* him?" I said, surprised.

"Well, I want to *know* him."

"That's better."

"Whatever time I have left, I want to spend some of it with him."

I picked up my sandwich and took a bite. I'd been ravenous the last few days and my breasts were swollen, both sure signs that my period was on its way, I reassured myself.

"I feel like a girl," she said. "I'll see him five times a week for the next two weeks." She leaned in and lowered her voice. "I got the receptionist to schedule the two of us together."

"That mean one?"

"She's not so mean."

"She's nasty," I said. "Remember how she barked at us when we were late?"

"We *were* late," my mother said, defending her.

"Five minutes." I picked the napkin up from my lap and wiped my mouth.

"Belinda gets impatient sometimes, but she's not so bad. She's much sweeter since I made her a couple of dresses."

"You made her two?" I said. "I thought you were going to make her one."

"One's a very pretty aqua. She wanted a darker color for evening."

"That was nice of you."

"People soften up when you give them a chance, Rachel. The hair falls off their cheeks," she told me.

"Or when you give them things," I said.

She stared at the small bowl in the center of the table. "Do you want the last of that hummus?"

I shook my head. "What else about Gilbert Wolff?"

She picked up a piece of pita bread and rubbed the side of the bowl with it. "He likes my legs," she said, chewing and talking at once. "I saw him looking at them. He thought his eyes were hidden behind the magazine, but I saw them."

"Did you talk to him?"

"Mostly I listened to him talk to the man next to him."

"Better hurry."

"No kidding," she said, laughing.

"I didn't mean it like that."

Her voice was serious. "I should hurry—and you should too. Everyone should hurry."

The waiter came up to the table then and refilled my iced tea. "You two doing okay here?"

"More hummus?" she asked me.

I nodded.

He smiled, turned away from us, and my mother picked up where she'd left off. "A lot of people at the clinic want to travel—see the world, they say. They sit there waiting for treatment with these glossy travel magazines across their laps, talking about their trips. They've touched the sands of Egypt. They've eaten *real* Italian food. Before they die, they'll see this or that cave, some mountain they can't wait to climb. I don't want to waste time schlepping up some mountain."

"I might," I said.

She shook her head. "One woman postponed therapy to sail around the world and dropped dead at sea."

"I understand that."

"You do?"

"She was thinking about quality, not quantity—about experience."

"I think she was giving up," my mother said. "She was floating around the world waiting to die. She was in a cramped cabin, I'm sure. It was probably a lot like a coffin itself."

"I don't think so," I said.

The waiter put the second order of hummus between the two of us and picked up the empty bowl. "Enjoy," he said, turning back to the other customers.

My mom picked up the lone olive in the middle of the hummus and popped in into her mouth. "You seem to like traveling, too. Not for yourself, though, but for the men you meet. Where's that Rex now?" she asked me.

"Let's just eat," I said.

3.

She was standing at the sink, washing green onions. Next to her sat lettuce leaves piled high, drying on a paper towel, a glass jar of chopped garlic, dark mustard, and honey in a container shaped like a bear. She was planning a sweet salad dressing, which normally I would have refused, but today I wanted to return to her, agree with each final thing she said and did, so from the dining room table I said, "Sweet's fine with me."

And it *was* fine. I'd had cravings lately for sugar and salt and yellow cheese, but the smell of coffee and meat bothered me. I'd been throwing up in secret, kneeling in the bathroom, my mouth pressed against an old towel, the radio on. When I appeared in the hallway, my mother asked why my face was flushed and I shrugged. "When you're ready, you'll talk," she said, sounding like a cop.

Earlier she'd limped into the kitchen, touching my cheek on the way, smiling and cheerful. Now, I sat at the dining room table, watching her, wondering how she could smile when the gray chunk was pushy, persistent, having returned for the third time to that spot in her hip.

Her first recurrence was in that hip, in that very spot, and I remembered her businesslike demeanor the morning after it was confirmed. She had carried the phone and phone book outside to the balcony. She sat there for hours, calling her stores and shops, her dry cleaner and favorite restaurants, her shoemaker, the bakery, and drugstore. She asked to speak to owners and managers all over town by their first names. *May I speak to Bob? May I speak to Dennis? Will you please put Katy on the phone?* She explained her metastasis, assuring Bob and Dennis and Katy that she was theirs to the very end—a loyal patron through all of it. She'd deliberately start coughing just before it was time to ask the favor, the reason behind her call. Would he or she mind responding to her horn? Would it be okay if she just pulled up in the alley or at the curb? Would someone come out and bring her what she needed?

But the radiation worked, at least temporarily. Within weeks the limp was gone, but still my mother pulled up to those curbs, honked the horn in those alleys or parking lots. Salesclerks and waiters, Bob and Dennis and Katy, too, came running outside with things: her clean clothes, shish kebabs and rice, a fresh baguette, a little white bag full of Demerol or Ativan or some new steroid.

"It's amazing, Rachel," she told me, smiling mischievously. "I've turned all of Belmont Shore into one big Jack in the Box. *Everything's* a drive-through," she said, beaming.

Now, chopping those onions, she was humming. I listened to her, felt the nausea coming on, and thought about Rex thousands of miles away in his studio, painting or sculpting, making something new.

When the phone rang, I answered it with a dull hello, a thud from my throat that made Claire laugh. "Rachel," she said, "come on. You act like she's gone already."

I looked at my mother, whose hum had turned into quiet song lyrics. She was tapping her foot on the tile. I watched her hands, the green onions flowering from them, and wished my friend hadn't called or that I hadn't answered the phone.

"I've got good news," Claire said.

"Tell me," I said, though I knew that any news she had wouldn't be good enough. I wondered how I was going to muster up the enthusiasm to respond to her news. I thought of stopping Claire midsentence but understood that it was impossible to slow people down—their lives moving right ahead, jobs, new friends, spouses and homes—while my life, even when I appeared to be outside in the world living it, was right here, watching her.

"I wasn't sure if I should tell you today. You've got your own things to deal with," she said, wavering.

"It's okay," I said.

"Maybe it's selfish that I called."

"*Come on,*" I said, growing impatient.

"I know Angela's taking you to the clinic this weekend to take care of it." Claire whispered the last five words.

"An abortion, Claire. You can say what it is. *Taking care of it* would be letting it go full term, giving birth, and sticking a bottle in his or her mouth."

My mother swung around from the sink. "*What?*" she said, taking a step toward me. She flapped those onions in my direction, then turned around. "Oh dear," she said.

I put my palm over the receiver and looked at my mother. "It's not about me," I lied, getting up from the table, taking the phone with me into my bedroom. I sat on the bed, then kicked the door closed. "An abortion, Claire," I said again. "I'm not taking care of anything but myself here."

"Okay," she said.

"I didn't support those clinics, escort those girls inside, so I could be ashamed of myself."

"Of course, Rachel."

"You were an escort too, and now you can't even say the word."

"Abortion," she said quietly.

I laughed, hostile and irritated. "You don't *really* believe in anything," I said meanly.

"I believe in things. I'm a liberal, a vegetarian," she protested.

"You're not a vegetarian if you eat tacos—even if you only eat them in Mexico."

"I eat them twice a year."

"Okay, even if you eat tacos in Mexico *twice a year,* you're not a vegetarian. You shouldn't call yourself one. You should just say 'I'm a person who doesn't eat chicken or fish, but I eat red meat in Mexico twice a year. I'm a woman who can't refuse a taco.'" My voice cracked into the phone.

"I shouldn't have called."

"Vegetarians don't eat meat—that's all I'm saying. They don't give a man a dollar, then watch him carve something from a bone," I said, starting to cry.

"Okay, okay," she said. "Don't cry, Rachel. Please. I'm sorry," she said.

I lifted a pillow from my bed and held it over my mouth to stifle the sobs. I gripped the phone. Neither of us said a word.

"Rachel," she said finally. "Are you there?"

"I'm here," I said, weakly.

"Are you okay?" she asked again.

"I'm so damn sorry, Claire," I said, sniffling.

"It's okay."

"My mom's dying. She's making a salad I don't want to

eat. I'm so damn sorry," I said again. "Please tell me your good news."

"No, Rachel. Another time." Her voice was soft.

"Talk to me, Claire. I need good news right now."

"Lora and I are moving in together," she said.

4.

My mother had been on seven dates with Gilbert Wolff. He was dapper, she said, witty, and as optimistic about his lumps and limitations as she was about her own. They'd been out for Cuban and Ethiopian cuisine. They'd been to a Russian ballet. They'd seen a Chinese film with subtitles. "See that, no need to travel, Rachel," my mother said. "He's taking me around the world right here in our city—right where we are now."

"It's not really the same thing," I said.

"It's better," she said. "There's no picking out a week's worth of clothes, no packing and unpacking, no taxis, no bellhops or unknown streets, there's no getting lost, no waiting."

"No strange beds," I added.

"*Well,*" she said, smiling.

Because Gilbert was a tree doctor—a surgeon, he insisted—lately my mother had been peppering her conversations with tree tidbits, trivia about redwoods and pines and sycamores and palms. *Did you know that when a palm gets sick its fronds might come down unexpectedly and kill a sunbather? Did you know that a young woman died just last year in Laguna Beach? Sitting out there in a string bikini and then bam, dead on* the sand, just like that. Did you know a sick tree dies so slowly that it can take forty years for it to go?

I knew nothing about trees, their trunks and saps, but I knew about her, my mother—how soon we could expect her eyes and the palms of her hands to turn yellow, which would mean that the tiny tumor they found on her liver was growing, affecting things.

The cancer was in three spots that we knew of. In addition to the recurrence in her hip, which was making her limp, there was a cherry-size lymph node in her neck, and the spot on her liver. Lesions, the doctor called them. "A couple zaps of radiation and she'll be okay," he said.

I doubted him, and the expression on my face told him so.

"It's true," he said.

"For how long?"

"That's not a question I can answer."

"Can you answer questions about the limp?"

"The limp will go away," he said.

The trees that took forty years to die were plenty sick; they peeled away bit by bit for four whole decades. I thought about that. I drank a cup of coffee at a bookstore in downtown Seal Beach and thought about how long an afflicted tree sits there dying. I went to the mall and shopped for shoes, wondering what the soles were made of. I tapped the soles with my finger and smiled at the puzzled shoe guy. "Can I help you?" he wanted to know.

"No," I said.

"Let me know if you want to try those on. They're very popular," he said. His shirt and tie were the exact same color, light blue, and if it wasn't for the dark stain on the tie I might not have been able to tell where one piece of clothing stopped and the other began.

"You've got something on your tie," I said.

He looked down. "Damn," he said. "Chocolate. I can't seem to eat it fast enough in this heat. It just melts all over the place." He was unknotting the tie as he spoke to me, pulling it over his head. He looked across the way at Yates' Yogurt as if the store itself were to blame.

"The mall's air-conditioned," I said.

"Yeah, I know—I ate it outside." He held the tie in his fist. "About the shoes," he said. "Girls say they're comfortable."

"They don't look comfortable," I said, still tapping.

"How about trying on a pair and telling me otherwise?" He was smiling, flirting or just selling shoes.

I shook my head.

"Come on," he said, pushing. "What size?"

"You should put the tie away," I said, looking down at his fist. "And I'm a seven."

He walked away then and when he returned, he had three boxes stacked in his arms.

I bought the shoes because I thought he deserved a sale, dealing with a woman like me.

I carried my bag of shoes to the car. I drove down Main Street and up First. I stopped and got out at the ocean, stood there for a couple of minutes, but decided against sitting on the sand. I ended up in the park, where I sat down under a tree that looked healthy, but what did I know? I didn't even know what kind of tree it was. And whatever it was, sycamore or pine, it might have been very sick. It might have had a killer fungus. It might have been sick for thirty-five years, ill before I was even born, dying there in that very park while my mother got morning sickness in the morning, like the rest of them.

5.

I was standing in front of my poetry workshop reading Anne
Sexton, reading from *All My Pretty Ones*, going backwards in
the book and finishing up with "The Truth the Dead Know."
No one said anything when I was through, when I asked for
comments. "'When we touch we enter touch entirely,'" I said.
"What do you think Sexton meant?"

Molly, the girl with maroon hair and gold studs in her
nose and tongue who hadn't responded to me in weeks, finally opened her mouth. "Isn't Anne Sexton the one who tried to
have sex with her daughter?" she said.

"No," I said.

"She did. She tried to sleep with her daughter. She had a
creepy crush on her own kid. My friend Edna read the daughter's autobiography," the girl said, looking around the classroom at the other students.

"Maybe so, but that part about trying to sleep with Linda
is untrue or at least undocumented," I said.

"Who's Linda?"

"The daughter you're talking about."

Molly shrugged. "Edna read the book," she said to the girl
next to her. "You know Edna, right?"

The girl nodded.

"She didn't try to have sex with her daughter," I said again.

"Well, she masturbated with the kid in the same bed,
didn't she?"

I was silent, looking around the room for an ally. Daniel
looked up at me from the front row, shaking his head.

"Tell the truth," the girl said. "Didn't Sexton masturbate in her daughter's bed?"

I nodded.

"And wasn't her daughter in the bed right next to her?"

"Something like that." I sighed. I looked at the tree outside the classroom window and decided its fronds didn't look well. They were yellow and dry where they should have been green. A couple was sitting under the tree eating lunch, obviously unconcerned about the tree's health. The young woman's head rested in the young man's lap. She lifted her head and sipped something from a straw. The young man took a bite of his sandwich. Perhaps I'd get Gilbert to check the tree out. Perhaps I'd drive him back here at dusk, when the couple would certainly be finished with their lunch, when surely they'd be gone, and ask him just what he thought of that tree outside my classroom.

"I don't want to read that pervert's poetry," Molly said, smacking the book shut.

And it seemed that all of the students in the room were nodding their heads, agreeing with her, except for Daniel, who was shuffling the papers on his desk as though he was looking for something important.

"Stop it," I said, maybe to the whole damn class.

"Something's wrong with you lately, Rachel," Molly said, and she gathered up her books and stood up. She bent her hip, balancing the books there, and looked at me. She shook her head, a strand of that purple hair falling over her face, direct-ly in the middle, cutting her in half. She was two girls then, and I didn't like either one of them.

"You're probably right," I said, sitting down at my desk.

"It's three," she said, staring at the clock above my head. And it seemed everyone stood up at exactly the same moment. It seemed everyone followed Molly, the girl who was cut in half, the girl who was two girls. Or maybe they left because it was time to go—I wasn't sure. Either way, my feelings were hurt. I was being abandoned; they were walking out on me. They were gathering up their books and pens, pulling jackets from the backs of chairs, straightening their jeans and skirts, and hurting my feelings. They followed the girl out the door as though she was in charge of something, as though she was a general or officer, and maybe she was, maybe she was in charge of everything, the goddamn President, and maybe I should have listened to her too, should have gathered up my own things and joined those students in the hall. That's what I was thinking about when I felt his fingers in my hair.

"What are you doing?" I asked, but I didn't move, just sat right there with the boy's hand in my hair.

"I'm sorry," Daniel said, taking his hand away and putting it in his jacket pocket.

"I'm pregnant," I said.

"It's okay," he said softly.

"It's anything *but* okay," I told him.

"*You're* going to be okay, Rachel—that's what I mean." Daniel crouched down in front of my desk so that we were eye level.

"I'm pregnant," I said again, looking right into the boy's eyes.

"Do you love him?" he wanted to know.

"He's far away. On a farm."

"I don't picture you with a farmer."

"I'm not *with* him. He's not coming back and I don't even think I want him to."

"I'm sorry."

"I'm getting an abortion," I said flatly.

"Can I help?"

I shook my head.

"I want to help you," he said again. "I'll drive you where you need to go. I'll wait for you."

"*Please,* Daniel."

"I'm serious."

"You can't be."

He paused, then continued. "Afterwards, you'll come back to my place and I'll take care of you. I'll make you soup."

"Soup, huh? What kind of soup?"

"Chicken or vegetable. I make tomato, too," he said.

I shook my head.

"I want to help you," he said again.

"Are you a doctor? Because that's what I need," I said.

"I'm not a doctor," he said weakly.

"Then you should just go." I looked around the room at the empty desks. I looked at the floor, what the students left behind: an empty Coke can on its side, a cupcake wrapper, and three balls of rolled-up yellow paper. I thought about the trees that made the paper and the students who couldn't find the trash can.

"I won't tell anyone, Rachel. It's just between us," he said.

"I know," I said.

Daniel stood up. He took a blank piece of paper off my desk and wrote his phone number down. "Here," he said. "Call if you need me. It's not the worst thing in the world, Rachel, to need someone."

"Just go," I said again.

"Okay," he said, gathering up his books, stuffing the books in his backpack, tossing his backpack over his shoulder, and leaving the room.

6.

The night before Rex went back to London we'd met up at a diner on Second Street. It was ten P.M. but he was eating breakfast. He'd found a place with bangers and eggs, his favorite. He was telling me his ideas about art and what he planned to work on when he returned home. "Chickens rotting behind Plexiglas, a hamburger on an exceptional plate—anything can be art," he said.

I smiled, but in my head I was thinking that art like that isn't art at all. "Interesting," I said.

"Ah, 'interesting,' that's the word reserved for pieces that are not interesting at all." With noticeable skill and help from his fork, he fit a whole banger into his mouth. He chewed and chewed. He looked at me. The grease was visible on his lips and I smelled the banger from where I sat. Maybe it was fine that he was leaving in the morning.

I drummed my nails against the side of my coffee cup. I tried to smile and said, "Where do you get the chicken?"

"The grocery store, Rachel. I wouldn't kill a bird for a project. I hope you know that. What sort of a man do you think I am?" He lifted his cup of tea to his mouth, held it there, but didn't take a sip. He was waiting for an answer.

"A fine one," I said.

He didn't believe me; I could tell. "Maybe this is separation anxiety—how we're getting along now," he said.

I wanted to change the subject. "What do you do with the chicken's legs?" I said.

"What do you mean?"

"How's the bird sitting or standing? What do you *do* with it?"

"The legs are pinned back," he said, and then he leaned over the table and held one of my arms, pinned it back so that it touched the plastic booth. He was gentle, playful, whispering sweet things about my mind, which he said was sharp. "Going to miss you."

"I hate it when people don't use pronouns," I said, pulling away from him. "'Going to miss you' isn't the same as 'I'm going to miss you.'"

"I disagree."

"It's insincere," I said, knowing that I shouldn't go too far with my theory, but unable to stop myself.

"Bullshit," he said.

"I'm telling you, it's the pronoun that makes the difference. Ever notice how people who don't quite love you, at least not yet, they might like you a lot, they might really, really like you, but they don't love you, they're the ones more likely to say 'love you' or worse yet 'love ya'?"

"I hate 'love ya' too," he said. "But it's the *ya* I hate—I'm not so sure it's the missing pronoun."

"It's important, identifying yourself in a declaration."

"I hate 'gonna' too," he said.

"And 'see ya,'" I added.

"Yes, that's right," he said, happy that we were finally agreeing.

"It's not just the 'ya' though, it's the missing pronoun, too—it's admitting things and being honest. It's adding yourself to the statement."

He sighed. He shook his head. He stabbed a yolk with his fork. "I don't know about you," he said.

"Sorry," I said.

"Where's *your* pronoun, Rachel? Who's sorry?"

* * *

Later, in his rental car in front of my mother's apartment building, he kissed my neck and shoulders, and I was imagining that grocery store chicken behind Plexiglas, rotting, its legs pinned back, but still, when he stuck his fingers into my underwear, I came with a cry, and it seemed I could come forever and cry forever there in the front seat with his hand half in and half out of my skirt.

7.

Daniel followed me all around campus. I saw him when I drank my iced tea at The Pub, standing behind a pillar. I saw him in the English building during my office hours, looking at a bulletin board for things I imagined he didn't need. I saw him on my way to class, and he offered to help me with my books. I let him. I was just that tired; I let a boy carry my books for me and didn't even try to hide it. I took the books from him once we were inside the classroom and thanked him out loud.

He played soccer for the university. A star player with broad shoulders and a small waist, with white teeth that spread from one end of his wide face to the other when he smiled. All the girls liked him. They stared at him in class, and he stared at me, a woman old and sad enough to be his aunt. He'd taken classes of mine before, class after class, sitting in the front row, writing things down, nodding at my points and laughing at my jokes. He'd left kind notes and rare books in my box. Recently he left a note card that said: *Sorry about your mom I know what that's like a mom sick and sore and you unable to fix a thing.* He didn't sign his name but I recognized his cadence and lack of punctuation.

After class Daniel followed me to my office. He stood behind me at the door while I fiddled with my keys. "Can I talk to you?" he said to the back of my head.

I was nodding, pushing the door open with my hip.

I sat down behind my desk. The desk was big and heavy, and I wondered how many trees it took to make such a desk, and if the trees were healthy or terribly ill, afflicted with something I couldn't pronounce. I played with a piece of string I couldn't remember finding. I didn't know where the string came from, only that it was in my hands, and that I was making tiny knot after tiny knot, and could barely look at Daniel.

"I'm older than you think," he said, and he had his hand out and was waiting for something—what? I didn't understand.

"Are you having trouble with Anne Sexton?" I asked.

He shook his head.

"What then?"

"I read your book," he said. "Twice."

I made another tiny knot.

"My mom died of breast cancer, too."

"My mom's alive," I said.

"She died fourteen months ago."

"That's terrible," I said.

"Do you need a ride to the procedure?" he said.

"It's an abortion, Daniel—it doesn't bother me to say it."

"I'm not going to tell anyone," he said.

"I know," I said, backing away from him, and my chair

squeaked, and I thought that next week I'd bring in some oil, and I'd crouch down on my knees even if I wore my new shoes, I'd oil the goddamn chair. I'd fix it.

Daniel leaned forward. "I'm older than you think," he said again.

"I heard you the first time."

"It's not about sex," he said.

"What's it about, then?"

"I want to spend time with you, that's all."

"I don't believe you," I said.

"Maybe I want to be your friend."

"*Please*," I said.

He put out his hand, his open palm one more time, wanting something. I didn't understand people lately. I didn't understand myself. And I didn't understand the boy, what he wanted.

"*What?*" I said, tired and cranky, the late afternoon nausea coming on strong.

"Give me the string," he said.

"What?"

"The string," he said. "Give it to me."

And I did.

8.

Tonight after *Hazel* is finished and my mother falls asleep, I move from the chair to her bed and watch her for nearly an hour. Her beard is soft and pale, but above her lip are several darker, wiry hairs that are stubborn and grow quickly, hanging on and returning despite her repeated waxing and expensive creams. She's spoken to me bluntly, joking about *turning into a man*—the steroids and hormones meant to slow the cancer affecting her femininity—not only changing her appearance physically but deepening her voice. Finally, she feels me staring and wakes up. "You're still here," she says. "Shouldn't you be asleep?"

"I'm not tired," I tell her.

"You're not going to believe it, Rachel," she says, "but my clitoris is growing."

"*What?*"

"It's true," she says. "It's bigger than it should be."

"Than it should be?"

"It was one size and now it's another." She looks like she's going to both cry and laugh at the same time.

"Are you sure?"

"At first I thought it was my imagination, but now I'm certain."

"Maybe it's menopause."

"It's the hormones. They said I might have to shave my chin. I thought I'd get a few stray hairs here and there, but no one mentioned this." She props a couple of pillows behind her and sits up. "I hope Gilbert doesn't notice—that would be terrible."

"*Mom.*"

"What?"

"I don't want to think about the two of you," I tell her.

"I'm sorry," she says.

"Maybe you should tell the doctor."

She shakes her head. "They're trying to keep me alive."

"And they *are*," I say, trying to sound positive.

"Sit by me," she says. "Put your head here." She pats her shoulder. "Come lean on your mother while I'm still a woman." She is smiling. "A big clitoris, one real tit and one fake one—what a prize I am. I'm lucky he likes me."

"Gilbert's the lucky one. You *are* a prize." I lean my head on my mother's shoulder.

"I know you're pregnant," she says softly.

"I'm sorry," I say.

"You don't think I'm aware of these things, but I am."

"I can't believe I let this happen."

She touches my face, lifts it up so that she can see me. She holds my chin with two fingers, inspecting it. "Smooth and perfect, not one stray hair," she says. She sighs. "The chemo ends and they promise me hair, those doctors. I grow hair, sure, but I wanted it on my head, not my chin. I didn't want a goddamn mustache," she says, laughing.

"You don't have a mustache—not a full one anyway," I say, teasing. We are quiet a moment. "Angela is taking me to the clinic in the morning," I finally say.

"Angela's a good girl, a good friend. Claire, too. They'll be with you forever." She pauses. "That boy, Daniel, called yesterday. Twice," she says.

"He shouldn't call here," I say. "I'm not giving out my home phone number to students anymore."

"Maybe you should give it out more often."

"He's a kid."

"He didn't sound like a kid."

I shake my head into her shoulder.

"He sounded very mature. We had a nice talk," she tells me.

"Oh, no," I say.

"About his writing, Rachel. Nothing else. It's your job. I wouldn't embarrass you," she says.

"The medicine is working, Mom. You're going to be okay," I tell her, wanting to believe it myself.

"Oh, hell," she says, "they're turning me into a man. Just call me Mom *or* Dad," she says, laughing and crying at once, and then the both of us are laughing and crying, and I am crawling into her sheets, and she is holding up the blankets, opening them wide, like a door or mouth.

Angela Burrows

1997–1998

What Angela Did
to Fuck Things Up

1.

She bought the biggest bed she could find—a huge, king-size pillow-top from Mary's Mattress House. She charged the bed on a new credit card without worrying about the interest, then headed next door to Bedroom Outfitter to buy sheets. She stood in the back of the store and pushed her fingers through the packages' plastic windows. "Ah, yes," she said to herself, finally deciding on a pale yellow 320 thread count by Stearns, "these will do fine."

The bed arrived on a Friday afternoon. Angela asked the deliverymen to set the massive thing up in the middle of her tiny bedroom. Forget about a dresser or matching nightstands. Forget about bookshelves, fresh flowers, or a place for candles. Forget about a magazine rack, armoire, or reasonable light.

Six nights out of seven, Angela slept alone, and though she was five feet ten inches tall and a hundred seventy pounds, the big bed minimized the young woman's physical strength—in it, she was a small and unprotected creature.

In addition, it severely limited her mobility, and getting from one place to another in the room was a feat; she held her breath and sucked in her stomach. Thinking about each step she took, Angela balanced herself carefully, scooting between mattress and wall like a woman on the ledge of a building.

2.

She snored in front of Hunter early on. And everyone knows that a woman who snores too early in a relationship reveals too much—her hot breath, her slack mouth. In the middle of the night, the most curious men have been known to fall into a woman's open mouth and never be heard from again. Obviously, the threat of falling, a red tongue and quaking uvula, and finally, the dark highway of a sleeping woman's throat, is terrifying.

Her best friend, Rachel, warned her. "Asleep, you sound like a wounded animal, like something hurt or trapped," her friend said, "something with a hole in its chest or a twisted leg, which should be reason enough to stay awake."

"How can I not sleep?" Angela said. "What if I'm tired, drunk, or full of food or full of him—what if I'm so damn sleepy that my eyes close on their own?"

"Fight it," Rachel said.

"How?"

"Think about things that trouble you."

"The calories I've consumed trouble me. My allergies. The men I've slept with," Angela said.

"But it's counting—don't count," Rachel warned, adamant.

After having silly, fumbling sex with Hunter, where, on the way into her, he accidentally (she hoped) tagged her asshole twice, she tried to stay awake. He was sleeping in the middle of her big bed, beside her, taking up more than his allotted space. He was not only snoring, but doing these little snorts that ended with puffs of air being shot out of his mouth. Angela, doing as Rachel advised, thought about various diets: the Grapefruit, Protein, and Pasta Magic. She thought about her third graders and she thought about Rachel's sick mother—how many months the woman might have left—but that quickly turned into the counting Rachel had warned against, so Angela started thinking about exercise and the indiscriminate number of laps she should do in the morning, knowing damn well she'd never see the blue pool, and as she was thinking about the swim she wouldn't take, Hunter's puffing grew faint, and Angela closed her eyes and imagined herself diving into that blue pool, doing the breaststroke or swimming underwater. She imagined herself coming up for air, and then, just then, she fell asleep and began to snore.

3.

Periodically, Angela suffered from anaphylaxis, a severe allergic reaction that made her lips swell to ten times their normal size.

It was after two in the morning the first time it happened, and she was startled awake by the strange feeling that her lips were being suctioned right off her face. She touched her mouth first, her lips like two pulsating pillows, then kicked off the sheets and blanket and jumped from the bed. She scooted between wall and mattress without giving a damn about knocking into things.

Finally in the bathroom, she looked in the mirror and gasped.

Angela called Rachel. "Help me," she said to her friend. "I look like a fucking vagina."

"A *what?*" Rachel said, sleepy, yawning into the phone.

"A pussy, a cunt, a twat—come and get me, Rach," Angela said. "You won't believe what I look like."

"Are you drunk?" Rachel said. "Is someone there? What's this about?"

"I'm alone."

"Tell me what's wrong."

Angela, despite her affliction, spoke slowly, deliberately. "My lips are swollen," she said. "They're huge, ridiculous. I've got some freaky disease, I'm dying, or maybe it's an allergy. Help me," she said again, starting to cry.

"I'm on my way," Rachel said.

The two women rushed to the All Saints Hospital emergency room, where a pimply girl behind the counter smacked her gum and looked at Angela blankly. She pushed a clipboard though the little window and said, "What seems to be the problem?"

"Look at me." Angela glared at the girl and pointed at her mouth.

After she had filled out the forms and answered the doctor's questions, it was decided that the offending substance was probably dust mites. When pressed, the doctor admitted that it was not really the mites themselves but the waste they leave behind.

"I don't understand," Angela said.

"You're unwittingly ingesting it," he said. "We're going to give you a shot of epinephrine—your condition should clear right up." He was smiling.

"You mean to say that I'm eating shit?" Angela asked, horrified, her huge, fat lips flapping.

"You could say that, yes," the doctor said.

Angela, for the second time that evening, started to cry.

The doctor leaned forward and touched her shoulder. "We all do it," he said. "We all eat their waste—only some of us are allergic, though."

"Is that supposed to make me feel better?" Angela said. "Where's that shot? Get me that shot now," she demanded.

4.

Angela believed that the last boy she loved who loved her back was smart little Larry J. from the first grade, and if she'd known that her relationships were going to lose power and depth from then on, she would have followed little Larry J. around forever.

After losing a game of tetherball to Larry J., Angela, leaving her brown bag of lunch on a patch of dry grass near the court, stuck her tongue out at the boy, called him a faggot without knowing what the word meant, and stormed off with two little girlfriends who'd been standing on the sidelines in matching blue skirts, watching the brutal game. All day Angela was hungry and unsettled, which she mistakenly attributed to leaving her lunch behind.

For the next hundred recesses she ignored little Larry J.,

and when it was time to pick partners for the spelling bee, Angela walked right by the smarter boy and picked a different boy, a lesser speller who didn't even know her name.

5.

Angela slept with Hunter before their first dinner date technically began, which Margot, her coworker, suggested, said was okay. Margot married the man she did that with, and she wanted Angela to have the same good luck.

"Look how happy *I* am," Margot said in the teachers' lounge, during recess. "Look how fucking lucky." Angela loved the word *fuck,* but wondered if putting it in front of the word *lucky* might be an omen, a warning against following Margot's suggestion. Still, she found herself unhooking her black bra and slipping out of her panties before she and Hunter made it out the front door, before they even decided where to go for dinner.

Afterwards, she asked him how he felt about his first name. "You know, *Hunter,*" she said, "what it implies."

He looked at her blankly.

"You're a vegetarian, right?"

"Oh, yeah," he said, shrugging, his skinny shoulders coming up to meet his ears, which made Angela wonder why she did the things she did. "Forget it," she said.

"Why's this bed so fucking big?" Hunter wanted to know.

6.

Angela helped Hunter put the condom on, which is something a woman shouldn't do, at least right away—and when
he's putting it on himself, a woman shouldn't stare; she should
seem disinterested in preparation—unless, of course, he's
making her dinner, say, getting the salad together.

Then, a woman should rise from the couch and offer to
help, telling him she's good at chopping things into pieces.
Here, hand me that tomato, she should say. And when he
hands it to her, she should let her fingers touch his fingers. She
should hold the tomato up and marvel at its smooth beauty.
A woman chopping that tomato should be sure to leave the
oily seeds in, those slippery yellow stars. She should hum a
song she knows he loves and try her best not to over-identify
with what's before her on the cutting board—the fruit's red
pulp.

7.

Angela stared too long at Hunter's bookshelves. She pulled a
dusty novel from its snug position and ran her finger over its
spine. She held the book like a baby to her chest, which made
him fear that she was overly anxious to become a mother.

When Hunter found her holding the book to her heart, he
said, "You're on the pill, aren't you? I love being an uncle, but
I'd hate being a dad. I'm not dad material."

Angela, whose lips had only recently returned to their natural shape and size, gave him the smallest smile possible.

"And you," he said, "you don't seem like the motherly type."

She was about to ask him what the hell he meant by that, but he was looking at the mantle at a photograph of his three nephews and one niece. "That one there," he said, gesturing with his chin at the pretty boy on the left, "he's going to kill the ladies."

Angela leaned forward and looked at the kid. She imagined him with a knife, a gun, or a fierce bare fist. She put the book back on the shelf and looked at Hunter. "What do you mean?" she said.

"A lady-killer, you know—a stud with the girls."

"Oh," Angela said. "Yes," she said, "I understand."

8.

When Hunter fell asleep she kissed his closed eyes, which scared him awake—and a man who starts his second morning with you, startled, who starts the day with your mouth that near his temples, always leaves without brushing his teeth or sharing a pot of coffee.

9.

It was their third date, and knowing Hunter was a vegetarian didn't stop her from ordering roasted chicken. When he talked about going vegan, giving up his leather shoes and jacket, giving up butter and eggs, Angela nodded. She picked up a chicken leg and ate right from the bone.

10.

She let Hunter see her drunk early on.

11.

She let Hunter see her weep.

12.

She let Hunter see her weep when drunk.

13.

She introduced Hunter to her now unhappily married coworker, Margot, who was also a vegetarian and whose husband was not, and let them spend time together in her living room, knee to knee on the couch. Angela put on music, a tape she'd recently made of Beth Orton, PJ Harvey, and Cat Power, and went into the den to call her mother.

Angela's mother, a woman who refused to forget the past, was talking about Angela's birth, some twenty-eight years ago. "Six weeks early," her mother said. "You were *born* impatient."

"You act like being premature was my first bad decision," Angela said.

"Well," her mother said, first as a statement, and then as a question. "Well? *Well?*"

"Well *what?*" Angela said.

Soon, the women were fighting and Angela found herself ignoring her guests in the other room. She found herself yelling into the phone, knowing that Hunter was probably looking at Margot's legs and chest, and that even over the music he would hear Angela's angry voice.

As the argument between mother and daughter reached its peak, Angela pictured Hunter leaning closer and closer to Margot, laughing with her, believing each remark she made. She pictured Margot tossing her hair over a shoulder, expressing sympathy for rats and cows and bugs and wasps, and smiling at Hunter, and Angela understood, of course, that she was losing two people in the process.

14.

Angela said, "Sure, Hunter, go out with her, we're not exclusive," her tone suggesting that exclusivity was far from her heart when really it was right there inside its red chambers.

15.

She agreed to go out with Hunter's friend Bucky, even though his name was Bucky, and she agreed to go out with him on the night that Hunter went out with Margot, and she pretended to be so okay about the whole thing and even suggested that the four of them meet up at midnight at the Blue Café downtown.

Angela didn't order the meatball appetizer right away even though she wanted it. As she sat across the table from Hunter, she gave him a friendly smile, which was different from a sexy smile, and made a conscious effort to keep her feet to herself.

After three glasses of wine, she caved, ordered the meatballs and, using the colored toothpicks to pick them up, ate them one at a time.

After four glasses of wine, her right foot shot away from her, but by then Hunter was too busy nuzzling unhappily married Margot's ear to care that Angela's foot in its black leather shoe was making its way up his pant leg—in fact, he was probably crediting unhappily married Margot for this bold act.

16.

Angela slept with Bucky even though his name was Bucky.

17.

After saying a rushed good-bye to Bucky in the morning, Angela called Hunter, got his answering machine, and hung up. Ten minutes later she called again. And ten minutes after that she tried once more.

18.

Angela called her mother, who had completely forgotten their fight from three days earlier, and told her the whole story, and asked her if she should call him again. When her mother said no, she called him anyway and threatened to throw away his CDs.

19.

When Hunter came over to pick up his CDs, Angela steered him into the dining room. Earlier in the day, she'd bought herself flowers, purple and yellow tulips. And as Hunter checked them out, bending at the waist and leaning toward them, she told herself that the gesture meant he was wondering where they came from, when everyone knows that tulips are a flower a woman buys for herself.

20.

There was a park near Hunter's house, and sometimes she'd go there on her lunch break, sit on a bench, and eat her sandwich. Sometimes she sat there, skipped her lunch, and wept.

21.

Angela wanted to forget about Hunter, who hadn't called her in two weeks, and she wanted the dust mites dead. She decided it was time to meet someone new, although she'd been warned that as a rebounding woman she was particularly vulnerable. She decided she'd try bombing her bedroom with insecticide, although she'd been warned that dust mites were invulnerable to the fumes.

She set the mini-silo on her dresser, pulled off the red cap, and closed the bedroom door. She got down on her hands and knees, scooting a thick towel between the bottom of the door and the hallway carpet. She darted into the den, where she stayed for two hours watching the news, the same stories over and over—this girl kidnapped, that boy angry and shooting his teacher and three students in history class, that man stole a bundle and that woman left her twin babies in a hot car to die. Faintly, on the other side of the wall, spraying from the silo, she heard the hissing poison. She imagined the gray fumes falling on her things—her big bed, her strewn clothes, jeans and white T-shirt, a smelly mist blanketing the hardwood floor.

While Angela had been trying to kill the dust mites, Rachel's mother had undergone reconstructive breast surgery, so that night Angela, Rachel, and Claire went to Ruby's Room to drink. Even though it was the middle of the week, they drank shots of tequila and chased that tequila with big, cold beers.

Eventually, Angela left a drunk Rachel at the bar with a former boyfriend and went off with a man whose name she'd never be sure of, while his pink face, gruff manner, and the unlit cigar hanging from his lips would be forever etched in her memory.

22.

Even though she barely liked the nameless stranger, she carried the phone around the house for weeks and prayed for the damn thing to ring.

23.

Angela baked cookies with walnuts, even though the allergy doctor wasn't a hundred percent certain about the dust mites and suggested that nuts might be offending substances, too.

Still, Angela mixed the sugar and flour and butter and eggs first, then ripped open a bag of walnuts with her teeth. She poured the nuts into the batter and folded it all together with a flat spoon.

While the oven preheated, she ate several spoonfuls of raw

cookie dough and decided that her mother was right about one thing at least: her lack of patience, her unwillingness to wait.

Angela sat at the kitchen table, within feet of the oven, feeling the heat and smelling the burning sugar.

24.

Two mornings after the walnuts and one morning after Rachel's mother's breast reconstruction, Angela woke up at her friend's mother's apartment, in her friend's bed. The man whose name she'd never be sure of was gone, and she heard Rachel puttering about in the kitchen.

Angela sat on the couch, drinking coffee with Rachel, who was asking all about Brad's exit. "Do you remember him leaving?" she wanted to know.

"I'm not even sure his name's Brad," she said.

"Really?"

"His friends called him Chuck."

"Lovely," Rachel said.

Angela sipped her coffee and looked at her friend, then away.

"Maybe you should have brought him to your place," Rachel said.

Angela shrugged.

"I've always wondered why you bought that bed anyway," Rachel said. "I mean, isn't it too big for your room? I think you should have bought a full-size."

"Maybe so," Angela said.

"You know, you could sell it. You could put an ad in the newspaper and get rid of the thing," Rachel said.

Angela sipped her coffee. She was only half listening to her friend talk, her friend could have been talking about anything, really, she could have been talking about her mother, about the ocean outside the window, about her own troubles with men. Angela sipped her coffee. She sipped it again and again, becoming aware of her lips and the tingling that had begun there. She knew it was time to get to the hospital, that a shot of epinephrine would be waiting for her, and that without it, this time, her lips would grow and grow, surely they'd grow and grow, turning into red pillows or ridiculously big mattresses, this time they might just be the end of her . . .

Rachel Spark

2000

Egg Girls

1.

I was in Los Angeles, at a dingy clinic on Sepulveda Boulevard, with all these very pregnant girls. Being over thirty, I had ten years on them, at least. We were lined up on the couch, a couple of girls reading magazines or pretending to, another few looking at the television, and every so often one girl tried to talk to another girl, asking some innocuous question, and was grudgingly answered or rebuffed, so Ms. Friendly went back to her magazine or book or whatever.

We were in waiting room number 4, our final stop before the procedure, which meant we left our husband (doubtful) or parent or boyfriend or best friend in number 1, waited in number 2 to give blood and urine, waited in number 3 to be ushered toward a cubicle—behind a thin wall, and within earshot of the others—where we answered a stranger's questions about our sexual history in hushed tones.

This was the place they sent problem cases. That's what I was, a problem. "We're having a problem, Rachel," they said last Saturday morning at The Family-Choice Center in Long

Beach, two miles from where I taught at the university and ten blocks from where I lived. In all fairness to the center, they'd warned me, told me that I'd have to wait at least six weeks from conception, but, having found myself pregnant by the traveling British journalist—my green-eyed five-night stand, my Hampshire farmer—I couldn't wait. "Yes," I snapped at my student Ella, who, to my surprise, worked at the clinic and whose voice I heard before I even saw her. It was Ella calling me to the little window, and Ella handing me the papers to sign, and then, to my horror, it was Ella sitting across from me in the cubicle, asking those personal fucking questions. It was almost enough to make me fail my star student.

"Is there someone *else* I can talk to?" I said.

"There's a wait," she said. "If you'd rather talk to someone else, I understand, but it will be a while."

"How long?"

"Maybe an hour."

I wasn't happy and I'm sure it showed.

"I'm a professional," Ella said weakly.

"It's not you," I said, throwing my hands up, frustrated. "Or maybe it is. It doesn't help, you know?"

Ella nodded, sympathetically. "I know, Dr. Spark."

"I'm not a doctor, Ella. I'm anything but a doctor. Call me Rachel. I don't even have a doctorate degree."

"I'm sorry, Rachel. I forgot." Ella paused. She looked down at her clipboard. She tapped her pen on her knee and looked at me. "It's been six weeks, then," Ella said. It was more a comment than a question.

"I said six—maybe it's been seven," I said. I calculated, counted in my head, and okay, I was early, a liar on top of everything else, but just by four days. I didn't think it would make a difference, but apparently it did, because now it was my second abortion—or attempt—in a week, because there I was on that couch with these ridiculously pregnant girls, and I was the only one not showing. I mean, they were big—not the kind of pregnant that's a secret, but visibly, stomach out, swollen breasts, the whole thing. They came back three days in a row for what they called insertions.

"I'm just here for an insertion," the biggest girl of all told me. She had a white bow on top of her head. She was huge, massive, tall and fat, with long legs like trees. One tree leg was crossed over the other, or trying to, and because she was sitting next to me, the bottom of her blue bootie was just inches from my bare knee. In addition to the bow, she was wearing little baby barrettes, pink, one on each side, holding back her hair. The barrettes were extra tiny, absurd on a girl like her. Her hairdo was way too busy. Just *who* would be with her, I was thinking, who'd make her pregnant, who'd pull those barrettes out, who'd set that silly bow aside and fuck her, that's what I wanted to know, which wasn't nice of me, I understood, but I was thinking it nonetheless. I was blaming my hormones. I was blaming Rex. I blamed myself and the condom I didn't use. I blamed my mother's breast cancer, which had recurred, popped up, chewing and chewing at her hip and neck.

I wondered if the big girl hadn't been aware of her pregnancy, like a woman Angela told me about who gave birth in the toilet. The woman thought she was taking a shit like any other shit, Angela said, and then *wham*—a baby boy. I wondered if the big girl next to me had the same problem, if she kept growing and growing, from Monday to Monday, thicker and thicker, like a balloon or cream puff, without a conscious idea of what was happening. Like a woman with a breast tumor who convinces herself it's benign, who goes into denial *before* her diagnosis, and so she waits and waits, months, a year perhaps, for a biopsy. Had the big girl next to me made excuses when her pants wouldn't zip, when the button popped off her best skirt?

There were a half dozen of us sitting on the couch, which was beige or gray, a cardboard color, and we were wearing white paper robes, and most of us, everyone but me, like I said, were obvious and round. We were watching *General Hospital* on a tiny television, the sound turned down low, quiet until the commercials began. A commercial for eggs came on, an animated thing, where a dozen eggs with faces popped out of their crate and danced around. They had eyelashes, these eggs, and lipstick. They were blushing pink, singing a song. "Scrambled or fried, poached or baked," they squealed. A voice-over declared that eggs weren't nearly as bad for you as the healthy-heart people claimed. His voice was deep, serious, when compared to the squealing eggs, and he was saying that they were all wrong about cholesterol, that four eggs a week was good for you. I was thinking that we looked like eggs, us swollen girls in white, sitting on a couch the color of cardboard. I was thinking that maybe I'd go home and write a poem about us egg girls when the biggest egg of all, the girl next to me, said, "You know what they are?"

"Dancing eggs," I answered.

"Not them," she said, rolling her eyes.

I shrugged. I wanted to be left alone.

"Insertions. I'm talking about insertions."

"Oh."

"You know what they are?" she said again.

"No, I don't want—"

"It's seaweed or something," she interrupted.

I nodded, but didn't look at the girl. I stared hard at the

television. *General Hospital* was back on, and I was pretending that the story line was more important than real life, that the pretty couple on TV and their impending divorce outweighed what we egg girls had going on there.

"It's supposed to make me, or it, easier to get to. I've been here a couple times already. Someone said my vagina might be open enough today, but I doubt it."

"It's your cervix," I told her, still not looking her way.

"What?"

"They want your cervix to dilate."

"Vagina, cervix, what's the difference?"

"There's a difference, believe me."

"Well, anyway, like I was saying, that nurse who took my blood, she said I might be open enough."

"That's nice," I said.

"Don't get too excited," the girl said, sarcastically.

"I won't."

"Because I'm not lucky that way. If everyone but the lucky ones come back here three days in a row, then I'll be here four, maybe even five, you watch."

"Maybe not."

"It's true. I'm unlucky—well, that's obvious, isn't it?" She let out a small laugh. She patted her stomach and sighed.

"Guess so."

"This is how it works. They've got you on a table, legs spread wide. I mean, they could stuff a TV in your honeypot if they wanted to." My new friend was working with her hands and arms now, elbows together, making a V. "They take this stuff, it's seaweed, *I think* it's seaweed, is it seaweed?" she asked the girl on her left. The girl shrugged. She wet her finger with her tongue, then used it to turn the page of the magazine in her lap. She lifted the magazine in the air, blocking the biggest girl from her view. "It's seaweed," my pal concluded, "and they've got your legs spread—"

"Look," I said, turning to her for the first time, "I'm not here for an insertion, okay?"

"Suit yourself," she said.

"I'm early," I said.

"So?"

"I'm barely pregnant." I turned back to the television.

"I'm just telling you what they do."

"Thanks for that," I said, sarcastically.

"Don't you like to know what goes on behind closed doors?"

"No, really—"

"They stick this stuff inside of you and—"

"*Please,*" I said. "Stop."

"You're weird," the girl said. "It's all over your face, how weird you are."

I thought about my face then, what it was or was not giving away. "Can't we just wait our turn?" I said.

"We *are* waiting."

"I mean, quietly."

"Oh," the girl said, sneering now, "you're one of those."

"Yes," I said.

"And you even admit it."

"That's right."

"You're not embarrassed about being a snob?"

"No."

"*Well.*" The girl took her leg in her hand, the one that she'd been attempting to cross over, and set it down, next to the other leg, which now had a bright red splotch and was maybe asleep because she was rubbing it. "I never . . . You should be ashamed of yourself," she told me, still rubbing.

"For other things in my life, yes. For wanting you to shut up, no."

"Look at you," the girl said. "What a freak. And what a snob, too. A freak and a snob."

"I'm fine with it, the snob part, the freak part might be inaccurate, but say what you want."

"Freak, *freak.*"

"Look," I said, turning toward the girl again, noticing for the first time that the other eggs, even the one next to her, were staring at the two of us, excited, enjoying our fight. "I've got problems worse than you not liking me. You understand?"

"*Well,*" she said again, breathless.

"I'm not here to make friends."

"Maybe the rest of us are."

"Come on," I said. "The rest of us have friends at home. I bet a friend or two of ours is outside in the waiting room right now. You see what I'm saying?"

"I *see* that you're crazy," she said.

"That's right."

"I *see* that you're whacked."

"You should be afraid of me, then."

"I *see* that you're a little old for an abortion, don't you think? You may be *early,* but you're old."

"Thank you, that's lovely."

"What are you, twenty-seven, twenty-eight?"

"Fuck you."

"Fuck you too, old lady."

"That's fine."

"Fuck you, fuck you," she said, and then, thank God, a door opened and a woman called her name. "Pamela?" the nurse said.

"*Pammy,*" the big egg corrected her, almost yelling.

The nurse frowned. She gave Pammy, who was focused on me and hadn't given any indication of getting up off the couch any time soon, a puzzled look. "It's your turn," the nurse said.

"Call me by my right name," Pammy demanded.

"*Please,*" the woman said, exasperated. She let the clipboard fall against her thigh. She sighed. She stared at Pammy.

"Say who I am or I'm not moving."

"Good God," the nurse said. "I should have stayed in bed."

Pammy shrugged. She fiddled with one barrette, then the other, unsnapping and snapping.

"*Pammy,* it's your turn," the nurse finally said, giving in. "You coming or you just going to sit there?"

Pammy ignored her.

"Fine," the nurse said. "I'll call on someone else." She lifted the clipboard in the air and stared at it. "Let's see here," she said, picking the next girl from her list. "Georgia, we're ready for you now. You ready, honey?" she said sweetly.

The girl who'd been protecting herself from Pammy with the magazine stood up then. She was a tall girl, pretty, with strange little bangs that framed her face.

"Sit down, Georgia," Pammy said, jumping up. "It's my damn turn," she said. "I didn't go three days with seaweed in my cooch to lose my damn turn."

Georgia sat back down. There was one less egg on the couch now, a noticeably blank space, some forty inches of beige couch where Pammy's ass had been. Georgia turned to me with a sympathetic smile. "You're not old," she said. We both looked at Pammy, who was moving her fat ass away from us, clutching that paper gown, hiding the ass. She was huffing and puffing, taking heavy steps in her blue booties. Before stepping inside, Pammy turned to me. "You better not be here when I get back, old lady," she said.

2.

I was at that dingy clinic, in that sort of trouble, because I lied, like I said. Four days early and the embryo was too tiny to reach. Last Saturday at Ella's clinic I woke up from what I thought would be my first and only abortion, and the doctor, a gray-haired man with a long white beard that actually touched my pillow as he spoke to me, said, "The procedure was unsuccessful."

"Who are you?"

"Dr. Wheeler."

"What are you saying?"

"It was empty—you're empty," he said.

"Tell me something I don't know," I said.

"Seriously, uh, uh—" he began, looking at my chart, searching for my name. "You're Rachel, right?"

"Yes," I said.

"I couldn't find anything. In your uterus, I mean."

"You're joking. Is this a joke?" I was drugged, slurring my words, trying hard not to.

"No, not at all, I'm terribly serious," he was speaking loud-ly now, enunciating each word.

"I have cramps, though. Here, *here*." I touched myself under the sheet, pointed out the places that hurt most.

"How about some codeine, Rachel? Want some codeine?"

"I *want* an abortion," I said, my voice cracking.

He patted my arm, that beard getting closer and closer to my cheek. He motioned to my student, Ella, who was standing across the room, half of her face obscured by the open metal cabinet. "Get her something for the pain, would you?" he said.

"Right away," Ella said.

"I *want* an abortion," I said again, starting to cry.

"I tried," the doctor said. "I worked and worked at it. There was nothing inside. Like I said before, I couldn't find a thing."

Ella walked up to my bedside, holding a Dixie cup of water, two white pills in her open palm.

"Give me those," I said.

Dr. Wheeler thought that the embryo was in a fallopian tube, stuck there in between, which I figured was fitting—my embryo lost, inches from potential nourishment, indecisive, unable to commit. He mentioned the threat of rupture, bleeding, death, and was sending me to a clinic on Third Street, a fertility specialist. From my grimace and sigh, Dr. Wheeler and Ella could probably tell that I didn't appreciate the irony. "It's the only place in town with an ultrasound machine available on a Saturday morning," Ella explained.

"Wonderful," I said.

"Dr. Baker is waiting for you. I've already called her."

"Lovely."

"She's opening the office just for you. It's a Saturday," Dr. Wheeler said, stating the obvious.

"I know what day it is," I said.

"It'll all work out," Ella said, sweetly.

"I wanted it to *work out* today," I said. "What's wrong with this place?" I wanted to know.

Ella shook her head. "You'll be okay," she said.

234

• • •

A half hour later, I was sitting with Angela at the fertility clinic on yet another couch. I was bent over in pain, on codeine, and trying hard not to throw up again. Angela held the plastic bag Ella had given her at the clinic in her lap. "If you want to throw up again, just do it," she said. "I've got this bag, and it's just waiting."

"I see the damn bag," I snapped.

"Okay."

"I saw my student give it to you. I was standing right there," I continued. "I'm drugged, medicated—not stupid," I said.

"I know, Rachel," she said, rubbing my back. "You're going to be fine," she said.

Against my wishes, Angela had called my mother, and now my mom was bursting through the door, her face scrunched up with worry. She limped toward me, a hand on her sore hip. "Oh, dear," she said.

"Why did you call her?" I asked Angela. "Do you think she needs this right now?"

Angela picked up a magazine from the coffee table and tried to ignore me.

"You've got enough going on," I said to my mother.

"Look at you," she said. It wasn't just that I was past thirty, unmarried, but where was my boyfriend? What about precaution? Didn't I know better at my age? All the things she wanted to say to me earlier, but didn't. She motioned for Angela to make room for her and then sat down right next to me. "What about condoms?" my mother said.

I said nothing.

Angela looked at me. "You used a condom, didn't you?" she said.

"Please, I'm in pain," I said.

"A condom can break anyway," Angela said. "I knew a girl who used a condom and the guy was so big—which isn't always a bad thing, of course—but he broke right through it and—"

"Never mind," my mother said, interrupting her. "None of this matters. Where does it hurt?" she asked, and for a moment we were mother and daughter, just that, and she was going to make it better.

"Everywhere," I said.

"We should have talked more about this," my mother said.

"I'm an adult," I said, starting to cry again.

"That's fine, that's fine . . ." She patted my knee. "You're a grown-up, that's right. I forget sometimes."

"You do," I said.

"You've got to stop worrying about me, though, acting out."

"What?"

"You know, it's always on television. The talk shows are always talking about *acting out*."

"They're talking about teenagers," I said.

"It's about behavior, as I see it," she said. "It's not limited to one age group."

"Is that so?" I said, sarcastically.

"As a matter of fact, yes," she said. "You can't worry about me all the time, that's what I'm saying."

"Fine."

"A little bit of cancer is nothing. A couple zaps of radiation and I'll be okay. You know me," she said, looking at Angela to back her up.

"Absolutely," Angela said, looking up from the magazine. She was nodding, trying to look hopeful.

"Where's Dr. Baker?" I said.

• • •

Dr. Baker, a short, stocky woman with red hair and freckles, helped me onto a table—the same table, I imagined, that other women wanted nothing more than to hop onto pregnant. I thought of those women, their loving men crouched beside them, holding their hands, waiting for heartbeats, dying to count fingers and toes, looking for little penises or tiny vaginas. Dr. Baker moved the sonogram thing, which was cold and metallic, across my stomach, the way someone else might have ironed a shirt. "Let's see," she said. "Let's take a look."

"I live with my mom in her apartment and she's sick . . ." I began.

"Eureka," Dr. Baker said. "Right here. In your uterus, where it's supposed to be."

"How'd Dr. Wheeler miss it?"

"Who?"

"The doctor from the Family Center."

"That's right—he sent you here." She was staring at the screen. "He or she is in the corner," she continued, "clinging to your uterine wall."

"Clinging, huh?"

"Do you want to see?"

"No," I said.

"I'm sorry," the doctor said. "I shouldn't have asked you that."

"I'm not like the rest of your patients, I guess. I've got different problems."

"Yes, well, I should be sensitive. My husband is always telling me that I'm not sensitive enough."

I nodded.

"I'm sorry," she said.

"It's okay," I said.

"What was that you said about your mother?"

"Nothing," I said.

Last week, driving down Atherton, a familiar one-way street I used all the time, several times a week, I found myself going the wrong way. My first clue was going through an intersection and realizing that the cars opposite me were stopped. My traffic light was turned around, backwards, which I thought strange, but still it didn't register. Within seconds I saw the cars coming toward me, screeching to a halt. Smoking, the cars, with their drivers hanging out windows, cussing at me. "What the fuck's your problem?" one man hollered. "Stupid fucking bitch," a woman shouted. I was turning my car around, trying not to see or hear them. Later, just before sleep, I kept seeing the image, all those cars, an SUV, a Caddy, a Jeep, that cursing man, his shoulder, one arm hanging out the window, and that cursing woman too, coming toward me. I listened to my mother breathing in the next room. I played and replayed my drive down Atherton, thinking, *Cancer is just like that.*

3.

I was turning between stiff sheets, coming to, with a terribly sweet taste in my dry mouth, when I saw Pammy's ass. They had us lined up on cots, and her ass could have been any ass at all, but it was hers, I knew it. The ass was white, wide, and flat, with dimples, and there was something very sad about an ass like that, and a girl, an obnoxious girl, but a girl nonetheless, alone, leaning over, vomiting into a plastic bowl. The barrettes were still there, but they had moved considerably toward the back of her head. She was holding the white bow in her hand, using it to wipe her mouth. She moaned, threw those big legs out of the sheet, and crawled from the cot. "I have to pee," she said. "Someone, help me," she said, and she was crying now.

I looked around the room for a nurse, someone, anyone, but it was only us, the egg girls from waiting room number 4. Georgia was to the right of me, eyes closed, snoring lightly. "Hey," I said, turning to the left, not wanting to wake her. "Someone here needs help," I called, but my voice was small, tiny in the room.

Pammy fell to the floor then, weeping, on her big knees. I sat up, pulled the sheets down, and stepped off the cot. I lost a bootie in the process, and the tile was cold on my one bare foot. I made my way to Pammy and stuck my hand under her arm. I tried to lift her, but she was heavy and wouldn't or couldn't budge. "Someone help us," I said. "*Please.*" But no one was there; no one was coming. "Come on, try to stand," I said.

"I can't," she said.

"I'll get you to the bathroom if you stand up."

Pammy took a deep breath. She sighed, then made an effort. Halfway up, knees bent, Pammy's eyes were level with my own. She looked into my face, squinting. "Which one are you?" she said.

"Don't worry about it," I said.

"I can't see without my contacts. Which one *are* you?" she repeated.

"It's me, the old lady," I said.

"Oh, you," she said, straightening up, holding her arm across her lower stomach, which I imagined, like mine, was pretty sore. My right arm reached around her thick waist, while my left hand cupped her elbow. She was a tower, a building, and I was helping her to the bathroom.

Halfway there, we stopped in the hall a moment to breathe, rest. "You lost a bootie," Pammy said.

"I know."

"Isn't your foot cold?"

"Yeah."

"Want to turn around and get it?"

I shook my head no. "It's okay," I said. "I don't need it," I told her.

Pammy took a deep breath. She exhaled. "I'm ready now," she said. And we continued down the hall, one foot in front of the other, taking little steps, baby steps.

Georgia Carter

2000

Geography of the Mall

Georgia Carter was sixteen that summer and working at the frozen yogurt shop in the mall. Frozen yogurt had made a comeback, was big again, and the cones she made for the boy who worked at the shoe store across the way were big, too, and he was big as well when finally his zipper was down and her hand was around him.

It was noon, too early for the act itself and the boy's spicy cologne, too early for the leather and canvas and suede she smelled on the boy's fingers moments earlier when he tried to touch her face with them.

She didn't know the make of his car, but noticed before climbing into it that it was wide and old, rusting in spots. On the passenger's side back door she saw a dent as round and perfect as her mother's favorite salad bowl. It was probably a bitch to park. She was with him in the front seat of that car for the first of many lunch breaks, where she'd skip food and juice, her own nourishment, and think only of the boy's satiation.

She pulled her long hair to one side and it hung down in a pale rope across her chest. She was balanced on one elbow,

243

palm to cheek, staring at her own moving hand, and at him too, the girth and length of him. With the window open she felt the sun's heat on one shoulder, her right cheek, where in just seconds the boy would try to land a kiss, and she would bend backwards, away from him.

The other boys were bossy, with aggressive hands and mouths, and she acquiesced, leaned back on a couch or football field, passive and inactive, hardly even there. There had been abortions and a recent bout with condyloma, so for this one, it was she who would make the rules.

Funny, she didn't say it out loud, rule number 1, but her body twisted away from him, went rigid at his touch, and the boy caught on quickly.

Perhaps he was smarter than the rest, she was thinking. She knew he was older, a boy who was really a man—the faint lines on his forehead, the lines framing his mouth like a set of parentheses, and the way he didn't flinch or cower when she used multisyllabic words. She'd said *clandestine*. She'd said *surreptitious*. She'd said, "I don't want you to *reciprocate*."

"You read books?" he said once.

"I read books," she said.

"Georgia, let me do you now."

"No."

"Come on," he persisted, his hand reaching for the buttons on her blouse.

She pushed his hand away. "Don't," she said.

"Your tits then. Let me kiss your tits, at least. What would happen if I just kissed your tits?"

She shook her head.

"It's your turn," he said, almost pleading.

"We're not playing Scrabble," she said.

. . .

Georgia's bout with condyloma had been persistent, too, treated once and a month later returned. It made her itch and squirm, and when she sat on the floor with her back against the side of her bed, her legs open and a make-up magnifying mirror between them, and looked inside, the warts were heads of cauliflower. Ella, her counselor at the clinic, called the condyloma insidious and threatened Georgia with cervical cancer. It didn't seem possible to get cancer from a wart, and she wasn't sure she believed Ella, thought she was exaggerating to slow Georgia down. And what was that dramatic smack of her medical folder? And that look on Ella's face, like Georgia had cancer already?

She lived alone with her father, a former high school math teacher, who was just forty-four years old but losing his mind and forgetting things like a very old man. There were things he still remembered, like Georgia's curfew and chores, like her mother who went out one night three winters ago with friends from work, met a rich man named Rich, and never came back to them, not even to pick up her clothing, but even those things would be lost to him within the year. "That's a woman who's willing to forget us completely," Georgia's father said, stating the obvious. "That's a woman without a conscience."

Through weekly phone calls and the occasional letter, Georgia learned that Rich bought her mother everything: a new wardrobe, a house on a hill two states away, and a baby girl from China they named Sam. On the front porch her mother sat on a wicker couch, feet up, talking to Georgia on the phone, describing things in theatrical detail. "The front lawn is landscaped," she said. "Gardenias, Casablanca lilies, and narcissus on one side, waxflowers and eucharis on the other. Waxflowers and eucharis smell like lemons," she told Georgia, and Georgia imagined flowers smelling like fruit, looking like one thing and smelling like something else entirely. Like a mother who asked you about school, who wanted to know if you liked the two new pairs of jeans she left on your bed, a mother who begged you to eat and tucked you in at night, while at the same time plotting her escape.

"There's a circular staircase that leads up to the porch," her mother said. "Very modern. You will love those stairs, Georgie," she promised.

"*When* will I love them?" Georgia asked, and her mother always said the same thing: when things settle down and we can plan a visit.

Her brother, Kevin, was off at college in San Francisco and her father didn't work anymore, just puttered around the house in mismatched clothing, talking to himself and rarely making sense. Sometimes, in a voice that was normal, not at all frantic, he called out her mother's name, as if the woman were still there, as if she hadn't left the state and were only a room away. Sometimes he talked about work, the students he left behind, and the subjects themselves, algebra and geometry.

"A circle's circumference is pi times double the radius," he said last week to no one. He was sitting at the round table in the backyard, drinking lemonade, and Georgia was watching him from the open kitchen window, waiting for her Aunt Alma to arrive so she could leave for work. "Double the radius," he said. "Double," he repeated emphatically, and he stood up then and stared down at the table itself, as if the circle of it were something to argue with, as if it were morphing into a square or disagreeing.

"The whole world is unreliable," he used to say, "but math is certain, fixed, it's made up its mind."

And Georgia, too, had made up her mind, had made it up from the first moment she saw the boy, down on one knee, slipping a sandal on a woman's foot. Georgia was on a break, sipping a Coke and standing at the store window, staring at a display of boots. She decided to start saving money for one pair in particular—dark brown and laceless. She'd need a shoehorn for those, she was thinking, and it was then that she looked up and saw the foot in its dark stocking pointing at the boy's chest. She saw an ankle, too, and a calf. She saw a bony knee and part of a thigh. A pillar obscured the rest of the woman's body, but Georgia wasn't looking for her then, but for him. His hand disappeared inside a shoebox a second and then came up with the sandal. It was orange—an awful color for a sandal, really—and there was a plastic daisy where the straps met. With one hand he clutched the shoe, with the other he held the back of the woman's ankle. That was it for Georgia—a boy on one knee steering a woman's suspended foot into a silly sandal; it was a smooth and deliberate gesture that decided things.

She took in his face and the dark bangs that fell in front of it. She took in his fingers pushing the bangs away. She took in his jaw and lips and chin, and after he returned the sandal to the box and stood up, she took in the whole boy. He talked to the woman behind the pillar, holding the box under one arm. He was nodding, smiling, obviously making a sale. And then he was looking over at the window—perhaps he caught Georgia staring—and she took in his eyes for the briefest second before turning away and heading back to Yates' Yogurt.

It was later at the food court that she saw him again, this time part of his face obscured by the ridiculously big pretzel in front of it. He was sitting at a table with four chairs. Georgia thought about walking over and introducing herself, but instead remained where she was: on a bench about ten feet away from the boy, behind a potted plant, her own face hidden behind the plastic leaves. She pushed two leaves apart with her fingers and watched him brush salt off the pretzel. She watched him sip his soda. She watched him until the pretzel was gone, until his whole handsome face was revealed.

Georgia's father had been diagnosed with a degenerative brain disease that even she couldn't pronounce, some five threatening syllables she gave up trying to say. She could say the other words, though, like *frontal cortex* and *temporal lobe*. She could say *inoperable, object recognition,* and *obliteration.* It was like Alzheimer's, only faster, speeded up, a disease in a rush, the doctor explained, and Georgia imagined a disease sprinting— a disease with feet, with toes and heels and soles.

Georgia, too, was in a rush, but apparently her noonday boy was not, leaning back on the car seat and taking his time. "Slow down," he said, and she willed her hand to do just that, which added a heightened awareness to the act itself that embarrassed her. She thought about stopping altogether, getting up and out of the car, but decided instead to finish what she started.

She introduced herself to the boy for the first time on a Tuesday afternoon. He was standing under the big clock, looking at the mall directory in front of him. She gathered up her nerve and walked over to the map, feigning interest in mall geography. He had his finger beside the red X, which told the boy where he was: You Are Here.

"You lost too?" she asked him.

"Sort of," he said, looking around. "I was supposed to meet someone and she didn't show."

"You look more sad than angry."

"Yeah, well." The boy looked at her. He ran his fingers through those bangs. "Do I know you?" he said.

"You work right across the street from me," she told him. "I mean, across the way from my store—well, not *my* store exactly, Mrs. Yates' store."

"The yogurt place."

"It's just part-time," she said. "I'm going to do other things—with my life, I mean."

"We all are," he said, smiling.

"Selling shoes is okay," she said. "At least you get commission."

"My name's Jim," he said.

"Hey, Jim."

"Hey."

They stood there a few moments, not saying anything, until finally he asked, "How long have you been working at Yates' Yogurt?"

It had been exactly three months, but she shrugged, pretending not to remember. "I'm Georgia," she said.

"How old are you, Georgia?"

"I'm eighteen," she lied.

He lifted his eyebrows.

"In June."

"You sure about that?"

"Want to see my license?"

"I like yogurt," he said.

There were things Georgia's father didn't know, never knew, and therefore could not forget. He didn't know, for instance, how often she imagined the gray-and-black image of his brain, and the doctor pointing, saying, *Look at that, would you just look at that.* He didn't know how many times she'd been to the clinic with health problems herself, sitting across from Ella, sometimes lying, sometimes telling the truth. He didn't know what she was looking for, and neither did she. He didn't know that she talked to her mother on the phone once a week and could nearly smell those lemony flowers. He didn't know that she was the kind of girl who would spend her lunch break in a car with a boy who was really a man of twenty-eight. He didn't know that she would lie about her age, that she would lead the boy out of the mall, through the big glass doors, and into the parking lot, that she would ask him which car was his and then steer him toward it like a puppy.

Maybe her father was standing in his closet now, she was thinking, not knowing what a shoe was. *Object recognition. Obliteration.* What exactly do you do with this? he might be wondering, while Georgia, on the other hand, had known exactly what to do only moments ago with what was in front of her—she tossed an empty cup into the boy's backseat and maneuvered her chest over the parking brake, leaning down and making her way to him.

* * *

One morning last month, before she left for Yates' Yogurt, her father, standing at the sink in his terry cloth robe and running shoes, was wiping his mouth with a piece of white bread as if it were a napkin. Georgia's Aunt Alma went to the sink and took the bread from his hand, replacing it with an actual napkin, saying, "Here, Denny, use this." Georgia's dad looked down at his palm, at the napkin sitting there, and didn't recognize its function. Georgia was thinking about functions now, what things are used for, their exact purposes, while she blew on the boy's balls, and the boy said, "Oooooh, cooling," like Georgia was a mint in his mouth, like her function was to freshen him up.

There were things she would not forget: like the boy's thighs and the car she didn't know the name of, like the cinnamon bird hanging from the rearview mirror, like the vinyl seats and his shiny shoes, and against her cheek the belt buckle, which was silver and small, almost dainty, which didn't match the gold watch he wore on his wrist, a wrist that was thick and hairy and unlike the wrists of the other boys she'd known.

She was going down on him in pure daylight, behind JC Penney's, her bobbing head and the boy's tense features obscured only by a short wall and dumpster. As she moved, his unforgettable thighs clenched, his muscles froze, and she heard delivery guys outside arguing.

"It's a fucking couch, it's heavy. You're a lazy motherfucker," one guy said.

"Shut the fuck up," another guy answered.

"Fuck you both," a third guy added.

Georgia imagined the three of them dropping the couch to the asphalt and moving toward the car. She imagined them peering over that short wall and getting a look.

The noonday boy was a new kind of boy, a boy who was really a man, a man in slacks and navy blue dress shirt, a man in a silk tie. Georgia understood that his silly garments were only his work clothes, a costume, like the blue jumper Mrs. Yates made her wear. She knew that when he left the mall and went home, he was, like her, a different person altogether—a guy in Levis and bare chest mowing the lawn or a guy in shorts and tank top running laps around the neighborhood park.

There was a band of white skin on his ring finger, and when Georgia jutted her chin in the finger's direction and raised her eyebrows, the boy said, "I don't know what you're talking about."

"I'm not talking," Georgia said.

"Well, you're looking," the boy said.

But it was Georgia's fault as much as anyone's, so she said, "I don't care if you got someone at home who cooks for you."

And he said, "She doesn't cook."

When Georgia opened the front door, she found her Aunt Alma on the couch, painting her nails. Her father was on all fours in the middle of the room, playing with Georgia's dog. "Hello, honey," Alma said. "You have a good day?"

Georgia nodded.

"Sit down with me, Georgie. Tell me what you think of this color. Is it subtle enough? I don't want anything too flashy. What do you think?" she said again, waving her fingers in the air.

"I think it stinks." Georgia wrinkled her nose.

Her aunt stretched her arms out, elbows locked, and spread her fingers apart. "You don't like it?" she said, pouting.

"The color's fine," Georgia said. "But they stink—don't wave them around like that."

"Oh, good, you like the color." Alma looked relieved.

Georgia walked over to the couch and bent down to whisper in her aunt's ear. "How long has he been like that?" she said, pointing at her dad's back.

"All afternoon. I didn't even know he liked that dog."

Obviously her dad had forgotten that he hated the dog, the dog Georgia had rescued from the streets months ago and begged him to let her keep. "Because of loyalty, because your mother's a liar and she's gone," he said finally, giving in.

Now her father was using a voice Georgia barely recognized, a sweet and sticky voice that came from somewhere inside him she hadn't seen since before she was a teenager. "Oh, baby, you're my pooch, my sweet pooch," he said. "Remember when Clara was a puppy?" her dad asked, turning to Georgia. And though the dog's name was Temper and she'd only been with them three months, Georgia said yes.

She made herself a turkey sandwich and took it to the den. She turned the television on but kept the sound way down low and thought about her father's forgetting, how today it led to love, or a sort-of-love, or maybe that wasn't love at all, because her real father, the man made up of actual memories, hated the dog he now thought he loved. Then Georgia decided that love wasn't a real thing anyway, only something people imagined or pretended to feel, and then she looked at her sandwich, sitting there with little bits of wilted lettuce hanging over the crust, and decided she wasn't hungry anymore.

Georgia didn't know what she felt and barely pretended when she met the boy who was really a man in his car at noon. She called him a boy to his face and he didn't protest, although they both knew the truth. Perhaps she called him a boy and wanted to believe it because he was more ordinary that way, more conventional, less original, and therefore would become less of a memory. He would be easier to forget if he was just a boy like the others, if, in her mind, he was ten years younger and not as experienced and didn't know how to smoothly accept the things he accepted: undoing his belt and unzipping his pants with one hand while lifting a lever and letting the seat fall back under his weight with the other.

On Sunday her Aunt Alma, who up until now only stopped by once a day with groceries and medicine and food, came to live with them for good. Georgia stood in the doorway and watched Alma in her parents' walk-in closet as she ripped her mother's dresses, blouses, sweaters, and jeans from hangers and dropped them into two huge cardboard boxes. Alma climbed up on a stepstool and swept the top shelf with her forearm, swinging her arm back and forth until the floor beneath her was covered with shoes: heels and clogs and slippers and boots. She stepped off the stool and picked up a black pump. "Look at this," she said to Georgia, holding the shoe by its skinny heel with two fingers, shaking her head.

"What?" Georgia said.

"This," she said again, louder this time, making a face and moving the shoe away from her chest like it was a dead animal, a rat or smelly fish.

"It's a shoe," Georgia told her.

"Yes, well," she said. "We should have known what your mother was capable of."

Georgia held the flaps shut while Aunt Alma taped up the

boxes. Later, after her father went to sleep, Georgia helped her aunt carry the boxes outside to the curb, where they sat until morning next to three fat green bags of trash.

It was noon again, and she should have been anywhere but there. She should have been at the food court sitting with a corn dog or milk shake or bowl of spicy chicken. She should have been doing anything but that.

She pulled her hand away from the boy, quitting at the exact moment he exploded. He dirtied the dashboard and steering wheel, and let out a huge sigh, a sigh that seemed to fill the whole car. "Fuck," he said. "Sorry." He pulled Georgia to his chest and hugged her tightly for several seconds before she wriggled from his arms. "Maybe we could go away one weekend," he said suddenly.

"I don't know," she said.

"I want to touch you too," he said. "It's not fair."

"To who?"

"To both of us," he said.

"Both of us?"

"Yeah," he said, "you'll never like me this way."

"I like you enough," she said.

The boy looked sad, like he did the day she introduced herself.

"Where would you want to go?" she said, feeling guilty. "If we had a weekend, where would you take me?"

"The mountains. I'd take you to the mountains. I'd rent a cabin. I'd build us a fire. We could roast marshmallows."

"I don't like marshmallows," she said.

"We could do whatever you like, then."

"I'd rather stay here," she said.

He looked around the car and shook his head. "I want to take you away from this," he tried again.

"Why?"

"*Why?*" he said, surprised, looking at her. The boy leaned back in the seat and let out a small, embarrassed laugh. "It might be cool, you know, to get to know each other."

"I've got work," she said.

"You're a funny one." He was shaking his head, leaning over Georgia and opening the glove box. He pulled out a pack of tissues, but before he cleaned things up or could say anything else, Georgia was out of the car and on her way back to the yogurt shop.

After two weeks of sleeping on the living room couch, Aunt Alma said she'd had enough. Her neck hurt and her back, too. She'd had a life before she moved in, you know. She had needs.

She moved Georgia's father's clothes out of the closet and carried them to the den. Georgia sat on what was her parents' bed and watched as her aunt lifted her own clothes from an old brown suitcase. She hung the blouses and sweaters in neat rows, trying to pat out the wrinkles by slapping at the fabric with an open palm.

Finally Alma turned around and looked at Georgia. She put a hand on her hip and said, "Your father doesn't know this is his bedroom anymore, Georgie."

"But it *is* his bedroom," Georgia said, her voice flat.

"You said yourself that he's been wandering into the den and sleeping on the sofa. Don't just sit there looking at me like that."

"Like what?"

"So judgmental," her aunt said.

"You could always take Kevin's room."

"Where's he going to sleep when he comes home for the weekends?"

"He doesn't come home for the weekends," Georgia said.

"Well, he might, and if he does, where would he sleep if your old Aunt Alma was in his room?"

"In the den."

"Your father *likes* it in there." Her aunt was emphatic.

"I just don't think it's right," Georgia said.

"So judgmental, Georgie," her aunt said. "You certainly didn't get that quality from *our* side of the family."

When the boy came into the yogurt store, she made his cone smaller than usual, but really it was standard and weighed what it was supposed to weigh, what it should have been weighing all along, the three fat swirls Mrs. Yates had demonstrated for her that first day on the job. He took the cone from her hand and looked at it, obviously disappointed. "I guess you're not coming out to the car anymore," he said.

She watched as he lifted the yogurt to his mouth, as his tongue went around and around in a circle.

"What did I do?" he asked.

And Georgia didn't say anything, just turned away and began stirring the fudge, which was hot and steaming, and she let the steam hit her face, inhaled, and didn't even turn around when she heard the sensor's little song, when she heard the bells under the mat outside ringing, which told her another customer was gone.

Rachel Spark

2000

Blur of a Girl

1.

It had been three weeks since my visit to the dingy clinic on Sepulveda Boulevard, and the cramps had mostly subsided, but the bleeding continued. I was standing in the kitchen in a black T-shirt and jeans, wearing two maxipads. I moved from sink to cupboard to stove, aware of the stacked pads between my legs, shuffling around like a very old woman. My hair was on top of my head in a messy ponytail and I wore my mother's apron, which at one time, years ago, said *Elizabeth* in black felt, but which now said simply *abeth*. She was in bed, too tired to cook the dinner she'd promised Gilbert Wolff earlier in the week, and I was attempting her specialty: eggplant with peanut sauce over pasta. If I cooked while she rested, I was hoping she'd be able to join us at the table.

My mother's skin was so slightly yellow that it was still something the two of us debated and questioned, but the fatigue was undeniable. She'd been sleeping twelve hours a night and taking multiple naps during the day. My mother was leaving me, letter by letter, and as I stood in the kitchen looking down at the open cookbook, I touched the remaining letters on the apron with a fingertip and imagined the fabric across my chest blank and white, those final five letters coming loose, falling to the floor or getting lost in the dryer.

In the last week she had stopped shopping, teaching, and going out with Gilbert, which is one reason the dinner invitation came about. If my mother couldn't go to him, she wanted him to come to her. She'd called the school district three mornings in a row for a substitute teacher, but refused to give up her classes completely. She'd promised the kids she'd be back as soon as the medicine kicked in. On Monday she'd be starting a new chemo, a drug that came from the yew tree, and if it worked, the doctor promised her at least a few good months.

I closed the cookbook and decided to rely on her instructions instead, which she was trying to shout to me from her bedroom. Her voice no longer carried down the hall, so I shuffled out of the kitchen and into her room. I stood above her with a notebook and a pen while she listed the ingredients: peanut butter, soy sauce, ginger, red pepper, and orange marmalade.

"You're wearing my apron," she said. "I love that apron, even if it only has half of my name on it." She was smiling.

"I don't remember you using jelly."

"It's not jelly," she said.

"Can I get you anything?"

She shook her head.

"Are you sure about tonight?"

"Yes," she said.

"Because I can call Gilbert and cancel for you."

"He's on his way, Rachel."

"I'll call his cell phone."

"I'm fine. Let me sleep ten more minutes, and then I'll come help you."

I shuffled back to the kitchen. I opened the refrigerator and hunted around until I found the jar of marmalade. I measured out a tablespoon. I banged the spoon against the bowl and watched the marmalade fall.

I'd met Gilbert several times before, but only in passing—the two of them always rushing off together. Tonight was supposed to be the next step in their relationship, the getting-to-know-the-family step. *I* was the family.

He arrived in a tweed sport coat, black button-down shirt, and jeans. He handed me a bottle of wine and a bouquet of irises. "I'm not supposed to drink—doctor's orders, so the wine is for you," he said.

"Thanks," I said.

"I couldn't decide about the flowers," he told me. "I was thinking about roses or lilies, but when I saw these—"

"They're beautiful," I said.

My mother was right; Gilbert *was* dapper and stylish, especially for a man in his sixties. He certainly didn't look like someone with advanced cancer, but I knew his ruddy cheeks and big smile were misleading, that inside of him terrible things were happening. I told Gilbert that my mom was in her room sleeping but that she wanted him to wake her.

When he headed down the hall, I set the flowers on the table, put the wine away, and searched for a vase. I arranged the flowers, stood back a moment and admired them, then followed to see if he was having any luck rousing her. I stood in the doorway, unnoticed, and watched them. He was sitting on the bed next to her, planting tender kisses on her cheek. He whispered something in her ear. My mother's eyes were open. "So handsome," she said. "Look at you all dressed up."

I saw it then: my mother was a dying woman in love with a dying man. I felt dizzy suddenly and held on to the door to keep my balance. I cleared my throat to make my presence known.

"Give me ten more minutes," she said to both of us. "Just a little more sleep," she said.

We gave her fifteen minutes. We sat across the table from each other, our conversation stilted and unnatural.

"How's school?"

"Fine, fine." I was nodding like an idiot.

"Good." A long pause.

"How's the tree business?"

"Things are okay," he said. Another long pause. "How's the poetry business?"

"There is no poetry business," I said, and we both laughed.

We gave her thirty minutes, then went to her room together to try again. My mother shook her head, shooed us away, and the two of us returned to the table rejected.

We gave her forty-five minutes, and Gilbert pushed his chair away from the table and got up. He walked to the window and looked out at the black ocean and lone oil tanker. He pointed at the cement patio ten stories down. "Your mother told me there was a suicide here a few years back."

"Yeah," I said.

"She said you saw the whole thing."

"It was awful."

"Said the girl didn't even live here, that she lived in a house across town."

"This building is famous."

He turned from the window and looked at me.

"It's the tallest building in the city," I said. "The woman next door has lived here for thirty years, and she told me—these are her exact words—it's just something that happens now and then."

"Like an earthquake," he said, looking back.

"Yeah, something like that."

A foghorn sounded in the distance. Gilbert turned from the window and came back to the table. He sat down with a sigh. I looked at the empty chair and wished my mother were sitting in it. I looked at the place I'd set for her: the plate, the knife and fork and spoon. I wondered if I'd be like those crazy, grieving women who continue setting the table for a dead son or a daughter who jumped off the tallest building in the city.

We gave my mother a full hour and then tried her a final time. He sat on her bed and rubbed her back. I stood at the door. "Gilbert brought you irises," I said over his shoulder.

She opened her eyes, then quickly closed them.

"Want me to bring them in here?" I asked her.

"I'll get up in a minute," she said groggily.

Gilbert watched the clock on the dining room wall, his stomach growling so loudly that I could hear it. He was obviously hungry, and I was too, but we didn't want to eat without her; it would be giving up, admitting all the dinners to come that she wouldn't enjoy. I used his growling stomach as a cue to get up from the table and go to the bathroom to check the pads. The blood was darker, richer than any menstrual blood. It was thick and surprising. I rolled up the two soiled pads and dropped them in the wastebasket, then covered them with toilet paper. I leaned over, reached under the sink and thought about doubling up again, but decided that one pad would have to do.

I washed my hands.

I washed them again.

I stood for a moment, holding onto the doorknob before moving into the hall. My steps were met with sharp stabs to my lower stomach, which made me want to open the bottle of wine Gilbert had brought with him. I imagined drinking a glass on my own, him watching me and wanting one himself, and decided against it.

I returned to the dining room and sat down at the table. "Well . . ." I said.

"Let's eat," Gilbert said. "We'll let your mother sleep and have some dinner together."

He twirled the noodles on his fork, gave me a sad smile, and I was wishing that she'd met him years ago.

"I love eggplant," he said. "It's meaty without being meat—not that there's anything wrong with meat. I told your mother how I feel about eggplant and she promised me this dish. And here you've gone and made it for me. What a good girl." He lifted the fork to his mouth.

"I'm sorry," I said. "It's sort of dry."

"Nonsense."

"It tastes much better when she makes it. She'll make it for you another time, I'm sure."

He was chewing and nodding appreciatively.

"When she makes it—"

But he cut me off. "It's delicious, Rachel," he said. "You've made a nice dinner."

"No," I said. "I didn't watch her enough in the kitchen. I didn't watch her enough anywhere." I felt my eyes welling up.

He put down his fork. "I want to tell you something."

"Don't," I said.

"Listen," he insisted, "you've got to get ready, prepare yourself." His voice was soft.

"I've been *getting ready* for years. Since she was diagnosed, I've known what was coming." I picked up my fork again and stabbed at a piece of eggplant. "And still I'm not prepared. How can anyone prepare?"

He shrugged.

"I thought I *was* preparing, imagining the inevitable scenario, seeing myself at her bedside, getting through it—holding her hand, the fucking morphine drip—I'm sorry," I said, losing my appetite completely and putting down my fork.

"Don't be sorry."

"I shouldn't say fuck in front of you."

"Hogwash. *Fuck* is a good word," he said.

"It's certainly better than *hogwash*," I said, smiling.

"Monday's chemo will probably work. It's from the yew tree. And your mother will have a few more months. Good months."

"It's just postponement," I said.

"What isn't?"

I thought about that a moment and then said, "Taking the elevator to the roof and jumping."

"Yes, well," he said. "Everything *except* that." He paused. "Let's have some wine with this dinner."

"But your doctor said—"

"Hogwash. I mean, fuck it."

"You're sure?"

"Absolutely. I want a glass. Or two," he said brightly.

I shot up from the table and went to the kitchen. "Is red okay?" I called out.

"Merlot, Chianti—whatever you want. Open the Bordeaux I brought, if you like."

I brought the Bordeaux and corkscrew to the table, then turned to get the wineglasses. "Your mother is the love of my life," he said to my back.

"Mine too," I told him.

"She wishes that weren't so." His voice was serious.

"It is what it is," I said, placing the wineglasses on the table.

Gilbert shook his head. "You'll have other loves, different loves." He picked up the corkscrew and began opening the wine. He was quiet while he twisted, a look of concentration on his face. "She told me what you went through—that man who left the country," he said finally.

"He didn't leave the country," I said.

"Oh?" He pulled, and the cork popped out.

"He was just here visiting. It's not like he lived here and then went away."

Gilbert nodded, splashing wine into our glasses.

"He's on a farm," I said.

"A *fucking* farm," he corrected me.

"A fucking farm," I said, lifting the glass to my lips and taking a sip. The wine was delicious—dry and bold and fruity. My appetite returned and I joined Gilbert in eating the dinner I had prepared. It tasted okay, not as good as hers, but better than I had anticipated.

We drank one glass. We ate our dinner and drank another glass. And then another. We opened a second bottle, and poured one more. Gilbert moved to the couch and I moved to the chair across from him. I was telling him about the tree outside my classroom window, how I thought the tree was sick.

"I'd take a look at it," he said, "but we're too drunk to drive."

"Angela! Let me call my friend," I said.

By midnight the three of us were standing on campus. It was dark and mostly quiet, except for the occasional burst of laughter coming from the dorms across the street. Gilbert was several feet away, busy with his black bag on a picnic table, searching for equipment. Angela scratched at the new hives on her chest and I told her to stop. She dropped her hand to her side, then leaned in to scold me. "I can't believe you got fucked up with your mom's boyfriend," she said.

"We're just buzzed."

"You tripped coming up the hill, Rachel—*twice.*" She scratched some more and I decided to let her. "He seems like a good guy," she said.

"I wish she'd met him earlier."

"And not bad-looking for sixty-five. Does he have any sons?"

"Daughters, two of them," I told her.

"Damn," she said. "All the good ones are taken, gay, or daughters."

Gilbert pulled a flashlight from his bag and came over to us. "Lead the way," he said. The three of us walked across the campus, passing the administration building and student union, up three flights of steps and one more hill. I didn't trip once and brought that to Angela's attention. "See, I'm fine," I said. And then the hiccups started.

"You don't *sound* fine," she said.

"I get hiccups even when I'm not drinking," I said, hiccuping.

"*Please.*"

We stood in front of my classroom, our backs to the door.

Gilbert handed me the flashlight and I pointed the light at the tree. "It's sick, right? I know it's sick. I had a feeling," I said.

"What do you know about trees?" Angela said, looking puzzled.

I shrugged.

"Let him do his job." She was scratching madly now.

"*Stop scratching.* You're going to start bleeding. You'll scar." I hiccuped, raised my hand to make her quit, but she sneered at me and quit on her own.

"Don't fight, you two." Gilbert held a metal wandlike contraption and moved toward the tree.

"We're not fighting. This is how we talk," Angela said.

"Then don't talk." He turned around and grinned at us.

"Your chest is red," I said.

Angela rolled her eyes and zipped up her sweater.

I hiccuped loudly.

Gilbert was inches from the tree now, looking closely. He used the thin metal tube to dig into the tree's trunk, pulling out sap. He held the end of the tube to his fingertip. He opened and closed his finger and thumb, like scissors, then lifted the finger to his nose and inhaled. Finally, he touched his tongue and tasted the sap. "This tree is fine," he said. "It's going to outlive us all."

By the time Angela dropped us off in front of the building, Gilbert and I were nearly sober and my hiccups had disappeared. "I want to come up and kiss your mom good-bye," he said at the elevator.

He went to her bedroom and I carried the dirty dishes to the kitchen. I was loading the dishwasher when he came up behind me. "She's yellow," he said. He leaned against the stove with his hands behind his back, his face drawn and tired.

"It's the lighting in that room." I turned from him and picked up a plate. I held the plate under the running water and shook my head.

"No," he said. "It's not the lighting."

"*I'm* sort of yellow in that room," I insisted.

"Come with me. Let's look at her." He took the plate from my hand and set it on the counter.

Gilbert stepped into her bedroom first and flipped the light switch. I stalled in the hallway. When he looked back and motioned for me to join him, I moved into the room. My mother slept on her side and was snoring softly. I stood with Gilbert and looked at her skin, her left arm outside of the blanket, her shoulder, neck, and cheek. He was right. It wasn't a tint, but a color, something true happening—a yellow from a child's box of crayons, a deep yellow, vivid and undeniable.

2.

After Gilbert left, I finished the dishes and turned on the teakettle. It was after two A.M. but I wasn't tired. I sat on the balcony with my cup of chamomile and a bowl of grapes and stared out at the black ocean. I picked a grape from the stem, popped it in my mouth, and looked down at the patio. It was well lit. A half-dozen gas grills stood in a horizontal row. I looked at the lounge chairs, the tables with their closed umbrellas, and thought about the suicide I witnessed years ago, just weeks after my mother's mastectomy.

I picked up the cup and blew into it. I took a sip of tea and imagined the girl falling, the way she continued to fall in my dreams for weeks after her death. She was tumbling through the air, and she wasn't quite a girl, but a blur of a girl, and she was falling right before my eyes, and when she landed with an enormous thud, the entire building shook.

She landed above the garage, four stories of cars underneath her, at nine A.M. on a weekday morning, and I remember thinking later that the drivers of those cars, at least a couple of them certainly, were probably holding their keys and opening doors and stepping inside and sitting down—their bodies answering yes to one more day, their fingers curled around steering wheels, feet poised and ready to go.

Her body was small and frail, and the force of her impact surprised me, and it surprised my mother as well, who had been sleeping in her room and was jolted awake.

The girl had been a blur, and perhaps I was a blur too, standing up and rushing toward my mother, who was standing in the hall, tying her robe at the waist, saying, *What was that?* And I blocked her view then, backed up with my arms outstretched. I stood in front of the sliding glass door, saying, *Don't look, it's a body, it's a body,* and she was covering the O of her mouth with her hand.

My mother held the phone to her ear and was asking for help, while I, despite my horror, was moving back outside to see what had become of her. The girl was no longer a blur, but a fixed thing, a curved and quiet thing, a comma on the patio.

"It's an emergency," I heard my mother shouting into the phone. "A suicide, I think. Or maybe a murder. Oh my God."

This is what we found out later: She didn't live in the building but in the house across the street. She followed a tenant inside and took the elevator to the roof. She was twenty-two. Her name was Bridgett. She'd had a heroin problem in the early nineties, but that was behind her now. Her parents lived in Riverside.

Men in blue suits stood around Bridgett's body, making a circle with their own bodies. They covered her with a black plastic sheet. They said things I could not make out. One man took notes. Another spoke into a recorder. A neighbor woman I recognized, clutching her housedress at the neck, stood in front of the patio door that led to the recreation room.

And there was the girl's pale ankle and bare foot sticking out from under the black plastic.

And there were her tennis shoes, one under the yellow awning and one several feet away, closer to our window.

And then I was on the couch, weeping, trying to catch my breath. And my mother was beside me, holding me. I was weeping for the girl and I was weeping for my mother and I was weeping for myself, for the many distressing moments in my life to come and how I'd have to live through them without the shoulder I was now sobbing on.

"It's okay," my mother told me. "I'm here. I'm right here," she said.

3.

Before she got sick, my mother was a woman who was always ready to leave me. When she visited my apartment, which was rare, she'd walk the halls with her purse on her arm, itching to go. She'd walk fast, the purse bouncing at her hip, talking and moving at once. It was impossible for her to sit and listen. After illness came, she moved slowly. She put her purse down.

She invited me to live in her apartment on the sand. She wanted to spend time. She listened. We ate dinners together, went to movies. I listed her men who weren't always nice by name and crude gesture. My mother apologized.

After the chemo from the yew tree had stopped working and the fatigue returned, we spent most of our time together in her bedroom. Once, the two of us were watching a ridiculous man on television, a man who claimed to talk to the dead, and I told my mother to talk to me now, to tell me everything I'd need to know now, so that I wouldn't have to follow a man like him around, so I wouldn't have to give him money and beg him to translate her wishes. "I'm tired," she said. "Haven't I said enough?"

She was sitting up in bed and I was in the chair across from her. I squeezed lotion into my palm and rubbed my hands together. "Please," I said.

"*What?*" She was impatient, sweating and cold at once.

"Tell me one thing, just one."

She sighed. She leaned back on her pillows and thought for a moment. "Finish your book. Make it good," she said. "And get a new screen door for the balcony."

"Okay," I said.

"Don't always obey the law."

I looked at her, puzzled.

"If no one's around and it's after one A.M., run the red light. Don't wait around, is what I'm saying." She paused, thoughtful. "But be careful. I don't want you joining me because of some car accident."

"Joining you?"

"In heaven."

Once she'd started she didn't want to stop. "Always buy plenty of socks and underwear. If a pan doesn't come clean, toss it out. Don't spend hours at the sink, that's what I'm saying."

I smiled.

"If the plants on the balcony die, take them back."

"What?"

"Take them back. I've been taking them back for years. Where do you think I'm going when I carry those dry pots out the front door?"

"To the trash chute?"

"Never."

"Where?"

"Back to the store, that's where."

"You return them?" I said, incredulous.

"Absolutely," she said. "I tell them they're dead. I show them their dead plants, and they replace them. They help me to the car with beautiful new ones, the same plants, only alive and green."

"You're kidding," I said.

She shook her head.

"Why don't you just water them?" I asked her.

"There's not always time. What sort of woman *always* has time to water the plants?"

"A lot of them," I said.

"That's right," she said. "Don't be like *a lot* of them."

My hands were still dry, so I picked up the lotion again and squeezed a small amount into my palm. I was rubbing my hands together and she was staring at them. "Want some lotion?" I asked her.

She shook her head no. "Come lie down with me," she said.

I got up from the chair and moved to the bed. I lay down, my head in her lap. "And get to know your father and stepmother. Sure, they live in New Jersey and you don't want to go to New Jersey, but go anyway. Sit with him and tell him about yourself. Let him tell you what his life is like."

I raised my head in protest.

"Well, at least call them more often."

"Okay," I said, resting my head again on her thigh.

"The divorce wasn't your father's fault."

"I never thought it was," I told her.

She laughed. "I was just too young."

"And the wrong woman."

"That too," she said. She had her hand in my hair now, was lightly scratching my scalp with her fingernails, which was something I loved, that I remembered her doing when I was a child.

"And I don't care if you call her Mom," she continued.

"Who?"

"Your stepmother."

"I'm in my thirties," I said.

"You'll always need a mom, it's in your nature. Most girls have had enough mothering at fifteen, but not you," she said.

"Great."

"It's true. You'll need a mom at eighty."

"What will I do at eighty without one?"

"I don't know," she said. "What *will* you do?"

Home

Today I want to move. It happens every few days since my mother died, this desire for big change, this urge to go. It has me looking in the newspaper, my new glasses halfway down my nose, yellow highlighter in my hand. I didn't realize I needed them, the glasses, attributed the headaches and faint type to stress, but now that they're here on my face I'm surprised at the black letters I see before me, their size and certainty. I check out one bedrooms and two bedrooms and three bedrooms alike, houses, apartments, a condo on a man-made lake. I highlight what sounds good, put little stars by my favorites. I'm not at all sure what I want. Anything is possible. Tomorrow or even tonight I'll look at my own apartment, the walls and corners, the view of the sea, my scrubbed floors, and I'll be grateful I'm here, relieved I didn't sign a lease elsewhere. But right now I want to move.

Several times I've talked on the phone to a real estate agent named Michael Brown. I told him I'm ready and want to buy something, a house with a yard and lawn, flowers, a place to park my car. I told him that I like big windows and closets, high ceilings and open spaces. I said the sound of traffic doesn't bother me, a busy street is fine. I said silence was okay, too. Both have their advantages. Great, he said, great. His voice was deep, sexy. I wondered what this Michael Brown looked like. Later, I touched myself, hearing his voice in my head.

This is what happens: I'll be in the middle of something, grocery shopping or teaching a class, and the urge to leave will hit me. I'll bolt from the gas station, my tank only a quarter filled, and speed off without my gas cap. I'll dash out of the market, ditching the orange juice and butter on a shelf next to the bread. Most recently I stuck a bag of green apples in the freezer, next to the ice cream. I was hasty; I had to go. I had houses to drive by and streets to explore.

Last Thursday, in the middle of a lesson, I left my students, who were surprised. I watched them get angry. They shook their heads, whispered. It was a college class, for God's sake. The cranky girl with purple hair and a shiny stud in her tongue said, "I got up early *for this?*" I heard Molly, and yes, I was sorry, but the urge was great and strong, beyond my control. I wanted to tell her about the abandoned apples, where I left them, and saw them in my mind, their green skins crystallized, their insides frozen, the flimsy bag gone stiff with ice. I wanted to tell her that I needed a new home, that leaving apples in a freezer isn't one more mistake, but indicative of my urgency, my need for cover. Can't you see? I wanted to say, but she didn't want to hear from me, I could tell. I rushed from the front of the classroom to the door, nearly forgetting my notebook and sweater. "I'll make it up to you," I said, remembering my belongings, turning back to my desk to get them.

"You're at work," Molly said.

"Yes," I said.

"Work comes first."

"We'll get to those poems tomorrow," I told her, gathering the notebook and sweater in my arms.

"Work is serious," she continued. She shook her head. Her jaw fell open. The sun coming in the classroom pitched just enough light on her tongue ring to make it visible. Even from across the room I thought I saw it glittering in the girl's mouth. Months earlier, when she'd first pierced it, she'd come to my office to discuss her grade. She'd tell me about the guy she'd been pursuing all semester, how that pursuit had taken time away from her studies. "Work comes first," I had said. The girl's tongue was swollen like a ball or eggplant. She asked me what she might do to bring her *C* up to an *A*. Was there extra credit, a paper or poems she could write? She would write those poems today, this very afternoon, she said, and they'd be good, she promised, because the guy she pursued didn't give a damn about her now, and the rejection inspired her writing, the work was coming easy; she was already writing those poems inside her head. "Is it ever like that for you?" she wanted to know. Molly was talking fast, and at the same time mumbling, struggling with the words, and I could see her fat tongue flopping side to side.

"Work comes first," she said again, clearly now, defiant, confident like a girl who'd never had a great, fat tongue.

"Yes, yes," I said. "I'm sorry," I told the class, rushing out the door.

That afternoon I went north, cruised familiar and unfamiliar neighborhoods: Westwood, Santa Monica, and Pasadena. I was looking for signs in windows, posted signs dug into lawns. I wanted to know about square footage and parking, the view and hardwood floors.

LISA GLATT

Today I want to pack my favorite things—plates and pots, pillows and books—in boxes and not look back. I want to hire a row of men, each one stronger and lovelier than the next, to lift those boxes and take them wherever it is I have decided to go. I'm not at all sure where I want to go. Occasionally I want to go far away to another country, Spain or France, but that thought passes quickly. Sometimes I imagine living on the East Coast, closer to my father and stepmother, where a person can wear a coat, a pair of gloves, a hat that covers half of her face. Most often I want to move a few cities north—say, the Hollywood Hills or Venice Beach. But today I'd like to find an apartment on the sand in the city in which I now live, and since my own apartment is on the sand, people question my motivation.

Daniel, who is my student once again, leaves notes taped to my office door. They're not even folded over, anyone passing by can take a look. They say things like, *I take you and your class seriously you should do the same for me,* or *I know you're having a hard time let's have a cup of coffee,* or *I've read your book ten times now and your poems rock,* or *You only want to move and change jobs because of grief I know about grief,* the boy writes.

My mother, who is now ashes in an urn, who is now pebbles and small particles in a cylinder, sits on a little table I've set up just for her. She wanted me to stay in her apartment on the sand and make a life. She wanted me to find someone to soothe me. She wanted me to see things through: the jobs and books and men I've started, but haven't finished.

Now I want to go where she is, just as I always wanted to go where she was going: to the store or school, to work, even to sleep when she'd climb into covers with men that frightened me, men who weren't always nice.

280

I wanted one of those leashes you see at the mall, the ones mothers wrap around their toddlers' waists so that the toddlers will not wander. But I was a grown woman when I wanted a leash like that, and I wanted to follow my mother everywhere, even into that midnight morning.

I changed things around, made the apartment mine before she died. I brought up my desk and futon and coffee table from the office I rented downstairs. I set the desk up in the living room. I pointed the desk at the sea so while I worked I could watch the boats and tiny swimmers.

One night, months ago, I kidnapped my mother from the place she then called home. I didn't get her doctor's permission. I hustled past the nurses' station, one skinny nurse twirling her hat on her finger, another one eating a fruity muffin. I could smell the muffin all the way down the hall. I could hear the nurses laughing, enjoying each other's company. I helped my mother out of the sheets, stuffed her swollen feet inside furry slippers. I brought a robe for her, a cherry-colored thing that months earlier she'd called *cheerful*. "I love that cheerful robe," she'd said. Now, though, she looked at the robe and at me, her daughter, wrapping her up like a gift, as if she wasn't sure what she felt. I helped her down the hall, my arm under her arm. I moved my fifty-nine-year-old mother, walked with her past the sleeping residents, who were in their eighties and nineties, who had come to this home to die, who were snoring and grunting, one woman howling like a wolf.

I brought my mother into her apartment that was now becoming mine. She said she was happy to be there, in that apartment she loved, even for just one night. She said I did a good job rearranging things, that the place was minimal and elaborate at once, an improvement over the way she'd had it. It sounds evil, I now think, to bring a dying woman to her home, showing her that even that is not quite hers.

 She was bright yellow by then, her liver half gone, and I slept with her in her bed, which I'd moved to the opposite wall. I'd bought a comforter full of feathers, one I hoped she'd think was pretty, with little roses and green leaves. I told her that the bed against that wall was better, that she'd never again trip over cords and the small table where she stacked her medicines, where she'd lean the bottles on their sides and balance them in a row, then stack them on top of each other, until they became a pyramid of pills, capsules, and tablets prone to disruption, an avalanche of drugs, from the slightest bump of knee or elbow. Now, I told her, there was a wall to back the bottles up. It would be easier for her when she came home. The two of us nodded at each other, knowing she would never leave that place.

 By nine P.M. she was on the phone with her roommate, the diabetic woman in bed B, Joanne, who shit in her big diapers every afternoon while I was visiting. My mother was assuring Joanne that she'd be home early in the morning. She'd called that place home, I remember, and then she was saying goodnight to Joanne, claiming to miss her. Joanne, a gruff woman with one leg, who admitted being mean before anyone took a saw to her limb. A woman who bragged about beating her children until they were tall enough to hit back. A woman with bad teeth, whose mouth I could smell from across the room when her diaper wasn't filled. A woman whose own daughter refused to visit. A woman my mother had met just days ago, and all they had in common was death rushing to fetch them both.

 "I'll be home in the morning," my mother was saying, and

I was looking around her room at my own clever changes, then tugging on her robe, the sleeve, as I might have done when I was four. "Talk to me," I said. "You're just here for the night."

"Bye-bye," she told Joanne. The phone fell from her hand onto her pillow, and even that I had to take care of.

I wanted to bring my mother home, and even though I'd changed things around, I wanted her to feel *at home,* safe and comfortable, but she was restless in her own bed, stirring in the night, saying in a sleepy voice, *Where am I?*

"You're home," I said, "with me."

"Who?" she said.

"Me," I repeated.

"Oh," she said.

When she had to pee, I helped her into the bathroom. The pee was pungent, dark brown and strong, not like any pee I recognized. It was late, the middle of the night. I tried to smile at my sleepy mother, helping her up. I tried not to look at the pee when I flushed, but caught a glimpse despite myself. I thought pee like that should be called something else, not urine, not waste. Something foul as that should have had its own name.

In the morning I helped her into the car. She insisted on the backseat so she could rest. I drove her car that was becoming mine. She was sleeping on her side, curled up, snoring and mumbling, incoherent back there, and every now and then I turned to look at her, staring at her one cheek and closed eye. She wouldn't like me driving like that. She wouldn't want me to stare and get upset. She wouldn't want me to swerve and weep going eighty miles an hour.

I removed my acrylic nails one by one with my teeth. I spit

the acrylic into my palm, then let the bits fall into the ashtray. I left little spots of red polish that I'd get to later. I decided to let my own nails grow—never again would I walk into that beauty shop where the two of us went together, where I'd make her pull up a chair and sit next to me.

"I'm right here," she'd say from the couch, a magazine open in her lap.

"Closer," I'd insist.

"How close can I get?"

"A lot closer than where you are now. Get a chair," I'd say. "Please," I'd tell her.

In a traffic jam on a side street I turned and looked at my sleeping mother again. Her wig was lopsided. She'd stopped snoring and was breathing softly. I stared at the empty passenger seat. I took the 710 North to the 405 North and then I got off at Durango, headed south, and drove my mother home.

That night at Safeway in the fruit and vegetable aisle, I saw Daniel. He was wearing a ridiculous outfit—tight black pants and a red and white striped shirt. It was the silly beret folded and hanging from his back pocket I saw first. "Daniel," I said.

"You look terrible, Rachel," he said, matter-of-factly.

"Thank you," I said.

"She's going, isn't she?" he said softly.

"No, no," I lied.

"You're going to be okay," he said. "I know it doesn't seem like you'll survive, but you will."

"What are you wearing?" I said, trying to change the subject. "What's with the silly getup?"

"I'm a gondolier," he said.

"You do those canals, right? It's beautiful out there."

"What's happening with your mom? Where is she now?" he wanted to know.

"She's home," I lied again.

"Are you going to buy that lettuce?"

I looked down at my hand and the head of red leaves I was gripping. They shot out of my palm like a bouquet of flowers. "I guess so," I said.

"Let me help you," he said, pulling a plastic bag from the roller above my head, leaning over and smelling good, like the water he worked on. Just then the store's timer went off, the silly recorded thunder, and the miniature lights blinking—a warning. Mist hit the bins of lettuce and onions, the peppers and tomatoes. Mist hit my cheek. "I've got to go. I'm in a hurry," I said, pulling the bag from Daniel's hand.

"I want to help you," he said again.

"She's waiting for me," I lied for the third time. I looked at his face. There was mist on his cheek, too. "Okay," I said, handing the bag back to him. "Will you pick out some tomatoes. My mother likes tomatoes. I'll make her a salad when I get home," I told him.

A graduate student had taken over my classes, so I was with my mom throughout the days. Gilbert was with her most nights. When I visited, I brought Chinese soup and begged her to eat. Instead, she'd lift the sheets and invite me in. The staff looked at me funny, nurses, the doctor, the ones who bathed her, the ones that brought her lunch, something smelly and unrecognizable, a chicken breast or slice of ham hidden under a plastic dome. *What's a grown woman doing in bed with her mother?* they wanted to know.

And my body was fetal, parallel with her body like in the beginning. I was holding her from behind, my arms around what was left. I was staring at the back of her head, the few stubborn hairs, then I was looking at her wallet and keys on the hospital nightstand—the keys, I couldn't help thinking, a reminder of the doors she wouldn't open.

Michael Brown wants me to buy this redbrick house on Seaside Drive. He thinks I can afford it. I've led him to believe such nonsense, talking to him on the phone about assets that don't exist. I follow him up the porch steps. I'm standing on the porch next to Michael Brown, who is dark and handsome, good jaw, wide chest. Moments ago, he helped me out of the car and shook my hand hello. I thought he held my hand for longer than was necessary. I blushed, felt the blood in my face. Now he's trying key after key, unable to find the one that fits. He sticks a key in the hole, twisting, twisting, unable to get it out finally. "Fuck," he says. Then, turning to me, "Oops. Sorry."

"It's okay," I say.

"I can't believe I said that. How unprofessional. I'm really sorry," he says again, pulling on the key, then giving up, hands at his sides.

"Let me try." I step closer to the door. I close my fingers around the key. I'm gentle. It slides out smooth and easy. I smile at Michael Brown, putting the key in his open palm.

He puts the key in his pants pocket. "Sorry about cussing. I shouldn't use words like that. It's just—"

"I like the word *fuck,*" I interrupt. "I use the word myself, more than I should."

"Still, I'm sorry," he repeats.

"I've used it in front of my classes and my mother. Lately, I've even tried it out on my dad. It's part of my effort to get to know him."

"Still," he says.

"I'm an English teacher, take it from me. The word means what it means, but it also means whatever you need it to mean."

"I don't understand."

"Right now, for you, it means *I can't find the right key* or *This key is stuck,* and depending on your tone it might even mean, *I've lost the key. We're locked out.*"

"You're right," he says. Michael Brown smiles at me. His teeth are big and white, his lips full.

"Now what?" I say.

"Yes!" he says suddenly, remembering something, making a discovery. "That's right, I put it in here." He pulls the key out of his shirt pocket and opens the front door.

It's the first of three houses he wants to show me today. I'm following him up the stairs to the master bedroom. It is where he wants to begin, what he wants me to see first. He's been talking about this master bedroom all week on the phone, the sunken bathtub, the skylight, the huge window and the palm fronds I'd wake up to if I lived here. He's a big man, this real estate agent, this Michael Brown, over six feet tall, with a broad back. His head is little, though, unusually so, and walking up the stairs behind him I'm amazed that a little head like that rests on such a thick neck, such shoulders, that a little head like that houses such big teeth. I imagine saying, *Hey,*

Mr. Real Estate Man, how about a little head? And then before he says *yes* or *no* or *you're crazy,* I imagine stopping him, saying, *Oh, I'm sorry, I see you've already got one.* This makes me laugh out loud behind him on the stairs.

"What," he says, turning, "do I have something on my pants? Did I sit in something?" he wants to know, and he is wiping himself off, and I am saying *no, no, no, no, no,* and I am laughing and I can't stop and I know that my laughter is strange, unusual, not like any laughing I've done before. I sit down on the stairs. Michael Brown is at the top, as many stairs away from me as he can possibly get. "Don't you want to see the master bedroom?" he says.

I shake my head no.

"Aren't you interested in taking a look?"

"My mother is dead," I say.

"I'm sorry," he says, "but—"

"Gilbert was there, my friend Angela."

Michael Brown is nodding, his eyes darting side to side as though he'd rather be anywhere but where he is and with anyone but me.

"Claire had stepped out, though," I continue.

"I'm sorry," he says again.

"I was in bed with her. I had my arms around her body and—"

"Look," he interrupts, "I can see you're really upset, but I'm not the best guy to talk to. I don't know you," he says.

"That's true," I say. "You're right about that," I tell him.

"Do you want to see the house at a later date? Maybe Monday?" he says.

"Your head is really little," I blurt out.

And Michael Brown reaches up to touch his little head, like that action alone might make it grow.

"It looks good," I lie.

"You like it?"

"Yeah."

"Are you okay?" he says.

"No."

"You don't look okay, that's why I asked. I mean, it's none of my business, and like I said, I don't know you."

"You don't know me."

"You should talk to someone who knows you," Michael Brown says.

"I'm going to get to know my student," I say, and as the words leave my lips, I realize how true they are. "Daniel is twenty-two—twenty-three, tops. Do you think that's a bad thing to do?"

"I think we should look at the house, that's what I think," Michael Brown says.

"I should wait until the quarter is over, until grades are in, shouldn't I?"

"You want to see the bedroom or not, lady?"

"I could spend some time with him now, though, couldn't I? He wants coffee, he wants lunches, he wants to go to readings in Los Angeles."

"Look," he says, shaking his head.

"I'll let Daniel know me—that won't kill anyone, right?"

"I don't know."

"Be serious. No one will drop dead because I enter into a friendship with Daniel," I say, believing it.

Michael Brown looks down at his shoes.

"Maybe I won't even wait."

"Do what you want," he says weakly.

"I'll go to coffee. I'll go to lunch. I'll tell Daniel everything." I stand up on the stairs and face him.

"Look, do you want to see the house or not?" He's shaking that little head of his, muttering something about other buyers and the cost of time.

"I've seen enough," I say, turning around, walking away, one step and then another, step by step away from Michael Brown. I go out the front door, take a deep breath, get in my car, and drive myself home.